Also by Ev Bishop

Bigger Things

Wedding Bands (River's Sigh B & B, Book 1)

Hooked (River's Sigh B & B, Book 2)

New Year's Resolution: One To Keep (A River's Sigh B & B novella)

Spoons (River's Sigh B & B, Book 3)

Writing as Toni Sheridan

The Present

Drummer Boy

EV BISHOP

Hook, Line & Sinker

River's Sigh B & B, Book 4

HOOK, LINE & SINKER
Book 4 in the River's Sigh B & B series
Copyright © 2017 Ev Bishop

Print Edition

Published by Winding Path Books

ISBN 978-1-77265-007-5

Cover image: Kimberly Killion / The Killion Group Inc.

Hook, Line & Sinker is a work of fiction. Names, characters, places, and incidents are either the product of the author's imagination or are used fictitiously, and any resemblance to actual persons, living or dead, business establishments, events or locales is entirely coincidental.

To my mom,

With fond memories and so much appreciation for all the special things you sewed for me over the years.

I will always miss you.

Chapter 1

AFTER THE MASSIVE LAX AND bustling YVR, Greenridge's solitary airport seemed tinier than ever, but it
was still too busy for Brian's taste. He scrubbed his
hands over his face, weary to the core and badly in
need of a shower, a shave and about twenty hours
sleep.

He strode toward the baggage carousel, where a
single chute served each flight, keeping his head down
and his eyes averted, hoping to avoid bumping into
anyone he knew. He already missed the anonymity of
the bigger cities and the solitude of the beaches he'd
explored solo the past few months. Ah, well. He
couldn't put off dealing with his parents' insanity
forever—unfortunately. Also, all that aside, it would
be nice to collect a paycheck again. He'd save for
another big trip, an even longer escape. Maybe he'd
travel permanently.

He shook his head at that last thought. He was as
prone to self-deception as anyone, but he couldn't deny
it. As much as he had needed the time away, a bigger
part of him longed for his own bed, his library, his

stereo and music collection, and art work he'd purchased, things that meant something to him personally
and weren't just decorations in some snazzy hotel. It
sucked beyond sucked that his own family had chased
him away from his home.

Sighing heavily, Brian sidestepped the gangly legs
of a bunch of teenagers plunked down in the middle of
the aisle. Then he almost walked smack dab into a
crying, blotchy faced woman and her two small
children. Her obvious upset contrasted sharply with her
very put together vintage look. She wore a formfitting
navy wool skirt with a matching high-buttoned jacket,
ivory stockings, and round-toed apple red pumps. Even
her suitcases looked more suited to Downton Abbey
than modern day British Columbia.

The family was huddled near one of the check-in
lines, no doubt fresh from seeing someone off. Such
drama. Brian held back a literal growl, reached out to
steady the child nearest to him, so he wouldn't bowl
her over—then, damn it anyway, had to stop mid-stride
again because a clerk rushed from behind the counter
to accost the woman. Between the frazzled clerk, the
crying family, and enough luggage to sink a battle-
ship—oh, so maybe they weren't seeing someone off,
after all—Brian's escape route was completely
blocked.

"I'm so sorry, but you have to understand. It's pol-
icy." The clerk was all big eyes and sleek hair, and
normally Brian would've taken a second look or

sparked up conversation, but his "normal" had split months ago. All he was left with was this miserable, lame ass version of himself, the one who couldn't find the energy to check out a pretty lady, let alone the drive to flirt, make small talk, or pretend to give a shit in the hopes of a bit of fun. What was the point? These days women always seemed to want more than he had to offer—and the more cases he handled at work, the more he realized he *never* wanted to offer more. Love? Pah. And worse, *marriage*. Don't even get him started. He'd rather eat glass. Why couldn't people hang out, have fun, slake their lust and call it good?

His face must've conveyed his mood because the bawling mom gave him a wary look and tried to shuffle her brood out of his way. The baggage cart had a rickety wheel, however, and when she moved it, a pet carrier on top of her pile of suitcases tottered.

"No!" the woman shrieked.

Brian managed to catch the container just before it fell. A scruffy rat-like dog—or at least Brian thought it was a dog—glared out at him and started to yip.

"Thank you." The woman took the caged muppet from Brian.

"Ma'am," the clerk tried again, and this time the mom didn't ignore her. She wheeled around furiously.

"Stop ma'aming me like you don't know who I am, Marie. And if you're looking for some sort of absolution, some word that it's okay, that I understand, it's not going to happen. You, as you said, were doing your job. Bully for you. Now leave me alone."

"But what are you going to do?"

"I have no idea," the woman said, fresh tears coursing down her already swollen features. "No idea at all."

The crated rat-dog whined. The smaller of the two children, a boy in a T-Rex T-shirt, whimpered. The little girl Brian had almost tripped over reached out and wordlessly patted her mother's arm.

Good night, what a gong show.

"Excuse me," Brian muttered, moving futilely to his left, then equally futilely to his right, trying to get past.

Suddenly there was a police officer in the fray. "Are you Katelyn Kellerman, ma'am?"

The woman rolled her eyes, then nodded. Katelyn Kellerman. Something about the name was familiar, but Brian couldn't immediately place it.

"I'm Constable Gerald Le Clair. Are you aware that you're in breach of your custody agreement?"

More tears. How did the woman have any saline left to shed? "Come on, Gerry. We live in Armpit, BC. Why does everyone keep pretending we don't all know who's who?"

Under his buzz cut and navy blue forge cap, Constable "Gerry" Le Clair was stone-faced and serious.

The woman—Katelyn—sighed. "I had a notarized letter from Steve, giving permission for the kids to travel. He changed his mind. It's that simple."

"But you are aware that the court ordered you *not* to travel out of the province?"

"I had a letter of permission! I thought if we both agreed—"

Le Clair held up his hand. "I only know what was reported to me. You're not to leave—"

Katelyn interrupted. "I know, I know." Something glinted in her eyes and Brian suddenly realized her tears weren't sorrow or weakness. They were barely contained liquid fury. Her whole body shook with it.

"Mommy, why is a policeman here?" the girl child asked. At the sound of his sister's voice, the boy jammed a thumb in his mouth and stopped whining. "Is it bad to visit Auntie Janet?"

"No, sweetie, of course not." The woman stroked her daughter's hair, a deep shiny mahogany that matched her own, and even managed a smile. "There's just been a misunderstanding."

"Because Daddy loves us and will never let us go?"

Brian cut a sharp look at the kid. Interesting—and awful—how words that should be lovely and reassuring were somehow creepy instead.

For a split second Le Clair's expression changed, revealing he shared Brian's opinion, then it went carefully blank once more. Brian scanned the woman's face again. He was sure he knew her. What was the connection?

"Okay, so this was a misunderstanding. You're not boarding, correct?" Le Clair asked sternly.

"That's right. We'll get it sorted."

The clerk inched away, murmuring that she had to "get back," and Brian noticed that the line of people waiting to check in had grown substantially in the minutes she'd been away from her post.

Le Clair raised his eyebrows at Brian as if they were in some sort of collusion. Brian nodded politely and the officer spoke, confirming Brian's suspicions that he'd recognized him—but also revealing a false assumption.

"Okay, Ms. Kellerman, *Katelyn*, so long as you understand you're not to leave town with the kids, there's no problem. And if Brian Archer here is your lawyer, you're in good hands. I suspect you'll get the best of your husband in court yet."

Brian shook his head. "I'm not her lawyer."

"Oh, uh . . ."

Brian could practically see the man's brain froth as he jumped to an even more erroneous idea, that Brian was her boyfriend or something. "No, man. I'm not her . . . anything. I'm just trying to get my bags. You guys are blocking the whole hallway."

"Oh." Le Clair nodded as if he finally understood something. "*Oh.*" He marched off, leaving Brian alone with the sniffling children, the stressed to the max mother, and the kennel of almost-but-not-quite-a-dog. He bobbed his head at Katelyn and felt that words of some kind were necessary before he too deserted her, crying and alone and apparently thwarted in her plans by some loser ex.

"Uh, sorry you're going through all this." He waved his hand at some general mess in the distance. "Seems rough."

The woman nodded. "Thanks, Brian," she said wearily and began straightening the luggage on the cart, making the stack of suitcases more organized, less tippy. "I'm sorry you had to witness all that. Totally humiliating."

Something in the way she said his first name, and how she commented casually on her humiliation, stopped him. Sure Le Clair had dropped his name, but it rolled from her tongue like she knew him.

"Are we going to stay at Daddy's house or at our apartment?" The girl's question barely registered with Brian until the woman replied briskly, "Neither, sweetie. We don't have our apartment anymore because we were going to live with my friend Janet for a bit, remember? But you don't need to worry. We'll find something."

Yep, every single day Brian saw one more thing that cemented his opinion: committed relationships were for suckers—or people who needed to be committed. His little inner joke didn't make him smile.

Katelyn rolled the cart a tentative inch or two. It was still wobbly. She lifted the dog carrier and handed it to her daughter. "Can you carry Monster for me?"

The girl obeyed promptly.

"Thanks, sweetie." Katelyn held a hand out toward

her son. He wrapped his fingers around her pinkie—
obviously a mode of walking together they'd worked
out some time ago—and she commenced pushing the
cart in an awkward one-handed grip. The cart veered
left as they went, and every few steps she had to stop
and kick the front wheel to straighten its path.

Brian looked over at the luggage carousel. A small
crowd had formed, but no bags spilled from the chute's
yawning mouth. He darted a look back at the young
girl, who was uncomplainingly trudging forward to
help her mom. He groaned inwardly. Damn it.

"You look like you have your hands full," he said,
"and my suitcase isn't out yet. Can I help move your
stuff for you?"

The rickety cart stopped. Katelyn raised her face to
look at him directly, and they made eye contact for the
first time since the whole debacle started. Large gray
eyes with thick sooty lashes met his—and Brian finally
put two and two together. Before he could stop himself, and before Katelyn nodded to accept his offer of
help, he exclaimed, "Katelyn, as in *Katie*, as in Janet
Smith's friend and shadow all through school? Holy
cow, I never would have—" He broke off, flourishing
a hand at her. "I mean . . . "

Katelyn, a.k.a. Katie, flushed. "Yeah, Janet's shadow as you so nicely put it. No one calls me Katie
anymore though—and don't worry, I didn't think
you'd remember me." Her shoulders jerked in a small
self-deprecating shrug. "I wasn't exactly the kind of

girl you noticed."

Brian took a step back, still mildly shocked. *Kate-lyn. Of course.* Crazy big charcoal gray eyes, large freckles on creamy skin, and a full heart-shaped mouth—that, if he remembered correctly, was quick to laugh and make sarcastic comments. She was apparently still obsessed with retro fashion, which her small frame and petite figure suited immensely. She'd been cute enough, but a year below him in school, which felt like a lot back then. Plus, Janet was a knock out. It would've been hard for anyone to shine next to her. Before he thought better of it, he grinned and winked. "What are you talking about? I notice *every* girl."

One of Katelyn's eyebrows arched and she shook her head derisively.

"So what do you say?" He pointed at the cart again.

The pink in Katelyn's cheeks intensified, making the puffy, mottled effects of her recent weeping even more noticeable—but at least there were no more fresh tears.

"I say, well . . . okay. And thank you."

Brian nodded and noticed a tiny crescent moon scar by her left eye, silvery-white against her heightened color. He figured under normal circumstances it was probably almost indiscernible. Embarrassed to find himself staring, he grabbed the handle of the cart. "Where to?"

Katelyn hesitated for a second then replied, "The cafeteria, please."

Chapter 2

ORDER PLACED, KATELYN WALKED BACK to the small cafeteria table where, of all the bizarre things, Brian Archer waited, one hand resting on her luggage cart.

She settled the kids into blue swiveling chairs, then rummaged for their water bottles in what would have been her carry-on bag, if life could ever, even once, give her a break. The kids slurped their drinks like she'd been depriving them of fluids for a year not an hour, and the counter girl brought out their food.

Both children grinned when they saw their dinosaur shaped chicken nuggets, and for a second it felt like a regular outing, one that involved a rare fast food treat. Then Brian cleared his throat and blew that fairy tale delusion all to heck. And why was he still at the table with them anyway? She'd already thanked him. He needed to go already.

She stole a covert glance at him. Why wouldn't he *go*? He may not have recognized her first off—and no wonder—but she'd known him the instant he appeared, seeming disgruntled by their very existence. His sandy blond hair was longer than he used to wear it, and it was tousled like he'd just come from bed or the beach or something. Stubble lined his square jaw, and the years since school had given him light creases on either side of his mouth and a slightly brooding wrinkle on his forehead, tempered by tiny laugh lines—all which suited him. His dress shirt was a little rumpled and untucked from his beige Dockers, and its top two buttons were undone. All that was surface stuff though; only his eyes were truly different. Oh, they were the same captivating color of stormy sea that she remembered, but they were tired or something. They didn't sparkle with intrigue or light up in teasing interest the way they had when she'd known him before, when he dated her best friend. Even when he'd made his flirtatious crack about noticing every girl, they hadn't lightened.

She suddenly realized she was staring at Brian like she'd never seen an attractive man before in her life. Cringing mortification flooded through her. She busied herself opening the kids' honey-mustard dips and doling out napkins, so Brian wouldn't see her face and possibly guess her thoughts. Even in the privacy of her own head she sounded like some sad, desperate nutcase. And good grief, it wasn't like she'd had that huge a crush on him back in the day or anything. She'd just been aware that she really liked how he looked. And now she was noticing that she still did.

Focus, she commanded herself. You've got bigger issues to worry about—like what on earth are you and the kids going to do? Where are you going to stay?

Before she could think on it more, Brian shocked her further. He slid into a chair beside Lacey. He was going to sit with them? Why? Her heart jumped a little in panic. She tried to keep her face neutral, to not glower, to not show nervousness or fear.

Stop it, she muttered to herself again. He's not Steve. Not every guy acting nice is just acting. Not every man has a hidden agenda.

"So, uh, when you were ordering food, Lacey here introduced herself and said you don't have any place to live."

Katelyn's face flamed yet again. Lacy had said what? Well, of course, she had. Great, just great. One part of her felt relieved. She always worried that through example she might have taught her kids to keep too quiet, or to feel shame over things they should never have witnessed, let alone feel responsible for.

In the early years, she'd tried her best to counteract those unspoken lessons through words: *You can share any story. You can tell any detail. You can talk about anything. Nothing has to be secret.* And now, or for the past two years anyway, she'd tried to teach it by example, but it was hard to know, to believe, to trust, that she could undo the damage that had been done and could keep a sense of silence and shame from being a life sentence—especially if she couldn't get her kids away from Steve permanently. So no, she'd never fault Lacey for being open and truthful or tell her not to talk about certain things . . . but honestly, was it too much to ask that she escape this day with one shred of dignity left?

Katelyn shook her head briskly. "I wouldn't say that exactly. I mean we gave notice on our apartment, and—"

"There's a zero percent vacancy rate," Lacey piped in.

Shit. Katelyn bit her lip. How on earth had she overheard all that? It made her feel like her heart was caving in to hear it relayed so matter-of-factly. That was the worst part of this whole mess of trying to break free of Steve's control—how much the kids picked up, how much of their innocence was robbed, how many adult cares it put on them, despite her best intentions. Lacey must've eavesdropped the last time she and Janet talked on the phone.

"Is that true?" Brian asked, frowning.

Katelyn shrugged. She needed to get rid of him. Her affairs were none of his business. "Look," she said. "I appreciate your kindness, but the kids need to eat and I need to adjust my plans and get stuff organized for tonight. I can handle things from here."

He looked at her for a moment, then nodded. As he stood up, her phone rang. She forced a smile, waved, and looked at her call display. Unknown caller. Biting her lip, she pressed Talk. "Hello?"

"Katelyn, honey, I hear there was a mix up at the airport and you couldn't take off as planned. What happened?"

Steve. She let his concerned (oily and fake) voice finish his sentence, then nodded as if considering something. "Yes, there was some confusion. I can't talk about it right now though. Thanks for calling." She clicked End before he could get another word in, hoping beyond hope that she had sounded genuinely unfazed.

She'd read somewhere that people like Steve thrive on knowing that they're getting to you, that you're afraid or intimidated. That all they want is to continue being in a relationship with you, no matter what, so any form of engagement—arguments, fear, begging, warning, reasoning, bartering—all feels like a win.

Katelyn recognized the truth in the advice, but honestly, it was a lot easier said than done.

She popped a fry into her mouth, but could hardly chew and swallow. Brian was *still* standing there.

"How are you getting to town? Do you need a ride to a hotel?" he asked.

Her eyes narrowed. "It's disconcerting to have someone refuse to take no for an answer," she said. "I have no idea why you're being so pushy, and I don't care if I seem rude. I appreciated your help with the cart, but that's enough. It's not gallant to force aid on someone who has told you they're fine. It's inappropriate."

Brian stepped back as if slapped and his face reddened. "Uh, yeah, sorry. I thought . . ." He didn't bother to elaborate on what he'd thought exactly, just apologized again and left.

Lacey looked down at her plate.

What now? Katelyn thought. *What now?*

"I might have accidentally told him that you quit your job and sold our car for extra cash," Lacey blurted—again quoting Katelyn's words to Janet almost verbatim.

"I'm sorry," Lacey added before her mom could say anything. "I know I don't need to tell everyone our life story."

Ouch, the kid really was a parrot!

"I just thought he was nice, plus he knows Auntie Janet. I was trying to be polite and talk so it wasn't all weird and quiet."

Katelyn exhaled and willed away the stupid tears threatening yet again. She smiled with sincere fondness at her daughter. "One: you can tell people anything you want. No secrets, remember? Unless it's something fun like a surprise birthday party or something. Two: Brian probably is nice, but sometimes *seeming* nice isn't the same thing as actually being a good or safe person, so always be careful, okay? Most people are safe and kind, but some are not. It's good you told me what you guys talked about—and never, no matter what, go off with *anybody* without clearing it with me first, right?"

Lacey nodded.

"And three," Katelyn smiled again, "like you could

ever go five minutes without talking."

Lacey giggled. "Yeah, that's true."

"Now eat up, you guys. I'm going to find us a place to stay tonight."

Sawyer made a small dinosaur growl, and both Katelyn and Lacey looked at him in surprise. He chomped a nugget.

Lacey grinned. "Grrr yourself!"

Katelyn took one of Sawyer's small hands and one of Lacey's, and squeezed them softly.

"It's going to be okay, right, Mom?" Lacey asked, squeezing back.

"Yeah, right, Mom?" Sawyer echoed, surprising Katelyn again.

"It's going to be better than okay," Katelyn said with forced optimism. "It's going to be great."

And inside her head, she said, Please, let that be true. *Please.* And please help me figure out what to do.

Chapter 3

BRIAN COULDN'T DECIDE WHICH WAS more irritating, the idiots standing in the queue to see where their missing bags were, or the airline for having only one— *one*!—customer service rep on duty. Could the line move any slower? *Could it?* The hairy, foulmouthed jerk ahead of him obviously thought so. He seemed to be on a personal mission to hold things up further by cursing a blue streak and generally being a douche.

By the time it was Brian's turn to step up, however, his temper wasn't much better than the jerk's. The woman at the counter, a curvy redhead with tired eyes, whose name tag identified her as Susan, explained that his suitcases had been held back in Vancouver. Then she lifted her hands slightly as if to ward off a verbal beating. Brian was sure the gesture was unconscious, but it made him feel badly all the same—and it took all the piss and vinegar out of him.

"And I thought *I* was having a bad day," he drawled.

Susan looked up at the note in his voice, cautiously curious. A wan smile played over her lips. "It's not bad news to find out your luggage didn't land with you?"

"Oh no, don't kid yourself, it sucks. I've been awake for over twenty-four hours, and I just want to be home, but it still beats being the person who has to tell irate Greenridgers they've been separated from their loot."

Susan's smile deepened. "It's true that I've had better days."

Brian sighed with mock seriousness. "I hear you, and I didn't even bring booze in my carry-on. What am I supposed to do without my duty free?"

"I have a feeling you'll survive." Her eyes twinkled a bit now.

"I guess I'll have to," he agreed.

"Thank you for being so understanding," Susan glanced down at his ID, "Brian."

"You're very welcome . . . Susan."

She grinned prettily once more and repeated her scripted apology, something about a last-minute change of planes in Vancouver because of a mechanical problem and less room in the cargo department.

Brian listened patiently, although the explanation didn't help him now. He checked his watch. He'd been on the ground, in this airport, for almost two hours. First the family of tough breaks. Now this. What a waste of time!

Why are you so worried about time anyway? a little voice nagged. It's not like you have anything to do or anyone to see, except your family. You should thank the airline for their ineptitude.

"So my suitcase will come in on the eleven-thirty flight?"

"Yes, but by the time they're unloaded, it will be closer to midnight. Do you want me to call you?"

"No, no, that's fine. Thanks, though. I'll come back."

He had started to walk away when Susan said, "Um, Brian?"

He turned.

She bit her lip and looked up at him from slightly lowered lashes.

"Yes?" he asked.

"I was wondering, if, well . . . I'm going on break in a few minutes. I could buy you a coffee if you wanted, or a beer and I'll have the coffee."

He wished he could scrounge up one iota of interest, but he couldn't. "I'm sorry, you seem really great, but it's not a good time for me."

She shrugged. "Can't blame a girl for trying, right?"

"Absolutely not, and thanks for the invite. You've boosted my ego for at least a week."

She beamed and wished him a good night.

He didn't bother heading to his condo. He was starving and he'd emptied his fridge before he left, knowing he'd be away for months. Instead he went to a country bar that he rarely frequented, figuring it was his best hope for privacy, and took a booth far away from the stage where live bands occasionally played.

He ordered a massive burger called the Big Bear with fries, then stared at some survival show playing in silent mode on the big screen above his head while he ate. His cell phone was going crazy with missed call alerts, but he decided not to listen to the messages. He'd been back in Greenridge for what, a couple hours? Give him a break. What was such a huge emergency that folks couldn't leave him in peace until he shook off the tarmac's dust?

It was hard to believe he'd been gone the better part of six months—and even more difficult to face the fact that he still didn't know what he was going to do. He'd taken an unprecedented leave from work, much to the irritation of his boss, a.k.a. his father, to think things through—or that's the excuse he'd given his mother anyway. Really he'd just been desperate to avoid, for once in his pathetic life, being caught in the middle of his parents' terrible relationship. Fat lot of good it did him. All he'd actually succeeded at was burning through his savings and backlogging his cases at his dad's firm. What should have been the trip of a lifetime was tainted by an endless reel of unhappy memories that moved relentlessly through his mind.

Duncan and I are getting a divorce. Our son Brian will be handling the details. Even now, almost a year since the farce of a thirty-fifth wedding anniversary party, where instead of a misty-eyed toast, his mother had made the shocking announcement that she was ending the marriage, the words were as sharp and freshly painful as when Brian first heard them.

What kind of mother assumed, without even asking, that her son would happily handle her divorce—from his own father? And what kind of father couldn't seem to care less whether his son acted against him in a divorce settlement?

"Truth is, I'm relieved. I thought she'd get someone better," had been Duncan's only response when Brian asked if he should do it, or if it would come between them and affect things at work. And Brian had laughed at the comment, actually *laughed*, knowing full well that he was a damned good lawyer—and knowing his father knew it too. No doubt this inability to feel things or to articulate feelings in a remotely human manner (a quality Brian sometimes feared he'd inherited) was just one of the reasons his mother had finally had enough of Duncan.

Brian scrabbled at his plate for another fry, only to find he'd already eaten them all. He closed his eyes. For months after the anniversary party, he'd agonized about what to do. Then, still undecided, he'd fled for a "holiday." And now? Now he was back, tanned but not rejuvenated, and still with less than no idea what the right thing to do was.

"That's not true," an inner voice intoned. "You know what to do, you're just a wimp."

When he returned to the airport just before midnight, his luggage, mercy of mercies, was finally ready for him. Even better, no crying women or children blocked his way. He was striding past the cafeteria, suitcase rolling smoothly at his side, when a now-familiar voice stopped him, and he realized he'd thanked luck too soon.

"You don't know how grateful I am." Katelyn had changed out of her fancy pumps into sneakers and was pacing near the airport café's entrance, almost yelling into her cellphone. "Thank you so much. I'll see you soon. *Thank you*," she repeated.

Brian wondered why she was still in the airport after all this time, and caught himself feeling curious about the identity of the recipient of all that gratitude. He gave himself a mental kick. Why should he care?

He was almost at his jeep when he heard fast feet sprinting up behind him. Someone was in a hurry. He stepped to one side, wheeling his suitcase out of their path. To his surprise, the runner didn't bolt past.

"Brian, thank goodness. You're still here."

"Uh huh?"

Under the grimy yellow glow of a nearby street-light, Katelyn looked jaundiced and even more tired and stressed than when they'd spoken earlier. She blinked rapidly and swallowed hard, as if trying to steel herself to do or say whatever was coming next.

"Brian, I . . . " She inhaled deeply. "I do need your help, after all. A ride, if you're still offering."

"I . . ." he started, then looked around. Where were her two appendages, a.k.a. children, not to mention that

22

pathetic excuse for a dog?

Apparently she read his mind. "A friend of mine happened by the cafeteria. She's grabbing a coffee before her flight and agreed to watch the kids and Monster while I chased after you."

Brian opened his mouth to speak, but didn't get a chance.

"I wouldn't bother you," she rushed on, "but that was before I realized there's only one business in this whole forsaken valley with space left for the night. I finally got that sorted, and then, just now, was trying to rent a car, but there are none left, if you can believe it."

She was babbling and Brian struggled to keep up. The first thing out of his mouth wasn't an agreement or a refusal to help, however. It was a ridiculously inane observation that made him cringe even as he made it. "I *can* believe it," he said. "Greenridge is so busy these days with hopes and dreams of natural gas pipelines and a big business boom that the existing infrastructure can't support the influx of people to the area."

Katelyn looked at him blankly.

"Oh, right," he said. "Not really the point. Yes, I can give you a lift. Where to?"

"A little place a bit off the beaten path, I'm afraid. River's Sigh B & B."

Brian gawked at her. "Seriously?"

Katelyn's eyes widened and her voice sharpened with concern. "What? No, don't tell me. Is it a total dive? Is it unsafe in some way?"

Brian shook his head emphatically. "No, nothing like that. Not at all. It's just of all the places you might end up . . . River's Sigh B & B belongs to my brother Callum and his wife Jo."

"No way!"

"Yeah, if you can believe it," he said, unintentionally echoing her earlier words.

"Oh, I can believe it all right," she echo-muttered too. "Greenridge really, really, really is an armpit."

Brian laughed. "Well, I don't know about that, but it is pretty small all right."

"So you know how to get there?"

"As easily as I can find myself in the dark."

She gave him a weird look, apparently finding his wording as awkward as he felt. "Okay, great. And thank you so much. I'll grab Lacey and Sawyer and our gear and we can be off."

His jeep was full to bursting as they headed out of the airport's parking lot and onto the highway. Katelyn's kids, safely secured in the back seat, were oddly quiet to Brian's way of thinking—though he was the first one to admit he was no expert on children. Plus it was after midnight; they were probably asleep with their eyes open. Katelyn was quiet too, leaving Brian to his thoughts and the formulation of some tentative plans.

He'd drop off his unexpected cargo, say hello to Callum and Jo—and maybe talk Callum into letting their parents know he was back, thus stalling his having to see them. There was definitely an advantage to being the baby in a family. Your older siblings happily—or at least routinely—took on responsibilities for you. If only Callum was still practicing law instead of being some baker-slash-bed-and-breakfast-proprietor, Brian bet he could've sweet-talked him into the chore of being their mom's legal counsel, no problem. But then again, though he'd never admit anything as sentimental to Callum, he was happy for him. Not only had his older brother escaped the talons of their father's law firm and the work he'd never enjoyed, he'd somehow found a love that seemed real and enduring. Time would tell whether Jo and Callum would make it over the long haul, but chances looked good. Their relationship didn't inspire Brian though, or give him false hope. They were outliers. Flukes that flew in the face of statistics. Their apparently genuine affection—and made for movies story of unrequited young love that got a second chance years later—did not a rule make.

Still, nice as it would be to see Callum and Jo again, what he was looking forward to most was hunkering down in his own space again. Maybe returning home wasn't the worst thing in the world. His phone buzzed with yet another incoming call, and Brian forgot his plan to leave all communications until the morning. He hit the blue tooth answer button on his dashboard, so he could talk hands-free.

Callum's voice, weirdly intense, blared from the

jeep's speaker. "Brian, your plane got in. I checked. You need to call me back."

"Whoa, big bro, it's not voicemail. I'm here."

"Thank God. Have you been home yet?" Callum still sounded bizarrely on edge.

"Come on man, where's the fire? They lost my luggage, so I went out for dinner before—"

"No, that's just it," Callum interrupted. "There has been a fire. Your whole place is gone."

Katelyn gasped, and from the back seat, Lacey revealed she wasn't asleep after all. "Is the fire at our cabin?" she asked shrilly.

"No, honey," Katelyn said, turning in her seat. "Close your eyes and try to rest. Everything will be okay. This is about Brian—"

"Not cool, Callum. I've got enough to deal with, without one of your lame jokes."

There was a moment of silence. Then Callum spoke again, more calmly. Somehow his lower volume and steadier cadence were more stressful than his panic had been. A hot knife of fear stabbed at Brian's guts.

"I'm not joking. I wish I were. The building went up early this morning, but I only found out about it myself a few hours ago because Jo and I were out in the yard. I called you a billion times. I think Mom and Dad have too."

Brian heard all of Callum's words, but he couldn't comprehend them. He was suddenly acutely conscious of the hum of his tires on the empty highway, Sawyer's heavy breathing in the back seat, and Katelyn's nervous fidgeting beside him. It was as if his brain, unable—or unwilling—to digest the real news, was seeking respite in trivia.

"It doesn't look like anyone was hurt, maybe a few cases of smoke inhalation, but that's pretty much it. We were pretty worried, though, in case you'd caught an earlier flight and were sleeping it off at home. You know how it is—how you're pretty sure someone's okay, but you're not one hundred percent at ease until you touch base."

"Sorry, wait. Can you stop talking a minute? I can't take it in. I have to think."

"Yeah, of course."

Brian noticed his speedometer and was shocked. He had decelerated to a crawl. Good thing there was no one around. He shoulder checked to confirm it, then signaled and pulled over to the side of the road. His knuckles were white on the steering wheel and he tried to relax his grip.

"Why did we stop?" Lacey's voice came again in the closest thing to a whine Brian had heard from her since they met.

"Shush, love. Brian needs a second. We'll be on our way again soon."

"Who's with you?" Callum asked. "Is there someone in your jeep with you?"

"It's a long story." Brian rubbed his face. "I . . . never mind. I'll explain later. What am I going to do? I don't want to stay at the house with Mom, and Dad probably wants to shoot me on sight—"

Callum didn't disagree. "It's already settled. You're staying at River's Sigh in the main house with us. Jo and I have plenty of room."

"But what am I going to do?" Brian was aware he had already asked that and been answered, but for someone usually quick on the draw, he was having a hard time. The conversation felt more like a dream than reality.

"We'll figure it out. Don't worry. Plan to stay with us for as long as you need."

"Okay, okay, thanks." Brian put the jeep back into gear, but kept his foot on the brake.

"When you get here, if we don't come out to greet you right way, just let yourself in. We got a last-minute booking for Spring cabin, some woman in a bind who couldn't get a place anywhere else."

Some woman in a bind. Right. Katelyn. Who, in the strangest of coincidences, was sitting right beside him. Brian shot her a look and she raised her eyebrows, her lips curving in the smallest of wry smiles.

"I'll see you in a bit," he told Callum and ended the call.

Brian sat, engine idling, for another minute. Then he pinched the bridge of his nose, took a deep breath, and slowly returned to the highway. He was homeless. Literally, figuratively, and in pretty much every way a guy possibly could be. *Homeless.* An iron band of sadness wrapped around his chest and squeezed.

Chapter 4

THE KIDS AND MONSTER, EACH completely wiped out by the past twenty-four hours, were still sleeping when Katelyn stepped out of Spring cabin. She left the door ajar so she would hear them if they stirred. A narrow deck wrapped the full perimeter of the skinny three-floored building. She looked up at the rows of tall narrow windows that filled the open concept kitchen and shared living room on the first floor, the bathroom on the middle floor, and the two tiny bedroom nooks on the top floor, with light. It was such an eccentric building, like whoever designed it had wanted his or her own lighthouse. She loved it.

She strolled around the small deck and surveyed her surroundings, which had been invisible to her when they'd arrived after midnight. The early morning air was chilly, bordering on frigid, and the sky was such a pale blue it was almost white.

Katelyn knew she was only a few minutes' walk from other cabins because Jo had pointed them out in the shadows the night before, but she couldn't see a single roofline from where she stood. It was like being alone in the wilderness.

With winter trudging away, sullen and resentful, and spring still non-committal, the yard was pretty dismal. But then Katelyn noticed the sheen. Everything she looked at was silver, from the wooden bench near her cabin's door, to the holly bushes beside the porch, to the bumpy carpet of yet to bloom pansy greenery at her feet.

It was too late in the season for this frost to last long. It was just a pause, a magical moment. The inevitable heat of the day would transform it back into a between seasons wasteland, a place where everything except the massive evergreens appeared withered and dead, as if nothing would ever live or grow from the earth again.

Katelyn descended the three steps from the porch to the ground, feeling, *really feeling*, the temperature. It was nippy against her skin, but no longer seemed frigid. Instead it felt invigorating and full of promise. Even if the barren earth around her didn't know it, if it was patient—and she was too—spring would come again.

A too-long unfamiliar emotion welled up within her. Hope. She walked a few more steps, still marveling at how private the world felt here. Massive cedar trees, most so wide it would take several people holding hands to form a circle around them, stood protecting her cabin, thoroughly sheltering her from any prying eyes.

She lifted her arms out to her sides and spun in a slow wide circle. She just had to hold on. Just had to keep focusing on the new growth, not the hard ground.

She had failed to get herself, Lacey and Sawyer away from Greenridge, away from Steve—but she had a secure place to stay, a bit of money from the sale of her car to hold them over for a few months, and no doubt that her old boss would hire her back. She would keep persevering. One day she would have a safe, permanent home for herself and her children, a place to live and grow and love that wasn't threatened by—or dependent on—the whims of someone else. *She would.*

Something damp and velvet soft nudged the back of Katelyn's knee. She shrieked softly and jumped, instantly startled back to the present. A skinny, gentle-eyed German shepherd looked up at her, then nodded and ambled away, as if she had only wanted to say hello and acknowledge the special moment too.

Katelyn stood stock-still as her breathing and heart rate returned to normal. Then she shook her head, smiling a bit, and headed back into the slumbering cabin to wake the kids and start her day. To her surprise, she found herself thinking the hippy-dippy thought she was always laughingly accusing Janet of: it really was the little things in life that got you through.

She reached the cabin door and stepped inside. While she'd been out, the coffee maker had done its job. The snug cabin was filled with the aroma of freshly brewed dark roast.

What would she do when Steve tracked her to this peaceful haven and had one of his moods? *What?* She'd enjoyed a brief respite while she was outside, but now her anxiety, never far off, attacked hard. She pushed against it just as hard.

She'd had a good morning. And she'd have another soon. And then, eventually, another and another—until it was her actual life.

On the tail of that thought, Lacey yelled from the top of the wrought iron staircase that spiraled up through every level of the cabin, "Mom? *Mom!* Where are you? Sawyer peed the bed again."

What could Katelyn do? She shook her head and had to laugh.

Chapter 5

THE WEAK MORNING SUN STRETCHED through the window and cast faint shadows across the big oak dining room table. Callum refreshed their coffees and settled into a chair beside Brian. "Not a very kind welcome home, hey?"

Brian grunted and Callum hesitated, then pressed on. "I'm sorry about your condo on top of, well, everything else." He waved an arm as if to say there weren't enough words to convey his sympathy. "And about that . . . how are you? Have you come to terms with Mom and Dad now? Are you going to represent her?"

The smell of frying bacon and fresh coffee that seemed so homey moments ago was smothering Brian now, heavy, greasy and laden with obligation to converse. But he didn't want to talk. Callum had worried he was having an emotional breakdown when he'd decided to go walkabout, and he hadn't been able to convince him otherwise.

"I'm fine. We all saw it coming. It should've happened decades ago, saved us all a lot of grief."

Callum took a big swallow of coffee. "I don't know. It was still a shock to me, a sad one. I guess I always hoped they'd figure things out one day and we'd be able to say, 'Ah, so *that's* why they stayed together, so we could learn this or see that.'"

Brian set his mug down too hard, and it clanked against the wooden table. "Well, we did learn something, right?"

"And what's that?"

"What we knew all along. That it's unnatural, unhealthy even, for two people to pledge to stay together forever. It just creates collateral damage—or what some people call children."

Callum shook his head, looking sad. "If that's what you truly think, that it's so natural, so unavoidable, for people to go their separate ways, why are you so broken up about it? And don't think I didn't notice how you avoided answering my question about being Mom's lawyer either."

Brian shoved his chair back from the table and wished he'd taken Jo's offer to eat at the sunny yellow table in their small personal kitchen, not in this big hall where they hosted the B & B guests' meals. He'd thought it would be easier for Jo though, and that there'd be other people around, thus saving him from the third degree. And maybe it did save Jo labor, but he'd been wrong about the last bit entirely.

"Also, if you're so anti-marriage and so vehemently opposed to 'collateral damage,' what on earth are you doing dating a woman with kids?"

"I'm not dating Katelyn. There's nothing going on."

"Yeah, right. I know your nothings," Callum went on, disregarding Brian's body language in the way only a sibling could. "You're never at a shortage for single girls. This Katelyn person has *children*. What if there's still a chance she and the dad could make it work, but you mess it up? Or even if that's not a possibility, you can't waltz in and out of a woman's life when there are kids involved. It's not fair."

No, what wasn't fair was being subjected to Callum's high horse bullshit. If this was what staying here was going to be like, Brian would rather live in the library park under a bench until he found a new place.

"And deprive a pretty maiden in need of rescue of my significant white knight skills? Besides without a place to live, I need something, or someone, to keep me busy," Brian joked, throwing Callum's earlier accusation—that he was a sucker for women with problems—back in his face.

A door clicked behind Brian. Ah, saved by food. He put on a big smile and turned, expecting to see Jo with plates of something delicious. Instead he looked dead into the flushed face of Katelyn Kellerman. She was trembling.

"The kids and I were just coming for breakfast," she said in a clipped tone, Lacey and Sawyer right on her heels. "Jo invited us."

Callum looked uncomfortable for a split second and Brian could almost hear his older brother's thoughts, knowing they matched his own: *Shit. She'd heard them.*

Then Callum's host skills took over. He smiled warmly. "Of course, of course. Have a seat. What'll it be? Waffles or pancakes?"

Katelyn's eyes narrowed.

Sawyer tugged on Lacey's purple shirtsleeve. She leaned her head toward him and he whispered in her ear. She grinned and nodded. "Waffles, please!"

Katelyn looked at her children, then back at Callum, shaking her head the tiniest bit. "Waffles would be lovely," she said.

Brian felt himself nod in sync with Callum. Relief. If she'd heard the conversation, she wasn't going to make a big deal of it.

"And do you guys like strawberries and whipping cream?" Callum asked.

"Yes, very much," Lacey announced, and Sawyer nodded like his goal was to make his head fall off his skinny neck.

Then Callum asked them if they liked dogs or swing sets and when he got affirmatives to both, he asked Katelyn's permission to introduce them to the property's pets after he let Jo know their breakfast requests.

Katelyn looked unsure, while the kids beamed at her with excited, imploring eyes that suggested they were jumping up and down inside, though they kept still and remained quiet. Weirdly quiet or good kid quiet? It was hard for Brian to know. "I guess that'd be all right," she finally said. "I'll enjoy a cup of coffee before we eat."

They took off without waiting another second, following Callum closely, listening intently to his descriptions of the dogs and what they liked. Just before the door shut behind them, Brian heard Lacey ask if she could go get their dog so it could be friends with the other dogs. The second they were gone, Katelyn stabbed Brian with dagger-eyes.

"Whatever you told your brother about me and my life or who I am to you, I want to be clear—"

"I didn't tell him anything. I said I just met you, randomly, out of the blue, and that you needed a ride so I gave you one. I explained that our showing up together was all a big coincidence."

"But he doesn't believe you?"

"No." Brian tried to make light of it. "He feels it's his duty to protect the fairer sex from me."

"I don't need protecting. And while I'm grateful for the ride—the ride I know I asked for, after being kind of rude to you—I'm not looking for a 'white knight.' I don't need to be rescued or helped. I don't need or want a man in my life."

Brian nodded and cursed the humiliation burning in his cheeks. "Uh, that was a badly timed joke. I was poking fun at Callum, not saying anything serious about you."

Katelyn's rosy lips flattened into a thin line, and Brian's gut churned. Why on earth was he noticing her mouth of all things right now anyway? Maybe Callum's lectures weren't totally out to lunch—or maybe this was actually Callum's fault. Brian hadn't been thinking of Katelyn much at all, let alone as date potential, until Callum had planted the stupid idea.

"And," Katelyn continued in an icy whisper, after shooting a glance at the door to make sure they were still alone, "I'm not getting back with my ex, ever. Period. Not that it's any of your or Callum's business, but we've been legally separated for two years. So yeah, if you and your brother could butt out of my life, I'd really appreciate it."

Brian hated that something in his stomach dropped at the information that she was separated, not divorced—but he also felt of twinge of defensiveness on Callum's behalf. "I know how it must seem, but please don't hold it against me—or Callum. And don't worry. It's an older brother thing. If you weren't around, he'd be giving me dire warnings about something else. He feels I'm incapable of managing my own affairs."

Katelyn shot him another sharp look.

"Wrong choice of words. No pun intended." Brian held his hands up as if in surrender—but then he winked. He couldn't resist.

She almost smiled, then picked up the ceramic pitcher of cream and poured a generous amount into an empty mug.

"I know it sounded like he was being totally judgmental and making some massive assumptions about you, but I promise, he's a good guy. He won't bother you or meddle or pry." Why Brian felt he had to reassure her of that, he wasn't sure. Her smile deepened though, revealing a dimple, and he realized he'd made a good call.

"Okay," she said finally. "Sorry. You must think I'm a complete psycho, especially when yesterday would've turned into a nightmare in every way if not for your kindness."

Brian grabbed another generous helping of bacon. "Not at all. And I apologize for the misunderstanding. I know you're not looking for a rescuer or whatever, and I promise I wasn't coming on to you—and I won't. Despite what my family always thinks about me, I'm not a huge womanizer. In fact, I'm thinking of taking a break from dating, period."

"Really? Why?"

Yes, *why*? Good question, but perhaps an even better one would be why had he blurted details about his personal life to this stranger?

The door clicked behind him again, and he was rescued.

"Sorry that took me so long," Jo said, reentering the room. "I was on phone duty—oh, good morning, Katelyn. Callum said you and the kids were ready for breakfast, but I didn't know if you'd gone outside with them for a few minutes or not."

Jo set a coffee carafe and a bowl of sliced oranges down in front of them. Her gaze touched on Katelyn, then rested on Brian. A question creased her brow—then quickly smoothed. Not before Brian's face heated, though. He realized the unspoken observation she'd made. There were almost twenty chairs scattered around the huge table, yet Katelyn had taken the chair next to him and was seated so close their thighs were practically touching. He opened his mouth, then shut it again. There was nothing to explain, but trying to say that would only make it seem like there was.

Katelyn didn't seem to notice Jo's scrutiny. "No worries, Jo. I just walked in. In fact, the kids—"

Whatever Katelyn had been about to say about the kids was cut off by their noisy return.

"Mom, mom!" Lacey yelled. "Monster doesn't totally hate Jo and Callum's dog, Hoover. He even let him sniff him for a second. And Jo has a sister named Sam, who's on a holiday, but her dog stays here when she's away—and Sam's dog is named Dog!"

Both kids broke into hysterical giggles, showing they thought "Dog" was the most hilarious name for a dog ever—something Brian considered odd since their own couldn't-hurt-a-flea, mouse-sized mutt went by the unlikely moniker of Monster. He'd never really understood dog people. While they were preoccupied by their mirth, Katelyn stretched her hand out toward Brian's beneath the table. "Let's start fresh," she

40

whispered. "I've been weird from the second you met me, but I'd like to be friends. Can we be?"

Brian laughed. This wasn't necessarily any less weird, but it would be nice to have an uncomplicated friendship for once. He gripped her hand obligingly and they shook on it. "Sounds like a plan. Nice to meet you, pal."

Katelyn's gray eyes warmed at his corniness, shining like slate kissed by the sun. Brian grinned back.

A throat cleared behind him. Jo was there, holding out a plate of buttery waffles. Brian hadn't even noticed his sister-in-law had left and reappeared again. Where was his head?

Chapter 6

KATELYN WOUND THE LANDLINE'S CURLY black cord around her wrist, then unwound it, then wound it again as she paced back and forth in the cabin's small living room. Her lawyer Marilee's next words made her heart thump so hard it physically hurt.

"You need to call Steve and let him know where you and the kids are, especially if he has some new bee in his bonnet. You don't want to give him any further ammunition for his ludicrous 'she's trying to kidnap my children' complaint."

Katelyn tried to take a deep breath, then fixed her sight on Lacey and Sawyer playing outside the window on the lawn. They were throwing a yellow and blue ball for an old bristle brush of a dog, while Monster looked on with wary excitement, his whole body twitching. That worked. She felt calmer.

"No judge in the world will fall for that. The signed letter of permission might not give me a legal right to take my kids on a trip in the face of the existing court order, but it does show that Steve not only knew about my plan, he was fine with it."

"I agree. He's just tormenting you, but all the same, you need to keep your end of communications with him above reproach. No angry text responses. No bitter outbursts. Nothing that can be construed as argumentative or uncooperative or that makes it look like you're trying to keep him from the kids."

"I know, I know. We're co-parenting. Some contact is inevitable. I get it, I do. It's just . . . I find him really hard to deal with."

Marilee sighed. "I know. And maybe that's the silver lining here. When we go to court we can ask for an order specifying how he's allowed to contact you, limiting him to text or e-mail, whichever you're more comfortable with, but until we have a court order saying otherwise, you're going to have to manage."

Katelyn nodded and closed her eyes. The white-yellow rays coming through the narrow windows felt searing, not comforting. "He won't really get it, will he? They won't give him part custody. They *can't.*"

Marilee sighed again and her voice grew forced, as if she didn't want to speak, but had to. "Honestly, Katelyn, it's so unusual nowadays to not have shared custody that barring some unbelievable event, I, well, I don't want to falsely raise your hopes."

"I . . . I understand. Thanks. I'll call him now."

Katelyn hung up without saying good-bye, keeping her eyes closed. It was pointless to rehash everything with Marilee who already knew—in ways that Katelyn was only just learning—how backwards and unfair the judicial system seemed. She knew this ultimate "respect" for both parents' "rights" was intended to correct past wrongs—to make amends for when the courts had, perhaps, too easily and too quickly severed parental rights and separated families. But now it almost seemed like they protected adults over children. No, Steve had never hit Lacey or Sawyer. Yes, he'd always kept a roof over their heads and food in the fridge. But he'd sure as heck hit Katelyn—and worse, he'd controlled and ruled every moment of her and the kids' everyday life. What kind of "unbelievable event" was needed? Did he have to actually kill Katelyn before they'd say, "Hey, maybe this guy shouldn't be parenting?"

Because of things she'd been able to prove initially—his heavy drinking, drug use and a history of battery—she'd been granted full custody, but he had unsupervised overnight weekend access because he had not, or so his lawyer argued and the court had agreed, hurt his children or shown he'd be a threat to them. If anything, the reverse was true. He was invested and concerned about them to a fault. He'd also been more than cooperative about taking the court ordered anger management and domestic violence classes, bowing his head as if momentarily overcome when the judge issued the order, then lifting his chin and humbly expressing gratitude for the "help."

And now, with enough time elapsed and enough smarmy assurances that he was "not the same man anymore," that he fully understood the ramifications of his past actions, that he no longer used any type of drugs "recreationally" (his favorite defense), she'd been notified that he was petitioning the courts for a new shared custody agreement—and, whether she could fathom it or not, he might succeed, which meant he'd have them a minimum of forty percent of the time, maybe even fifty. That's why she'd wanted to go on an extended visit to Janet's, with the aim of getting an apartment and a job once she was there. She had hoped that being out of sight would put her out of his mind. She knew it made her a bad person to wish him on anyone else, but sometimes she prayed he'd find a new woman to fixate on, a new relationship to obsess over. Or that he'd die in a car accident or something. The kids would be sad, but maybe at the end of the day it would be . . . better.

"I just don't get it. Why now? *Why now?*" she had moaned to Marilee when she'd first contacted her about the letter she'd received from Steve's counsel two months earlier.

"He, as you know too well, doesn't want to let you go. Since none of his other tactics have worked, he has decided that the work of taking care of his children half-time might be worth it because it's the one thing you won't be able to do: let them go. He probably thinks you'll go back to him just so they're not alone with him. Or that's my best guess about whatever he's thinking anyway."

Katelyn agreed with her lawyer's "best guess," and she'd marveled at Steve's canniness, though hadn't been surprised by it. At one time, just the threat of him gaining custody would've worked, would've gotten her to try again. But no longer. Just like how she never wasted time (anymore) almost wishing he'd hurt her really badly, in some way that couldn't be explained away, so the courts had to remove the kids from him and never risk putting them back with him. She had healed to a point where she knew she could successfully break herself and her kids free. She was playing a long game, yes, but she was playing to win. Eventually he'd grow tired or disinterested—or the kids would get to an age where they had the power to choose where they lived for themselves.

She chanted her mantra for strength under her breath, "Don't quit, don't give in, be yourself, believe in love." Then she opened her eyes, walked to the living room's bay window and tapped on the glass.

Lacey and Sawyer looked up. "I. Love. You," she said in sign language, something Lacey had learned in school and taught both her and Sawyer. Her kids grinned, signed back, and returned to their tireless delight in playing fetch.

Katelyn called Steve.

Chapter 7

BRIAN FELT SICK WITH EVERYTHING he'd seen the past hour or two and he wanted to talk to someone. Plus he needed to rip off the bandage and get calling his mom over with. Perhaps he could nail two birds with one stone. With that hopeful thought, he paced Jo and Callum's living room, phone to ear, listening to his mother's number ring.

"Hello?" Caren sounded vaguely confused, like she'd heard a noise but hadn't quite figured out what it was.

Brian had been increasingly sure he'd be sent to voicemail, so he was startled when she answered and fumbled for something to say.

"Hello?" Caren repeated.

"Hey, Mom. It's me. Brian."

There was a pause, then Caren's voice took on a bit more life. "Brian! Hello—took you long enough to call. You've been back a while now."

Brian opened his mouth to object, but realized he couldn't. She was right. He wanted to say, "Well, you know the old saying, time flies when you're having a shitty time," but what came out was, "Yeah, sorry about that. I've been busy getting things sorted with the fire and everything."

Caren inhaled sharply. "Yes, I was horrified by the news. It could've been worse though. Thank goodness you're safe."

That was very true, but Brian didn't find it comforting. "Yeah . . . anyway, I'm just calling to say I missed you while I was gone. We should get together for a visit." *And also, phones work both ways.*

"That would be lovely. I look forward to it—no hurry though. If you're swamped with little details, I understand. I can wait."

Brian lowered the phone from his ear, stared at it like it was an alien device, then lifted it back into place. "Okay, great. I thought maybe you'd be impatient to know my plans regarding your divorce proceedings or whatever."

"Actually, I've been busy with work and haven't let it distract me too much."

Brian shook his head and wished he'd been able to be so nonchalant about it. "Look," he blurted. "I totally support your decision, totally get why you want to end it, but I can't represent you. I just can't. He's my dad, my *dad* and my *boss*."

"And you feel it would be uncomfortable?"

There was another brief pause.

"Yes, Mom. I feel it would be 'uncomfortable,' to say the very least."

"Oh, Brian, I'm sorry. I didn't think . . . You should've said so from the very beginning—and you're right, a visit is exactly what we need. How about lunch sometime next week?"

Brian nodded numbly. "Sounds great. Okay."

"Good, we'll talk more then. Meanwhile, do you need anything? A place to stay, money to tide you over?"

"No, no, I'm good."

"Right then . . . just let me know if that changes."

Brian couldn't believe he'd been dumb enough to hope his mom would be a possible sounding board. He ended the Twilight Zone of a phone call and spent the rest of the morning trying to read, but for the first time ever, he couldn't concentrate on a book. Next he wandered the various paths surrounding River's Sigh, hoping to burn off his anger and malaise, but it didn't work very well. What he needed was a run—but he simultaneously felt too drained to summon up the energy for that. Instead, he plunked down on a huge white rock near one of Jo's perennial beds that lined a trail leading to the cabins furthest from the main house. The bed had been weeded and prepped for warm weather growth, too early and too optimistically. It was mostly cold dirt, with only odd bits of green poking through here and there.

Callum and Jo had left, thank God, for a bank appointment right around the time he'd returned from viewing his destroyed condo and called his mom, so he had a bit of time to try to process things and get a grip.

He pushed his fists into his eyes. He'd been sick with loss and dread ever since Callum gave him the bad news, but he'd still been unprepared for the shock of seeing the aftermath of the fire firsthand—which made him realize too late that a part of him hadn't truly believed he'd lost *everything*. Now, though his brain still reeled, he knew better. He knew fully. Half the building was gone—the half that had housed his home. Just *gone*. The condos on the left side were opened up for the world to view, like an angry giant had slid an evil blade into the seam between the units' outer wall and the burning hallway and cut everything away, drywall, insulation, framing and all.

The strangely revealed spaces were smoke and water damaged, but otherwise intact. One couch, bizarrely, had a book turned face down on its arm, like its reader had merely hopped up to grab a snack and would be right back. For some reason, that image really got to him.

Because of the ongoing investigation and probable structural damage, even the remaining units were off bounds, possibly forever. As he and the other displaced souls tread the outskirts of the safety tape barricade, he couldn't imagine which was harder: knowing, as he did, that there was nothing left, or seeing a semblance of your home standing, as if waiting for you, but not knowing what, if anything at all, you'd be able to salvage.

When Brian overheard some officious looking person trying to calm an increasingly hysterical woman who he recognized as his neighbor from two doors down, he strode back to his jeep and left abruptly, feeling all too much like he might join her in falling apart.

His condo, his house, his *home*—totally destroyed. And the worst bit? That he couldn't adequately explain to anyone how much it sucked because he'd always made such a big deal of being "footloose and fancy-free" to quote his dad, or "not in a hurry to grow up," to quote his mom, which was mildly insulting. Good grief, he was thirty-years-old, had a career, and made good money. It wasn't like he was living in her basement, smoking spliffs, and playing endless hours of video games. Even his brothers always made a big deal about his perpetually single status, asking him when he was going to get tied down instead of just tied up—har, har, har.

But what did his family expect? Of course, he'd never blathered on about how much he loved his place, enjoyed collecting things, and took pleasure in decorating—and not, as his old friend Dave would've said, just to create a good place to get laid. Privately, in his own head, as embarrassing as it was, he'd always considered his home a nest, this totally safe place where he could just . . . be.

Neon threads and lines waved against the black background of his mind's eye. He'd find a new place, of course. And he had good insurance, so financially he'd make out all right. He was always careful with details like that. But it hurt. It hurt a lot. Especially coming as it did, so closely after accepting the hard truth about his parents. It made the loss feel cataclysmic.

That puzzled him too—the continuing extremity of his grief about his parents. But Callum's latest words on the subject had triggered some clarity. Duncan and Caren were never going to get their act together or learn to love each other properly. Somehow, maybe because they'd hung in there and tried to make it work for so long, ending the marriage now made everything they'd suffered as a family seem extra pointless. It was almost like their divorce hurt more now that he was an adult and no longer expecting it. Maybe if they'd split when he was a teenager, he would've been like, "Dudes, so called it," and just shrugged it off.

Abruptly, the yard quieted. Brian hadn't even been aware of the birds calling and chattering around him until they suddenly weren't. From the direction of the main house, a crunch of heavy tires on gravel broke the new silence. Simultaneously, from behind a row of towering cedars, came the sound of a cabin door opening.

Seconds later, Katelyn, oblivious to Brian's presence, appeared from behind one of the big tree trunks. She stood on the path, shielding her eyes from the sun with one hand, and stared toward the driveway.

The rumbling of the approaching vehicle grew louder. Katelyn moved in quick jerky steps toward the parking area. Something about her gait, as uneasy as the silent birds in the treetops, made Brian climb to his feet and follow her.

"Hey," he said softly.

She looked startled, then gave a small nod and returned her focus to the driveway.

Just as they reached it together, a shiny red extended cab with all the bells and whistles rolled up and lurched to stop ignorantly close to Katelyn. She took a step back and gave no greeting to the large guy who climbed down from the driver's seat. She stood to his mid chest, maybe, and he probably had a hundred pounds on her petite frame. If Brian hadn't already guessed, the flint glinting in her eyes would've given it away. This was the ex.

As Brian made the connection, the guy noticed him. Something almost imperceptible changed in the way he was carrying himself. His shoulders softened and he shrugged a little, his head bobbing in a friendly manner. He stuck his hand out. "Hi, I'm Steve."

Brian clasped the proffered hand and shook it warmly. "Nice to meet you. I'm Brian." Inside his head, he muttered, *You can't play a player, Stevie-boy.*

"So how do you know my wife, old friends or something? I sure appreciate you helping her out the other night. A real life saver." Steve's face was open and his tone was jovial and casual, but Brian didn't miss how Katelyn inched another step back. Or how the idiot still referred to her as his wife. Any urge he had to be a smartass or give ol' Steve something to be jealous of died before it was born.

He shook his head. "I dated a friend of hers back in high school. It's a total fluke we met at the airport and were going to the same place." Brian gestured at Jo and Callum's house behind him. Steve's eyes narrowed as he took in the home's cobalt blue door, old-fashioned multi-paned windows and cedar sided charm.

Brian continued, "Well, she's in a guest cottage, of course. This is my brother's spread. I'm staying with him and my sister-in-law for a bit because my place burned down."

Steve's eyes widened and his head jerked a little. "Whoa, no shit? You had a condo in that building that went up in smoke?"

Brian couldn't help but notice Steve's voice carried more lurid curiosity than sympathy.

"If that was me, if it was *my* place that got torched?" Steve shook his head and let out a low whistle. "I'd find the little bastard responsible and make him pay. No one messes with what's mine. You know what I mean?"

Brian nodded. He did know what Steve meant. Knew exactly.

Chapter 8

AS THE THREE OF THEM walked toward Spring cabin together, Katelyn looked back and forth between Steve and Brian and listened to their small talk with growing distress. Stony resignation hardened in her stomach, weighing her down, squashing her voice, making her mute. Everyone bought Steve's act. He could just seem so . . . down to earth, like such an everyday normal person. She wanted to scream. And weep. She knew his wide-eyed concern was an act. Steve didn't care about what happened to anyone except in relation to how it affected him. In fact, he'd no doubt find some way to resent the condo fire because it had brought her into contact with Brian.

When they reached the cabin steps, Brian and Steve's bizarre long-lost best friend conversation wound down, but Brian surprised her by not saying good-bye. Instead, looking all shamefaced and embarrassed, he shuffled his feet and asked, "Is it okay if I still come in, like we talked about? I can't believe I locked myself out of the house. What an idiot!"

Brian was inviting himself into the cabin to keep

her and Steve company! She could hardly believe it.

"You've got a lot on your mind, buddy," Steve said kindly. "Don't be too hard on yourself, but if you don't mind, I need to talk with Katelyn alone for a bit."

"We can talk in the kitchen. He won't disturb us. If anything, he'll distract the kids—and what if it rains? He'll get soaked if he stays out here." Katelyn could've kicked herself. Brian had sounded so casual, so perfect, so just right—and she was a babbling mess of nerves. Steve would see through the ruse in a red hot second.

Except he didn't. He came in and firmed up the plans for his weekend with the kids—which could've been done over the phone. This was just a power play, a way of him proving yet again that he could have access to her, via the children, pretty much anytime he wanted.

He finally left, though not before giving Brian a solid cuff to the shoulder and saying, "Thanks again for helping out my family, buddy. Takes a village and all that. I hate the idea of Kiki being all alone in the middle of the night with our two kids. She's just a little woman, you know? Anything could happen."

Katelyn bit her bottom lip, hard. Brian rubbed his shoulder and shrugged as if to say his "help" was nothing. His expression was friendly but blank, and if he'd heard the threat in Steve's words that Katelyn did, she couldn't read it on his face. "Good to meet you too," he said.

When Steve's truck engine rumbled to life outside, Brian finally looked at her. "*Kiki*?"

Katelyn glanced past the kitchen's breakfast bar to the tiny living room; the kids were absorbed in a cartoon. She forced a small grin and hoped she didn't look as close to vomiting as she felt. "I know. Awful, right?"

"Well, not for a kitten or a bird or a very small child, maybe."

Their eyes locked and somehow she didn't feel like she had to joke or brush the comment away. "Yep, pretty much," she said.

"Who's your lawyer?" he asked.

Why on earth was he asking that? Katelyn wondered. "Marilee Weston."

He nodded slowly. "Good," he said at last. "She's good."

A beat later, still neither of them had moved.

"Okay, right . . . " Brian clapped his hands together like he'd come to some decision. "I should split too. I have a ton of stuff to do."

"Yes, of course. Me too."

Katelyn trailed after him to the door, then stopped as he opened it. The bright sun framed his broad shoulders and lit the ends of his hair with gold. Damn. All he needed was a white horse and he *was* a stinking knight. A sigh of mingled desire and sadness quaked through her. The desire part was obvious, look at him! As for the sadness . . . well, what good did it do to

entertain stupid romantic fantasies? She had no time—
and no heart—for any potential risk.

He turned back to her, like she'd spoken aloud.
"What?"

"I . . ." She shook her head. "Nothing." But she
couldn't refrain from asking the question gnawing at
her. Brian had seemed to buy Steve's act, so—

"Why did you do that?"

"Do what?"

"Volunteer to witness a potentially super awkward
confrontation?"

Brian winked and for a second Katelyn felt like the
girl she used to be, like she was answering the door at
Janet's house and should be calling her to come
downstairs, but instead was standing there jelly-legged
and totally enthralled. "What do mean? You were
doing me a favor. I locked myself out of Jo and
Callum's, remember?"

He jogged down the steps and headed along the
trail toward the big house. All Katelyn could do was
shake her head, a sudden realization leaving her
stunned. She'd endured an encounter with Steve, and
in its aftermath, only minutes later, she was hardly
thinking about him at all. Instead she was smiling like
a fool at the departing—very attractive—back of a
totally different man altogether.

Chapter 9

ON ONE HAND, KATELYN COULDN'T believe she'd been at River's Sigh with the kids for a week already. On the other hand, they'd settled into the little cabin so quickly and completely, she couldn't believe they hadn't been there for months. Smiling at the thought, and grateful that the deluge of spring rain had let up for a bit, she removed the final heavy plastic tote from the backseat of the new-to-her Honda, a steal of a deal that she still couldn't quite believe she'd been lucky enough to get, and settled it on the ground beside the others.

She wasn't winded when she finished hefting the seven containers into the big dining hall, but she could feel the workout she'd given her biceps.

When she pulled the lid off the first container, the sound grabbed Lacey and Sawyer's attention. They sprang up from the tower of blocks they'd been building and ran over.

"Can we see too?"

"Absolutely, but no touching unless you go and wash your hands."

Jo and a young platinum blonde carrying a toddler on her hip came through the big swinging door from the kitchen just as Katelyn was unrolling the first bolt of vibrant cotton.

"This is going to be like Christmas," Jo exclaimed, taking in the print's mermaids, anchors, sailing ships and other antique marine things.

Katelyn grinned. That's how she always felt when she hauled out her fabric collection too.

"It reminds me of vintage tattoo art. I love it." The blonde leaned in to look more closely, and Katelyn was struck by how much she resembled Jo. She even had the same wild curls, though Jo's were much darker—a coppery honey to the girl's white gold.

The toddler seemed equally enthused and reached toward a ship.

"No touching, sweetie. Just looking," the young mom said and stepped back from the table.

"It is pretty cool, hey?" Katelyn agreed and stuck out her hand. "I'm Katelyn, by the way."

The toddler grabbed her hand before anyone else could, making all three adult women laugh.

"I'm Jo's niece, Aisha," the blonde said, "And my quick with the greeting daughter is Mo."

Mo was still holding Katelyn's hand and shaking it energetically. "Hi, Mo. Nice to meet you." This seemed to satisfy Mo's apparent need for acknowledgement and she dropped Katelyn's hand and squirmed in Aisha's arms to be let down. Aisha obliged and Mo wobble-sprinted toward the block tower, which captured both Lacey and Sawyer's attention. They galloped after her.

There was a loud crash and a chortle of manic toddler glee.

Oh no, please don't freak out, Katelyn begged her kids in her head. It could go either way.

Aisha was at the trio's side in a heartbeat. "I'm so sorry," she was saying. "It's Mo's favorite game. She doesn't play with a lot of other kids yet."

Lacey shrugged. "It's okay. Sawyer always used to do that too."

Sawyer was equally philosophical. "Yes, because I was also a baby before."

Mo looked around, as if trying to find the baby of which he spoke.

"We can build another tower for her to knock down, if you want," Lacey offered.

"Mo would love that. She adores big kids," Aisha said. "Thank you."

Lacey and Sawyer smiled with pride, then Lacey took charge and proceeded to issue commands regarding how the tower was to be rebuilt.

"Lacey reminds me of me," Aisha said, rejoining Katelyn and Jo.

Katelyn withdrew a second bolt of cotton: ivory like the first, but this time adorned only with swirling navy waves and sea foam.

"Okay, this one is awesome too," Aisha enthused.

"I knew the second she asked if she could use the dining hall, and said what for, that you wouldn't want to miss it," Jo said.

Aisha agreed heartily. "And not that I'm stalking you, but your suitcase collection is fantastic."

Katelyn cocked her head, and Jo was quick to explain. "Aisha does all the housekeeping for our cabins. She tidied up the morning after you arrived—before we knew you were extending your stay and would take care of your own cleaning."

Katelyn grinned. "That was you? Well, thanks. I thought it was a cleaning fairy or something."

"And Jo says you're a seamstress, that you make most of your own clothes?"

Before Katelyn could answer, Aisha continued in a rush. "Sorry, sorry, I'm probably being overwhelming. Also, Jo doesn't talk about you incessantly or anything, I promise. It's just that I want to run my own shop, an upcycling place, someday. I'm insanely curious whenever I meet people who do bespoke work or a lot of crafting or refurbishing or refinishing or whatever."

Jo shook her head at Aisha, but her fondness for her niece was obvious. Katelyn burst out laughing. She couldn't help it. "Wow, you actually remind me of Lacey, too."

A crash of blocks and three thrilled screams punctuated Katelyn's comment.

"Do you want to help me lay everything out?"

Katelyn asked.

Jo and Aisha both squealed, so Katelyn assumed they shared her idea of fun. "I sure appreciate you letting me use the dining room table, Jo."

"No problem. Do you have everything out of your storage unit now?"

Yet again, Katelyn didn't get a chance to answer. The main door bumped open and Brian entered, a large box in his arms.

"Oh, hey, if it isn't my scrumptious sister-in-law," he said cheerily, then nodded at Aisha and Katelyn. "And her equally scrumptious cohorts."

Even knowing he was just joking around, Katelyn was tongue-tied.

"I'm more like a minion," Aisha replied.

"Hello, silliest brother-in-law," Jo said. "What do you have there?"

Brian raised an eyebrow and purred in an exaggeratedly seductive voice. "*Sexiest* brother-in-law, hey? Jo, Jo, Jo, I honestly never knew you felt that way."

"Idiot," she said, smiling.

Brian grinned. "Now there's a description I'm more familiar with." He hooked a chair leg with his foot, pulled it away from the table, and lowered the box onto it.

"Books and DVDs" he said, suddenly serious. "About the only thing that's looking up. I happened across a Buy and Sell post meant for me. Some guy's moving overseas and we have similar tastes, apparently. This," he motioned at the box, "doesn't remotely replace what I've lost, but at least I have some of my favorites back."

Jo couldn't be much more than a couple years older than Brian, but she reached up and ruffled his hair like he was Lacey's age. "Well, that's something, right?"

"Yeah." Brian looked around, then plunked down in a seat beside his books. "What's all this? Have you finally found the solution to your bedding dilemma?"

Jo slapped a hand over her mouth and stared at Katelyn. "Oh. My. Goodness. I can't believe I didn't think of it myself. I've been boring Callum and Brian with my complaining all week!"

Katelyn lifted a questioning eyebrow.

"Oh, totally. *Of course*," Aisha agreed.

Katelyn's brow arched higher.

"Will you sew the bedding and curtains I need for our newest cabins? Callum and Brian's oldest brother, Cade, renovated them last summer, but I'm just doing the final touches now. Coho has three bedrooms, one with a queen-sized bed, one with a double and one with three sets of bunk beds. Sockeye's smaller, just one bedroom with a king."

"I, well—"

Brian commenced sorting through his new finds, tuning out of the conversation.

Jo looked stricken. "I'm sorry, I'm not trying to be pushy. You don't have to, of course. It's just I can tell I'll adore anything you come up with. I want each cabin to be unique, not feel like a hotel, you know?"

Katelyn recalled the glimpses she'd had of various cabins so far: Tiny, picturesque Minnow with its equally tiny deck, housing a huge black rocking chair that called for you to sit and dream a while. Rainbow with its whimsical twisted-wood porch and tinkling wind chime made from copper wire, colored glass and antique silver spoons. Super posh Silver and roomy Chinook with its private park of a yard. And the one she called her own: fairy tale worthy Spring with its three small floors and spiral staircase. Each place almost defied the label "cabin"—at least to her.

"I totally know what you mean, Jo," she said. "Each one's a special little home."

Jo beamed. "Thank you. That's exactly what I aim for."

"And you nail it," Aisha affirmed.

Katelyn pressed her clenched fist to her mouth. What must it be like to get to be part of a family, a place, like this? To never have to leave? "I'd be honored to make coordinating bedding and linens for your new cabins, if you're serious."

"Hooray! I'll pay you, of course, or we can take it off your rent so we'll both save."

"Won't Sam have a cow about you decorating without her?" Aisha asked.

Jo laughed. "Normally, I'd say yes, but I think we're safe. She's a lot more mellow now that she's married, with Charlie keeping her so happy in—"

"Gross," Aisha interrupted. "Whatever you were about to add, just remember, he's my dad. And it doesn't matter that she's my birth mom. It still feels like she's the other woman."

Jo laughed again. "A fact she no doubt loves. I was going to say *keeping her so happy in warm tropical places* and gallivanting off to writers' conferences."

Katelyn took in Jo and Aisha's banter with amused curiosity. Sam was Aisha's birth mom, but she'd just married Aisha's dad? There was definitely a story there. She didn't get a chance to ask about it though; Jo's face was transformed by another "I just had an idea" expression.

"What?" she asked.

Jo looked startled. "I'm that easy to read?"

Katelyn nodded.

"I don't want you to feel any pressure."

"Don't believe her. She wants you to feel at least *some* pressure," Aisha said.

Jo shrugged and grinned.

"*What?*" Katelyn said again.

"Greenridge's annual Spring Fling Business Fair is coming up. Its theme is A Blast From the Past."

"Uh huh?" Katelyn asked at the same moment Aisha said, "Oh, *I* see where you're going with this. I approve, I approve."

"And I was wondering," Jo continued, "if I paid for the fabric and for your time, if you'd mind making us all matching fifties dresses, like you, me, Aisha, Lacey and Mo. Just for fun. I mean, I'll run the booth, but maybe the dresses could have our logo? Callum's building a mini cabin for a display too."

Katelyn didn't reply. Instead she tore through the box in front of her at a quicker pace.

"So is that a . . . " Jo's voice petered out hopefully.

Katelyn looked up, but continued her frantic rummaging. "Oh, sorry—yes. A huge yes!" Her eyes lit on the subject of her search and she whooped in victory. "In fact, I have just the material."

She pulled out four bundles, each featuring bright red cherries with little brown stems, but on different solid backgrounds: turquoise, black, sunshine yellow and a soft pink.

"Oh, those are perfect!" Jo said. "This is so exciting."

Aisha chattered on too, and another wave of wistfulness washed over Katelyn. This must be sort of what it felt like to have sisters.

Across the room, Lacey yelled in a horrified tone, "Baby Mo fell asleep, just like that!"

They all looked over. Sure enough, Mo had zonked out, somehow managing to look comfortable and peaceful, despite the fact she was practically lying on top of a pile of wooden blocks.

"Oops, I guess it's naptime," Aisha said wryly, going to fetch Mo. "Can I pop by Spring for a visit?" she asked Katelyn on her way back across the room.

"Oh, please do!" Katelyn said, then felt a little embarrassed by her exuberance and added shyly, "I'd really enjoy that, and so would the kids."

"Is there a specific time that works better than another, like does Lacey have school or anything?"

Katelyn stammered, "No, er, well, she would normally, but I thought we were going on an . . . extended holiday. She's bright and we worked ahead. Her teacher said she'll be fine to enroll in grade three next September."

"Nice! I would've done anything to skip school when I was her age."

Jo shook her head, but Katelyn could tell Aisha was just being nice, trying to normalize the unusual circumstances.

"Okay then. We'll have coffee," Aisha promised and inched toward the door, Mo slumped and snoring in her arms.

A phone rang loudly from the office, next door to the dining room. Jo nodded toward it. "Well, that's my cue. Feel free to use this room as long as you want. We can chat about the sewing projects in detail another time."

Katelyn thought she might burst with gratitude as Jo, Aisha and Mo left the room. How kind they were.

"Now we can build a tower and not knock it down," Sawyer announced.

"You said it," Lacey agreed.

Brian had been so quiet for the sewing conversation that Katelyn would've forgotten his presence altogether—except that every so often she caught the lightest whiff of some yummy cologne that made her temperature rise. Now he laughed out loud and turned to Katelyn. "You probably already know this, but your kids are hilarious."

For some reason, his casual comment made Katelyn mist up. She swallowed hard and studied the DVDs closest to her to hide her emotion. How easily this virtual stranger observed and commented on her kids' good qualities. Steve would've yelled for her to shut them up several times already. But she didn't want to think about that right now.

She cleared her throat awkwardly and said the first thing that popped into her brain. "Miss Congeniality?"

Brian Archer, flirt and joker that he was, surprised her by blushing. Actually *blushing*. Then he picked up the stack of movies topped by the Sandra Bullock feature and fanned the titles. A whole assortment of romantic comedies met her eye.

"I don't know why I like them so much. It's a sickness."

"A disease even. They're so unrealistic and dumb—and completely predictable."

Brian's eyebrow lifted, a look Katelyn was already starting to consider quintessential Brian. "So you love them too?" he asked.

"Totally."

They both laughed, then Brian's face grew thoughtful, like he was pondering something.

"The scenery's great out here in the boonies, but the nightlife sucks," he finally said.

"Oh, yeah?"

"*Totally*. It's terrible. *Completely predictable.*" He shook his head, but the crinkle by his eyes gave him away. He thought it was the furthest thing from terrible and he was mimicking her on purpose. "Anyway, I was planning to hole up with a movie or two tonight. I could come by after the kids are in bed and we could watch one together. If you want."

"That would be very nice . . . thank you." Katelyn nodded, and, to her utter humiliation, her face heated and she knew she was probably bright pink. She *did* want. But she stopped that thought right there before she got too carried away, dwelling on all the details her "want" might involve. Evenings felt long when you were a single parent. That was the only reason she was excited about the prospect of Brian coming over— because adult company would break the monotony. It had nothing to do with the way he filled a shirt, had laugh lines she wanted to trace with her fingers, or how he smelled like heaven. Nothing at all. Not a thing. She also tried to ignore how her mind flew to ideas about what to wear.

Chapter 10

BRIAN KNOCKED ON SPRING CABIN'S door just as the sun dipped behind the mountains, streaking the denim sky with pink and orange. The days were getting longer, all right. Almost eight o'clock, but it wasn't fully dark yet. He hoped, much as he liked Sawyer and Lacey, that didn't mean a later bedtime for them.

The door opened and Katelyn was there, smiling up at him. As he looked down at her, he felt a stirring of surprise. She was wearing a baggy pair of gray sweatpants and an oversized hoody that had seen better days. She looked ridiculously cute, but it was definitely a change from her distinctive retro flare.

"If I'd known we were going to wear what we sleep in, I'd have shown up in my birthday suit."

Her cheeks flamed crimson like they had earlier in the day, which was interesting. Why did she blush almost every time he opened his mouth? A woman as pretty as she was had to be used to male attention—even the corny kind he specialized in.

Katelyn looked down at herself and her face scrunched. "I'm sorry, dumb, I know. I was obsessing about what to wear when you came over, but then I thought that was stupid. We're just friends and it's just a movie night, no special outfit required."

"So you decided to borrow a homeless guy's clothes?"

Katelyn's eyes flashed and for a second Brian worried he'd hurt her feelings, but no, to his relief, she giggled. "Something like that."

"Well, you totally rock them."

"Okay, well . . . " They stood for a moment, as if someone had hit a pause button. Then Katelyn shook her head. "What are we waiting for? Come in, come in."

What were they waiting for, indeed? He followed her in, and his stomach growled as the scent of hot chocolate and buttery popcorn hit him.

She grinned. "I'm glad I made snacks."

"Me too, apparently."

"On that note," she said as they settled into the small living room, him on the couch, her on the floor, bowls in hand, "you owe me."

"I *owe* you?"

"Yeah. Do you have any idea how many times I had to bribe the kids with the promise that I'd make them popcorn tomorrow in order to get them to stay in bed?"

"I can only imagine." Brian laughed as a memory hit him. "My brothers and I used to complain bitterly if there was even the slightest evidence of a snack party that we hadn't been privy too." Weird. He'd forgotten all about that—that his parents used to drink champagne and eat smoked oysters after he and his brothers went to bed. When had they stopped?

A blur of something furry caught Brian's peripheral vision. What the—?

"Don't worry. That's just Monster skulking around, not a rat. He'll warm up to you. Especially if you throw him the odd snack." As if to prove her words, Katelyn threw a piece of popcorn. The furry blur snatched it from the air and hurtled up the spiral staircase, disappearing into one of the rooms overhead.

"Well, I'm not convinced he isn't a rat, but I'll take your word for it."

Katelyn smacked his knee gently as if to scold him, and Brian caught her hand—then dropped it as if burned. Theirs eyes met, but they both looked away equally quickly. What was up with that? he wondered stupidly. He'd touched her fingers, hardly anyone's idea of an erotic zone. Why did it feel like a bolt of electricity had snapped through him?

Katelyn is a wife and mom and altogether not your type, he lectured himself, feeling a bit Callumesque. She is exactly what you don't look for in women: needs someone serious, has tons of baggage, is solid salt of the earth good girl stuff. Friend stuff, in other words. *Friend.*

His "friend" passed him a full mug of hot chocolate, complete with bobbing, half-melted marshmallows. He inhaled deeply. Definitely a beverage of buddies and pals, not hot romantic interests—well, maybe for some guys, but not for him. He definitely preferred an edgier type of woman, a harder kind of drink . . . so why did he feel so soft-centered and warm when Katelyn smiled at him?

"Moooom," Lacey shrieked from upstairs. "There's a monster under Sawyer's bed. Heeeeelp."

Crazy peals of laughter—Lacey's and Sawyer's—followed the impassioned plea.

Katelyn sighed and looked at Brian. "That's one of the reasons we got such a strange, obviously unthreatening little dog. Sawyer used to be really afraid of . . . well, a lot of things."

"Including monsters under the bed?"

She nodded. "I figured if we could turn it into a good thing to have a monster under the bed, it was one fear that would take care of itself."

"Did it work?"

Upstairs the kids were crooning, "Monster . . . *Monster* . . . come and get us."

Katelyn rolled her eyes. "A little too well."

Brian laughed. "What was the other one?"

"Sorry?"

"The other reason you got such a little 'obviously unthreatening' dog?"

Katelyn wrapped her hands around her mug and stared into her hot chocolate like it might have the answer—or like she was considering whether she should share the answer.

"A lot of people get dogs to protect their kids or yards or so they feel less fearful when they're out walking."

Brian nodded and sipped his cocoa.

Katelyn shrugged. "It probably sounds stupid, but I wanted to get my kids a pet that they would need to take special care with, that would show them that no matter how small you are yourself—or how big—it's important to be gentle and kind. I mean, I want them to be gentle and kind with any animal or person, regardless of size, but with Monster, they don't easily forget, and he adores them for it. I don't think we naturally know how to nurture things, even things we love. I think we have to learn. We need to be taught."

Brian lowered his mug and stared. Katelyn turned pink again.

"That's . . . wow. You're a really good parent."

"No." Katelyn shook her head. "I'm not. I hope, sometimes I even think, I do some things okay, but other things and in the past . . ." She shook her head again.

Brian sensed that her comment wasn't a ploy to garner an outpouring of flattery or compliments, so he didn't argue . . . much. "Well, from where I sit, from what I've seen, you are. And anyway, maybe only shitty parents and complete narcissists feel confident that they're doing an awesome job."

That brought a small smile, finally. She dipped her

chin. "Well . . . thank you."

"You're welcome." Her smile deepened a tad more.

As Gracie Hart embroiled herself in the beauty pageant world, they laughed at familiar lines and munched popcorn—tossing the occasional piece to an increasingly brave Monster who had reappeared downstairs again—and Brian relaxed fully. Katelyn was easy company; he didn't need to overthink their friendship. When the movie ended, they let the credits roll, each lost in their own thoughts.

Finally Brian broke the silence. "Have another one in you?"

Katelyn yawned and stretched. "I wish I did, but I have an early start."

"Okay." He got to his feet reluctantly. Ten-thirty felt too early for bed and too late to go into town to visit anyone else. Also, he didn't really want to see anyone else. He was so comfortable *here*. It had been such a nice low-key night. He wondered if Katelyn read before bed. Maybe he should've brought a book and after they'd read for a bit, then he could've headed out.

You're losing it, Archer, he muttered in his head. You've lived alone for years, but now you want a *reading buddy*?

He scooped up the bowls and mugs they'd used and put them on the kitchen counter on his way toward the door.

"Thank you," Katelyn said softly.

"You made the food, thank *you*."

She twinkled at him. "No, I meant for coming over. I don't enjoy adult company at night very often, and I haven't enjoyed male company in like, I don't know, forever."

"Well, I'm honored you let me invite myself over. I enjoyed it too—though the latter is totally your choice, of course."

Katelyn squirted dish soap into the sink and turned on the hot water. "What do you mean?"

"You're beautiful, funny, nice . . . you could have a guy any night of the week."

"Um . . . thank you?"

"I'm serious."

She killed the tap and picked up a dishrag. "We'll have to agree to disagree. I have two kids, no money to speak of, and a very complicated life. I'm not exactly a catch, but regardless, I don't want a guy any night of the week, so it's a moot point."

There were so many things Brian wanted to say that his mind stumbled over them. He wanted to tell her she was wrong, that yes she was, stupid word, a "catch." He wanted to insist that he meant all the nice things he'd said and more, even though he hardly knew her. He liked how kind she was to her kids and how sensitive she was about their feelings, thanking them for things they did for her, involving them in her day-to-day plans, and genuinely seeming to enjoy them. He appreciated how she was comfortable enough with herself to wear her least flattering outfit when she was having company. And he loved that she offered him cocoa, not alcohol—which was weird, because he loved booze—but again, this small action made him feel like she was accepting him into her real life or something, not pretending her evenings were something they weren't. But trying to put any of that into words might sound like he was hitting on her and that's not how he meant it—and it would wreck everything. He settled for, "So I don't have to worry about losing my new movie friend to some hot date? Excellent!"

She flicked soapsuds at him. "I think you're pretty safe."

He grinned. "I'd better be—and I'll hold you to it."

Chapter 11

KATELYN SAT ON SPRING'S PORCH steps in her leggings and well-loved, almost worn out runners, studying the check marks and cross outs that filled the current page in the spiral notebook on her lap. She inhaled deeply and as her lungs filled with sweet, slightly damp air, renewed hope and vigor danced through her. Even rolling her eyes at her inner geek couldn't squash her satisfaction. She was fond of lists. Liked how they gave her a feeling of control. She could plan what she wanted to do and needed to accomplish, short and long term, then see those goals come to fruition, or at least track herself getting closer in a tangible way. Yes, she still faced a plethora of problems, but the past weeks had gone better than she ever could've imagined they would after that dark night at the airport.

Just a few of the things on her list making her smile as Lacey and Sawyer kicked a ball nearby:

Call Jayda at Got the Notion and see if her job was still available—check. The girl they'd hired to replace her worked well enough, but she was struggling with the work-school balance and had actually given notice.

Katelyn could start back at the little fabric shop in two weeks. Jayda encouraged her further by telling her she could be as busy as she wanted after shop hours too, doing bespoke orders and alterations. "There's no one in town like you!" Jayda had finished, which was probably more kind than true, but Katelyn found it incredibly cheering nonetheless.

Find a good second hand car, cheaper than the old one, if possible—check. She'd gotten it within days of arriving at River's Sigh, actually, because Callum knew someone who knew someone, but she'd written it into her notebook anyway. She wanted a record of her good fortune and to remember to be grateful. The Honda sedan was twenty years old but had less than 100 000 miles on it. Plus, it had literally been owned by a little old lady for its whole pampered, parked in a garage, regularly maintained life. At five hundred bucks, it was not only a steal, it left her with a couple thousand dollars in her account.

And best of all? Find a place to live and arrange childcare. Check and check! She couldn't believe her luck.

Jo and Callum, though Katelyn had hardly been able to articulate the hope even to herself, had agreed to a month-by-month rental. And in the freakiest, most awesome bit of coincidence or blessing or whatever you wanted to call it, Aisha, who actually *had* come for a visit, and was now frequent company, was looking for some extra work that wouldn't take her away from Mo. She had a built-in, on the property, babysitter!

There was something else behind her current sense of well-being too, she knew, something that hadn't made it onto the page, but still topped it: Steve had been wonderfully quiet and absent. She'd enjoy the respite while it lasted, trying not to overthink why or worry that it was merely the calm before another storm.

From somewhere across the parking area, Katelyn thought she heard a door slam—and her heart skipped. She set her notebook and pen down and shifted positions, moving a good two feet, but still couldn't spy around the shield of cedar trees. She stood up, dusted off her butt, and strode down the path. She hadn't gone far when Brian appeared around a bend thirty paces in front of her, dressed in a ragged blue T-shirt, moisture wicking shorts, and neon orange running shoes.

The soft breeze that had been caressing Katelyn's bare arms suddenly roughened, becoming a windy gust that raised goose bumps across her flesh. A black storm cloud dodged in front of the sun, seemingly out of nowhere, and the sky darkened. Oh, they were in for it now. Spring in Greenridge—weather that could change in a heartbeat.

Brian lifted his arm in greeting.

"Are you still going?" Katelyn called.

"Of course," he yelled back. "If you won't run in the rain in Greenridge, you'll never run."

He jogged off slowly, but Katelyn knew from seeing him run daily the past week, that his regular pace,
which he'd commence soon, would be what most
normal people considered a sprint. She gathered Lacey
and Sawyer up, shushing their protests with the assurance that they could go back outside the minute the
rain stopped, and headed toward the cabin. They
scooted up the stairs and reached the shelter of the
porch's overhang, just as the clouds broke. Rain
pounded the ground like someone was throwing
buckets of water from the rooftop.

Katelyn glanced at Brian's retreating figure. His
worn shirt was already damp right through and cling-
ing to the muscles in his back. She caught herself
chewing her bottom lip in appreciation of the view and
something long dormant uncurled and stretched in her
belly.

Get a grip, she lectured herself. Poor Brian. The
last thing he needs right now is to be ogled by you. For
a moment the shine rubbed off her peaceful glow.
They'd exchanged enough tidbits of conversation over
breakfast, while watching movies—the Bullock night
had kicked off a semi-regular habit—and during their
newest shared activity, running together, for Katelyn to
know Brian wasn't enjoying the string of good breaks
she was.

Katelyn's glow brightened again, almost instantly,
however, when Aisha trotted into view, golden-haired
Mo in tow. Aisha was holding a sweatshirt over their

heads to fend off the worst of the sudden downpour, and Katelyn wondered if she'd ever been happier to see someone in her life. Only because of the anticipated exercise, of course. Nothing more. Definitely not because Aisha's presence meant she'd get to see more of Brian.

"Sorry I'm late," Aisha said.

"You're not late at all—and thank you."

Aisha gave a thumbs up and little Mo flashed a drooly grin, which Katelyn returned.

"I'll be back in forty minutes, an hour max?"

"Perfect. I'll be here."

Katelyn practically flew down the path. She and Aisha had decided that rather than shock the kids' systems with full eight-hour days right off, they'd do a few short babysitting stints here and there first, so they could get to know each other. So far, it was turning out wonderfully. Both Lacey and Sawyer took to Aisha right away and seemed to adore "the baby" as Sawyer still called Mo, despite her delight in destroying whatever he built. And as for Katelyn . . . well, she really enjoyed running outside again. It was so fun!

Oh sure, it's the *running* you're enjoying, teased an inner voice that Katelyn recognized as sounding all too much like a certain running partner. But it was the running, it really was—or was in addition to, anyway. Katelyn didn't think her smile could get any bigger.

Brian had been all the way to the highway already and was almost back to River Sigh's parking lot when

Katelyn caught up to him. "Sheesh, *finally*," he said.

"And here I'd been hoping you'd burned off the worst of your ego and cheekiness by now," she joked back.

"No worries there," he assured her, sounding very serious, running backwards just in front of her. "I always have tons of ego and cheek to go around."

Katelyn laughed. "So let's get the lead out, shall we?"

Brian pivoted so he was jogging forward again and she fell into an easy stride beside him. "Your wish is my command. Wanna take the lead today?"

"Sure, creek or forest?"

"Surprise me."

Chapter 12

BRIAN TOOK DEEP PULLS OF air, concentrating on filling his lower diaphragm and hoping the focus would keep him tethered to the ground. He hadn't had a running partner since he was a kid in university. He felt buoyant. It was so fun! And Katelyn was a champ. Not as fast as him—or not yet—and not as used to running trails, which was different than treadmill running, but they'd quickly, almost accidentally, fallen into a pattern. He'd resumed his running habit a couple days after his introduction to the creep, as he'd taken to calling Steve in his head. He thought Katelyn might have spotted him running before, but she didn't comment on it until the morning after their first movie night. He'd been doing a warm down, loping past Spring cabin, sweaty and feeling totally spent, and she'd looked at him longingly. "I used to run."

He'd stopped in his tracks and jogged on the spot by her porch. "So why don't you again?"

She shrugged. "The kids, mostly. Once I started using childcare a lot, I wanted to be home with them as much as possible when I wasn't working. Plus our old apartment had a treadmill that someone left behind. It was like a gift at the time."

Aisha, who'd been sitting in a lawn chair by the three playing kids, made a shooing motion. "Why don't you go now? It'll be good to do a trial run—no pun intended."

Brian groaned at Aisha's joke, but Katelyn found it funny and her eyes squinted in the cutest way. Then she'd slapped her hands on her thighs. "Okay, I will."

And the rest, as they say, was history. They'd been running together almost every day since, with Brian warming up and running full out for twenty minutes or so before she joined in. He was already trying to figure out how to keep her running with him after she returned to work.

He liked their movie nights, but he loved their runs under the protective evergreen canopy in the forest around River's Sigh. The time they spent exploring the soft duff trails was practically the only time Brian enjoyed peace of mind and freedom from depressing thoughts, since returning to Greenridge and finding his home destroyed.

And on that note, as if sensing the shadow that crossed his thoughts, Katelyn glanced over her shoulder at him. Her face was dewy with perspiration and she was radiant, like she herself was a source of light and life—

He shook his head at himself just as she asked, "So how did it go?"

"With?"

"You know, lunch with your mom and everything."

He did know, and what's more, he had no desire to pretend that he didn't. Shortly after his initial phone call with his mother, he'd ended up spilling everything to Katelyn: how depressed and angry his parents' relationship made him in general, how torn he felt about his mom, but how he'd ended up telling her he wouldn't represent her, even though it made him feel like he was letting her down. The disclosure had surprised him by feeling infinitely right, not scaldingly embarrassing. There was something he hadn't told Katelyn, however. Not because he was holding back, but because it hadn't come up.

"About that, funny thing. We ending up postponing our lunch date."

"Oh, yeah?" She sounded interested, but not pushy. An unfamiliar feeling wrapped around him: kinship. He was used to women reacting to him—or to who they thought he was, anyway. Katelyn seemed to respond to who he actually was, a subtle but critical difference. And when they were outside like this, working hard together, but also completely focused on their own independent progress, it felt natural to share things he usually kept bottled up.

"When you see her in person, are you going to stick to your decision?"

Brian raised his eyebrows and gave a small shrug without breaking his stride.

Katelyn glanced over and caught his response. Her pace didn't slow either. "I was thinking about all this the other night, avoiding my own problems, you know?"

Brian laughed. "It's always much more fun."

"Right?"

"And what did you come up with?"

"I don't know, not much. Just that I'm kind of furious at your mom, even though I get where she's coming from."

"You do?"

"Yeah. It's tempting because you get so lonely, but no parent should ask their kids to intervene in their relationship. They're *kids*, no matter how old they are. It's not their job."

Katelyn was breathing a bit heavily now, as if emotional exertion was far more winding than anything physical you could throw at her. Brian totally related.

Her voice was soft when she spoke again. "You try to take care of people, Brian, but who takes care of you?"

The question caught him off guard. "Who takes care of you?" he shot back.

"Me. I take care of myself, or I try to."

"Exactly."

They both stopped running for a moment and studied each other.

After a few beats of silence, Katelyn said, "Game to pick up the pace?"

"Thought you'd never ask."

They pounded out another two kilometers or so. Any time Brian wondered if he should inch ahead, it was like Katelyn sensed his thoughts and lengthened her stride just that little bit. She was a petite, like, what? Five foot two or three, maybe, so keeping up with him—not to mention *leading*—had to give her a pretty good workout.

"Don't your muscles ache when we're finished?" he puffed.

She laughed breathily. "The first couple days it was like they were on fire. It was awesome."

He laughed and slowed to a jog and then to a walk as they neared a jade green creek. It was moving hard and fast, just like they had been, and was close to overflowing its banks because of spring runoff. Katelyn stopped too, and using a large jutting rock as a stool, she propped a foot and leaned to stretch her hamstring, then did the same with the other leg. Her purple T-shirt was soaked to the point of transparency, the outline of her racer back bra clearly visible and somehow as erotic as any daring lingerie. Faded block letters on the shirt's front read "I run like a girl."

"Great T."

She glanced down, as if to remind herself what she was wearing, then shot him a dubious look, like she suspected he was mocking her. "You think?"

He nodded. "I do. You're kick ass fast and you never get tired."

She made a huffing sound that could have been a held back laugh, but maybe wasn't, maybe was something different altogether. Then she checked her wristwatch—she and he might be the only people in the world who still wore those, he thought—and exhaled explosively. "We should get back."

"Okay. Who should lead the way home?"

She hesitated only a second. "Whoever's not it!"

She smacked his arm, making it clear he was the "it" in question and bolted, jumping a fallen log like a deer and getting a good lead.

Brian sprinted after her, but the energy he'd expended before she'd joined him showed. Try as he might, he didn't catch her until they broke through the tree line that opened into a grassy clearing that edged Jo and Callum's house and the guest hall and office.

"Yes!" Katelyn fist pumped the air.

The sun, as if responding to her celebration, burst from behind an ominous black cloud. Suddenly the weather was doing the weird thing it sometimes did in their coastal-influenced rainforest. The sun smiled down hot and brilliant, while rain simultaneously poured on their upturned faces.

Without a thought, Brian swooped Katelyn up by her small waist and swung her around in a circle, reveling in the sensation of her sinuous muscles beneath his hands. "And the winner is!" he announced. "Kate . . . by a cheating landside."

She shrieked with unsuppressed glee—but then the

sound died in her throat and something in her face clenched. Brian set her down at once. Her head bowed, and she crossed her arms tightly over her ribcage, beneath her breasts, like she was trying to protect herself from a blow. A rock of apprehension formed in Brian's stomach. He turned to face the same direction she was staring.

Callum had descended the three wide stairs from the office's large cedar deck. It was obvious he'd witnessed their antics from across the expanse of green lawn. His eyes flickered over Katelyn, then fixed on Brian, and he shook his head, but looked amused. It wasn't Callum's obvious misinterpretation about what he'd seen that increased the weight lodged in Brian's gut, however. It was Steve, standing behind Callum, stone-jawed and ice-eyed, glaring at Katelyn as if Brian wasn't even there.

Chapter 13

ONE OF THE FIRST TIPOFFS to Katelyn that she was perhaps in an abusive marriage had been the realization that Steve made her feel intensely guilty over events, things said, things done or not done, where no guilt or shame was warranted. She—in a fact that still made her wince and want to slap her old self—had gotten so used to feeling chronically nervous and wary and guilty that she hadn't even noticed anything awry.

After all, didn't every wife worry that dinner might be two minutes later than whatever nebulous, random time her husband wanted to eat? Or that it might not be the type of food he was in the mood for?

Didn't every woman not want to rock the boat or make her mate feel insecure or unloved by smiling or greeting or conversing with another man—or, heck, even responding politely to a male grocery clerk?

Didn't every truly loving, committed female realize that her partner was only so controlling, so rigid, so intensely paranoid that she was cheating or looking to cheat, because he loved her so much and couldn't, or wouldn't, live without her?

It had taken a visit from Janet, a rare time where Steve had actually allowed her to stay at their house in the guest room, to open her eyes and make her see that no, not every woman accepted that kind of mental and physical tyranny as normal. When Steve finally left them to their own devices for a couple of hours because he couldn't, as much as he wanted to, stay away from the office all week, Katelyn had almost wept, hearing Janet's objections and her angry, shocked horror at how Katelyn was continually—casually, almost—railroaded by Steve.

It was like seeing her life and experiences through her friend's eyes allowed her to voice, to admit, to confront, what she had always hoped—or known—deep down. *It wasn't normal.* And once she acknowledged that and forced herself to do the horribly scary thing of calling his abuse what it was . . . well, she only saw it more and more. She also admitted to herself that, if anything, his behavior was growing worse over the years, not better, and if she was going to get out alive, she probably needed to do it sooner rather than later.

All this and more flashed through her mind as Steve's glare locked on her. But old habits die hard, and familiar—if hated—feelings of shame welled up in Katelyn.

What *was* she doing going for runs with Brian every day when she should be focusing on the kids and what her next steps were going to be? How selfish was she? And of course it would be hard for Steve to see her and Brian together. Of course he would read something romantic into it and see it as a betrayal. He still, unrequited though it was, loved her—according to what his idea of love was, anyway. Why flirt with danger? Why make waves? Why do that to him, if she really wasn't interested in dating? Why put him through that extra pain?

But then again, what was she "doing" to Steve? *Nothing.* When was she going to get over this sick, codependent weakness she had with him? Why wasn't she strong enough to recognize the shame she felt around him was emotionally and mentally unhealthy? What kind of role model and parent would she manage to be for her kids, if she couldn't get herself healthy and strong, once and for all?

Katelyn realized she was shaking and clutching her stomach. She forced herself to unwrap her arms from around her middle, as Callum grinned. "Looks like you two had a good run."

He had absolutely no idea about the rage that his cheerful observation triggered in the eyes of the man standing behind him.

Katelyn's knees trembled and she felt mildly nauseous. Then, suddenly, there was gentle pressure on her back. Brian had softly nudged her.

"So am I correct in thinking ol' Steve won't call me 'buddy' the next time we meet up alone?" His whisper was quiet to the point of being barely perceptible—but it was like the flashing beam of a lighthouse in a stormy sea. Her thoughts steadied and she found her way back to firm land.

"Yes, I think that's a safe bet," she said equally quietly.

Brian was here. And Callum. She was not alone with Steve. There were witnesses. She was safe. And the kids were with Aisha and Mo. They were safe.

"Yeah, it was a pretty good work out. Thanks, Callum." To her profound relief, her tone matched his: light, friendly, *normal.* "Steve, it's not your day with the kids. Why are you here?"

Steve advanced in long, angry strides. The friendly rain ceased and the sun took cover behind the clouds again.

Perhaps Callum saw something in Katelyn's face or felt a change in the air at Steve's movement, but for whatever reason, he pivoted toward Steve.

Steve's voice was low and furious. "Maybe I had a father's intuition. Maybe I felt my wife wasn't watching our precious children properly on 'her' days."

Callum's eyes narrowed in surprise, but it was Brian who spoke. "Whoa, that's enough. As you told me when we first met, Katelyn here is your ex-wife."

"What does that matter? I have a right to know my children are being cared for. That their mother's not out"—he practically spat the words—"cavorting with anything with two legs and a dick."

Because of his mellow temperament and gentle

demeanor, Katelyn sometimes forgot how big Callum was, but as he blocked Steve from moving any closer with a restraining hand, Steve seemed well aware of it. And then Brian stepped toward him too.

Steve reconsidered his audience and lifted his hands apologetically. "Sorry, Brian—Callum," he said. "I didn't mean that how it sounded. It's just, well, this break up has been really hard on me. I love my wife, I mean, Katelyn, and our kids. I'd do anything for them."

Callum snorted and Brian outright laughed. "Anything except respect her wishes, or let her go, right, *buddy*?"

Steve tried once more. "I don't know what she's told you. I wasn't perfect in the past, but—"

"I think you should head out, Steve," Callum said. "You're more than welcome when it's your day to pick up your kids, but other than that, well, this is private property and I have a business to run." He sounded calm, but Katelyn was sure his words were a warning—and not just to Steve. Her flesh burned. Callum and Jo *did* have a business to run. She couldn't bear it if her stupid family drama caused hassles for them or hurt their professionalism in front of their other guests. Yes, because she didn't have any place else to go at the moment, but also because they'd been kind to her and she didn't want them to suffer for it.

"Please, Steve. Just go. I don't want to get into this again, or to get anyone else involved. I'll see you

Friday at five."

Steve's eyes glinted and his fists clenched. "When we go to court this time, you'll be sorry."

All Katelyn could do was nod wearily. "I'm already sorry, Steve. That never changes."

He blasted her with another look, opened his mouth, then closed it with a sneer, and stormed back to his truck.

He roared away, spinning his tires and tearing up the carefully raked gravel. It was like a physical symbol of the embarrassment spraying through her: ugly and obvious, destructive and intensely *stupid.* That he'd shown his true colors to Brian and Callum was little comfort. Sometimes he could keep up a façade indefinitely; other times, like today, he had virtually no control. Either way, she was left with a throbbing, near tears awareness: because of her, River's Sigh B & B's peace had been disturbed and would be further threatened if she stayed. She could practically hear that thought run through Callum's head—so loud, in fact, that when he spoke, she shook her head and stared for a long minute before grasping what he was actually saying.

"I'm sorry, Katelyn. I should've stuck with the simple truth that you weren't around, but I didn't pick up any off cues from him when he asked me to track you down. Won't happen again."

"What? No. You don't have to apologize to me. I need to apologize to you. I'm so sorry."

Callum's face was sad. "*You* have nothing to be sorry for." He punched Brian's arm lightly. "Well, that pump won't fix itself. I'll see you later."

It was only as he walked off that Katelyn noticed the small toolbox he was carrying. She was left standing awkwardly beside Brian, all traces of the peace she had enjoyed on the trails totally obliterated.

"I'm really—"

Brian interrupted her before she could apologize yet again by taking her hand. Unlike when their fingers had connected during the first movie night, there was nothing remotely sexual or electric in the touch this time. It was just the solid grip of a friend, soothing and grounding.

"So how did that happen anyway?" Brian asked after they'd crossed the clearing and started on the trail leading to Spring cabin.

"What do you mean?"

He jerked his head toward the parking lot as if Steve was still parked there. "How did you two . . . come to be?"

She sighed heavily and dropped his hand. "It's an old boring story. You know, stupid naïve girl marries a charming monster. Ever heard it?"

Brian laughed, but it was a bitter sound. "More times than you'd ever believe. Relationships. They're for idiots, aren't they?"

Katelyn kept silent because after what he'd just seen and her own admission of naiveté, she couldn't say she hoped not. But she *did* hope not. Surely, good relationships, good marriages, existed for some people. Look at Janet. Look at her own parents. Their union hadn't been perfect, but it also hadn't been awful. She knew it would be a long, long time before she was free and safe to try again, but she did hope she got a chance sometime.

"Do you mind my asking—" Brian faltered.

"Mind your asking what?"

"Why did you stay with him as long as you did, long enough to have two kids with him?"

Yep, that was the question, wasn't it? The big one. The one she'd asked herself daily for a long time. The one she still didn't have a completely satisfactory answer to.

Brian misunderstood her lack of an immediate response. "I'm sorry." He shook his head. "That's incredibly personal. Forgive me."

Katelyn stretched her arms out in front of her and cracked her knuckles. "No apology or forgiveness needed. At all. It's not like you haven't shared some inner secrets of your own. It just doesn't have an easy answer—or if it does I haven't discovered what it is yet."

"That makes sense. I read somewhere that there's always some sort of psychological pay off for what we do, decisions we make or things we put up with."

Katelyn shot him a disbelieving look.

Brian held up his hands apologetically. "I'm an ass.

I was thinking out loud."

"No, not all," Katelyn said for a second time. "I'm just surprised. I read something similar once. It was really eye-opening for me." She took a minute to process her thoughts, and Brian walked quietly by her side.

"I think it's hard because that idea, that there's some overarching 'pay off' that explains why a person stays with an abuser, suggests if we can figure out what it is, presto, everything will be magically fixed. It tries to make something that's incredibly complex simple."

Brian nodded.

"And then other times, I think maybe the answer *is* simple, that I only want it to be complex because it would help assuage my guilt."

Brian's mouth opened, no doubt to share some platitude about how survivors shouldn't feel guilt—but she didn't need or want to hear that right now. She shook her head, and he held back whatever he'd been about to say. She knew full well she wasn't culpable for the abuse, but she still felt she'd been complicit in some ways—and dealing with the elements of her personality that opened her up to abuse, allowed her to put up with it for so long, was her way of making sure she'd never be in that situation again.

"But then, by thinking that, I realize again, no, it really is complicated."

Brian looked confused—and she totally related.

"I don't know what I got out of the relationship," she said, frustrated. "At first, of course, like most people erroneously think—and not just about abusers, but about anything they find unpalatable in their partner—I thought I could change him, that my love was strong enough to be a cure-all. And he'd say that too—that I was a 'rock.' That I would be his 'salvation.' That he didn't know what he'd do without me. That he didn't deserve me."

She took a deep breath. "Also, I had very elderly parents. My mom was forty-four when she had me and my dad was fifty-six. They were very traditional. He was the breadwinner and head of the house. His word was law and she, in every way, supported those notions. The difference was that my father was a very kind man, not a tyrant in any way, and though, yes, he was a chauvinist, he was the kind who thought that meant you needed to dote on, take care of, cherish the 'fairer' sex. Steve gave mouth service to similar ideas and I'd been too sheltered to not know the difference between chivalry and sexism."

Brian seemed a little shell-shocked.

"T.M.I?" Katelyn asked.

He looked blank.

"Too much information?"

He shook his head. "Not at all. Please go on, if you want to, anyway."

Katelyn sighed heavily. "My parents died in a car accident just after I graduated. I was vulnerable, lonely. Steve was there, protective and strong, wanting to take care of me—and in the beginning of our marriage, incidences were few and far enough between that I'd think, hey . . . it's working. I'm doing it. I'm fixing him." She stopped talking and shot Brian another look, but he still didn't appear shocked or disappointed in her. His expression was merely . . . compassionate.

"And also, he would be so sad, so seemingly genuine in his regret—and so flamboyant and passionate and over the top in the ways he'd try to make up for his 'failings' that I felt . . . " she broke off, feeling nauseous, "*loved*, like it was the price you pay for a huge, deep, passionate all-consuming love—that you get a little consumed."

A small choking sound escaped Katelyn before she could swallow it. She was shocked by the intensity of the shame, sadness, guilt and hopelessness that talking about this still triggered.

"It was hideously hard on me when I realized that the extreme highs and lows of our relationship were pretty much a cliché of every battering situation."

"Rough," Brian said. His voice held no judgment and no further questions, only commiseration.

"Most of all though, I just didn't recognize it for what it was. It took me a long time to realize that the elements of our relationship that were making me so crazy and sad were abuse. No one wants to think they're a victim—or can even see abuse as abuse, at first. Or I didn't and couldn't anyway."

They were almost at Spring cabin. Lacey's flute-like voice carried over to them, chatting about something to do with the swing set, though she was out of sight, around the corner of the building.

Brian's pace slowed. "Thank you for sharing all that. I'm honored you trust me with it."

Katelyn rolled her neck. "Oh, yeah, lucky you."

Brian's eyes creased and his voice was soft. "I do feel lucky."

She looked at him for a long moment. Then nodded. "Well, thank you."

Brian clapped his hands, then rubbed them together briskly, and Katelyn could see him mentally changing gears, getting ready to be back in Aisha and the kids' company again.

"So," he said, "you're going to write down what happened with Steve back there and send the details to Marilee, right?"

"Um, I hadn't thought about it yet."

"You should. Every run-in you have with him, no matter how small it seems, should be on the record. He wasn't happy today. Not at all. And if he thinks you and I have any sort of thing going on, it may finally hit home that you guys are really over."

Brian didn't have to finish his thought; Katelyn did it for him. "And he might stop holding back in the hopes he can lure me back. He might lose it once and for all."

Brian's expression was grim. "Yeah, you know the drill, hey?"

Katelyn's stomach dropped and she laughed inappropriately. "Right near the top of the chart for causes of death in women, right? Heart disease, cancer, husbands."

"It's not funny."

Katelyn bit her lip. Nodded. "I know. And I don't actually even believe that. I just don't know what else to do sometimes, you know? I have to laugh or I'll—" She stopped talking, didn't bother to fill in the blank with *go crazy, start crying and never stop, become homicidal*—all of which felt terrifyingly true from time to time. She cupped her palm over her left eye, a bizarrely simple but effective technique that staved off tears.

Brian stopped at the staircase to Spring's porch, patted her shoulder in a silent farewell, and left.

Before he walked five paces, however, he turned back. Katelyn tilted her head questioningly. She hadn't moved yet, had needed a moment or two to compose herself and transition from prey to protector and mom. Lacey and Sawyer had been part of too many awful scenes. Since they hadn't witnessed this one, she wanted to spare them its emotional fall out.

"What?" she asked finally, when he still hadn't spoken.

"I, well . . . " Brian pounded his fist lightly into his palm. "Ah, shit, I'll just say it. I'd thought a casual friendship might be nice for both of us, but I should've known it would be misread. I don't want to complicate things for you with your psycho ex, so maybe we should cool the running thing for a bit, you think?"

No, she didn't think that. Not at all.

Brian watched her, sad and patient, and she realized she'd only responded in her head. "No!" The word came out too loud. Katelyn darted a look toward her unseen children, but there was no break in the burble of conversation coming from the yard, and no small people came running. Katelyn closed the distance between her and Brian in rapid steps.

"Don't," she said. "Please. I mean, I totally understand if it's too much for you. I'm a friend with a lot of baggage, I get it. But this is what he does. Waltzes in wherever and whenever I make a new friend or I'm just starting to get a life of my own again and does his crazy thing and totally wrecks it for me. Scares people away. I've even lost jobs because of him. He wants me isolated, alone and dependent. That's all he has ever wanted."

She took a gulping breath. "I can—and I will—keep running on my own, but . . . I don't want to."

There was a moment of silence as deep and all-encompassing as the quiet of the woods and sky around them.

Then Katelyn reached out and placed her hand on Brian's forearm. Somehow this contact felt bigger than their casual handholding earlier—and maybe he felt similarly, because he flinched. But his flesh was warm and strong under her palm and she stayed her course. After a moment, he covered her hand with his, and Katelyn realized that her fingers had been freezing, but she hadn't noticed until she felt his heat.

"Okay," he said. "But I don't want to cause problems for you, you know?"

She nodded. "I do know that. And I appreciate it—but you don't cause problems for me. He does. Also, no one gets to dictate what I do anymore. Not him out of selfishness. Not you out of selflessness."

Brian's gaze rested on her, intense but comforting at the same time. Then he laughed. "You're something else."

The heaviness of the moment lightened, and relief or something like joy coursed through her. He was going to continue running with her. She couldn't keep from beaming. "Don't think compliments today will keep me from kicking your butt tomorrow."

"I'm not that big an idiot," he assured her with mock solemnity. Then he grinned and loped off. At the bend in the trail that would steal him from view, he turned and looked her way again. Somehow she'd known he would. She waved. He smiled, shook his head, and disappeared.

Katelyn inhaled deeply, then headed around the corner of the cabin to rescue Aisha and to listen to her kids' stories about their morning adventures.

Chapter 14

BRIAN STOOD IN HIS OLD living room, futilely grabbing at pictures and books and people that disappeared into oily smoke and flames the minute his fingers touched them. The acrid reek of burnt plastics and other manmade materials permeated his nostrils.

He jolted awake, breathing hard and sweating, from what was becoming a regular nightmare. He was sure his hair and clothes smelled as foul as the apartment building had. He couldn't get memories of the smell and the devastating sight of his demolished home out of his mind, waking or sleeping.

He checked his phone for the time, knowing he wouldn't rest any further, and was relieved it wasn't indecently early. He could start his day without looking insane.

As he dressed, he continued to obsess. He couldn't help it. He was supposed to be consoled that the insurance company had offered fair compensation from a financial point-of-view—but he'd expected nothing less. After all, he had a notarized list of his valuables and extensive photographs documenting his possessions, which he kept safe and sound in a safety deposit box at his bank.

"You're thirty going on eighty," an ex-girlfriend had teased years back. Later, when they broke up, she referred to it again. "You only play at being No Strings Attached Guy. Really, you're all about holding on— and until you realize you can't control everything, you're never going to possess the things you crave most." Her words rankled, but even then he'd suspected there was some truth to them.

He shook the memory away as he shaved and brushed his teeth in the guest room's en suite—another thing that was starting to press on him. No matter how he enjoyed staying at River's Sigh, he couldn't sponge off Callum and Jo indefinitely. He needed to start making plans, something more concrete than collecting boxes of new crap to replace his old crap.

The house was quiet and his socked feet were equally silent as he padded down the stairs. A flash of movement caught his eye and he heard a soft laugh as he walked past the open archway that led to the living room. He stepped back, shielding himself from sight, just as Jo and Callum moved into view.

Jo was twirling around in a bright cherry print dress with a flaring skirt. "Isn't it pretty?" she asked happily. "Katelyn made us all matching dresses for the Spring Fling, one for herself, one for Lacey, Jo, Aisha, and even a mini one for Mo."

Callum ran his hand along the sweetheart neckline

and fitted bodice. "Very nice," he said. "Very, very nice, in fact."

Brian felt like the world's biggest creep watching his brother and his wife have a moment, but if he moved now, they'd notice him and that would be even more awkward.

Callum's head dipped and kissed the curve of Jo's cleavage. "I've always been a supporter of easier access."

"Perv."

They laughed, but then Jo inhaled sharply. Brian didn't want to know why.

His feet unfroze and he backtracked as silently as he could, face burning, heart thumping. Yes, it would be embarrassing to have them hear him and realize what he'd already observed, but that would be better than seeing anything else.

On one hand, he couldn't care less that his brother was getting lucky and that he'd seen a little more than either Jo or Callum might be comfortable with. But on the other hand, it made something ache deep within him. Damn, he wanted that. Not the sexual relationship, or not merely. That was the easiest bit to come by. He wanted what they had. He craved the silliness, the friendship, and the obvious-to-all deep affection and love to go with the lust.

But his mushy longing was nonsense, of course. He was just rattled from the fire, feeling sentimental and a bit lost because he no longer had a place to call his own.

Nonsense or not though, a certain heart-shaped face and pixie grin flooded his brain and a specific tinkling laugh filled his ears, and Brian had to face facts. It wasn't that he wanted all those things Jo and Callum enjoyed that bugged him so much. It was that he wanted them with *Katelyn.*

But that was nuts. It didn't matter that he already felt like she knew him better than anyone else did. They hadn't known each other long enough for their attraction to be more than an infatuation. It was irrational, completely irrational—but even so, the desire intrigued him. He had never yearned for closeness and companionship with any other woman. He had never even believed that a relationship like that was truly a possibility. Friends were friends and lovers—well, lovers were temporary. This stirring, the temptation to blur the lines, was unnerving. Beyond unnerving.

Jo's merry voice in the hallway jolted Brian from his uncomfortable thoughts. "Oh, Callum, you poor boy—but I'm serious, and think of it this way. It'll motivate us to get our chores done. Just let me change and we can get out of here."

Callum grumbled something in a joking tone, but Brian couldn't make it out. A few minutes later, the front door slammed and he heard Jo's pickup start.

When he was sure they were really gone this time, he slipped into the kitchen. A note on the fridge caught his eye. It had a smiley face and his name was under-lined three times. *Full cabins this weekend. Season's starting with a bang!* (He had to give it to Jo. She really didn't seem to see the crazy amount of work she did as actual work.) *C and I have headed to town to do a massive grocery shop, then we plan to sneak a fancy lunch out—oohlala! Want to do steaks with us tonight? Hope so. Will buy plenty in case. Eat 6ish. ~ Jo.* (Another happy face.)

Yes, Brian wanted to eat dinner with Jo and Cal-lum. He pretty much wanted to eat every meal with them. He liked having a family around. In fact, the only thing nicer, more relaxing—and more distracting from his homelessness—was spending time with Katelyn. Just like that, his brain was back to its favor-ite obsession.

They had another movie night scheduled for later that evening, and it couldn't come fast enough. He wanted to see her now, in fact. But it was the middle of the day. The kids were awake. Would Katelyn mind if he jogged in and out of their lives, the way he did hers? He didn't want to be a nuisance, but he wasn't used to having so much time on his hands—and he still had another week of his leave of absence left.

He glanced out the big window. Katelyn's little beater was parked beside his Jeep. Score. She wasn't at work. He rummaged in the fridge for a worthy excuse and found a bag of nectarines. Good enough. He plucked four of the ripest ones, then bounded through a misty shower of rain—sometimes it felt like River's Sigh poured 24/7—to Katelyn's cabin.

Three knocks later, he heard a questioning, "Hello?"

"Hey, it's me. Brian."

The door opened and Katelyn appeared, disheveled but smiling. She wiped her soapy hands on the thighs of her wide-legged denim trousers and pushed away a strand of hair that had fallen from her messy bun. "What's up?"

"I, well, silly thing really." Brian held up his fruit offering and wondered why he was such a stuttering fool around her. "These are perfectly ripe right now, but they'll be past their prime soon, and I can't eat them all myself. Do Sawyer and Lacey like nectarines?"

Lacey, draped in a huge white shirt with streaks of yellow and red paint on it, appeared like a friendly ghost from behind her mom's hip. "We love them!"

"Okay, go wash your hands then," Katelyn said, then squinted up at Brian, amusement crinkling her eyes. "Did you really just use overripe fruit as an excuse to drop by and see us?"

Absolutely, Brian thought—and the weighty truth of the realization shocked him and made his stomach jump. "Um, well, yeah, actually." He grinned. "So what's the verdict? Totally lame?"

Katelyn shook her head, still smiling, and extended her palm. He dropped a nectarine into it, and she took a big bite. Juice trickled down her wrist. She licked it off. His feeling of bewildered shock—and something else—grew as he watched her.

"Not lame at all," she said with a wide-eyed earnestness that made him feel . . . weird. "*Sweet.* But also, just so you know, you're welcome anytime you want, no reason necessary. Bearing snacks is just a bonus."

"A *big* bonus," Lacey piped in, apparently finished washing up, though she didn't look much cleaner.

Katelyn opened the door wider and Brian walked into colorful chaos.

Every visible surface in the small kitchen and dining room, including the floor, was covered in newspaper. Sawyer, looking like he might be the skinniest little boy in the world, though maybe that was just a kid of a certain age thing, sported superhero underpants and nothing else. His bony ribs, like Lacey's shirt, were streaked with color.

"I'm starting Jo's curtains and bedding soon, plus I'll be bringing other work home," Katelyn started to explain, and Lacey continued, "so we have to get all our painting in now. Even with paper down, Mom doesn't let us finger paint when she has customers' fabric in the house."

Customers' fabric in the house. One day Brian would get used to this child's adult way of phrasing or mimicking everything. And note to self, he added in his head, don't say or do anything around her that you don't want to get back to pretty much everyone in the world.

"Right. No paint. No how. No way," Sawyer added sternly.

Katelyn blushed. "I don't have a lot of secrets with them around, do I?"

"Secrets are highly overrated."

"Mom would agree with that, right, Mom?"

Katelyn's cheeks flamed brighter.

"What is it you do exactly?" Brian asked. "I mean, I know you got your job back at Got The Notion, doing alterations and sales and stuff, but why do you have fabric for customers?"

"Because," Lacey announced with breathless pride, "our mom can sew *anything*!"

Katelyn laughed. "Not exactly a high demand skill in our off the rack, want everything as cheap as possible world, but yeah, what Lacey said. And it *is* a good thing in prom and prime wedding season. I knew Jayda would have hours for me, but I hadn't dreamed she still needed a seamstress for custom dresses. Turns out she hadn't found anyone to replace me yet."

"Mom's indie spent Sybil."

Brian looked at Katelyn for help.

"She means indispensable, but she's just parroting as usual, and Jayda was just being nice."

Brian scanned the room again. At least eleven shiny white pieces of paper were strewn around the room in various degrees of paint smeared completion.

Maybe he should introduce Katelyn's kids to his mother. She'd approve.

"It might not have been the brightest plan to tackle painting in tandem with unpacking," Katelyn said, "but, well, it's a fun rainy day activity."

It did look fun. And then, yes, Brian spotted three boxes in front of the couch.

"All our worldly possessions," Katelyn said, following his gaze. "Well, plus the massive suitcases that you helped us with that night—and my ridiculous fabric totes and serger and sewing machine that you witnessed in the dining hall."

That night. Less than a month ago. It felt like a momentous occasion. He shook it off. "What? You're serious? That's it?"

Katelyn laughed. "Yeah, we travel light these days. I used to have a ton of stuff, but I've been trying to stay easily transplantable. And if I had to I could've left my sewing stuff in storage indefinitely, or even let it go altogether and started fresh."

Brian removed a small Batman running shoe from one of the tall bar stools by the kitchen island and sat down. "Not me. I'm like a gnome. I want all my stuff around me, and lots of it."

Katelyn rested a hand on his shoulder. The gentle gesture made him feel like misting up or something. He looked away abruptly.

"Having your home burn, losing everything . . . that has to be brutally hard. I'm so sorry."

He shrugged. "Whatever. There's insurance."

"It's not the same though, is it? The new stuff won't have the attached memories."

"I guess."

Katelyn bit her lip. "I like homemaking, too—kinda messily, like a nest, actually, full of crafts and sewing and projects—but I'd live out of a packsack, so long as I could have my kids safely with me, with enough money to feed them and keep a roof over our heads."

Brian needed to lighten the mood, so he looked around exaggeratedly. "A messy nest, hey? Looks like you're succeeding."

"Ha ha, funny man." Katelyn moved away from him to help Sawyer open a container of green paint. Why on earth did he miss her touch already? "But I'm serious. I stressed about what I'd do for furniture and how I'd manage to keep toys, kitchen stuff and personal mementos when I first knew I had to leave Steve—but then a good friend of mine, in the most casual of comments, made me realize I was being nuts."

Brian pulled a spare sheet of untouched paper from across the counter so it sat in front of him. "How so?"

"She moved a lot with her kids, like every few years, for work, and I wondered how that was for them. I'm a really traditional person, and used to be even more so. I was married to the idea of the nuclear home, the mom, the dad, the picket fence and the family home that the kids could come back to with their kids." Katelyn sighed and studied her hands, maybe seeing the ring that was no longer there. "It was my dream and I still think it's a good one, just I married the wrong person for it."

An arm's length away, Lacey seemed absorbed in the purple swirls she was making with two fingers, but she was obviously tuned into everything that was going on—to the point that she'd even observed that Brian had set himself up to paint. She handed him yellow and red tubes without him having to say a word.

"But when I asked my friend if the kids minded, if they didn't miss having a home to come back to, she looked surprised and said, 'No, wherever I am, wherever we are *together*, that's home. I'm their home.'"

Brian had to smile. Katelyn did indeed . . . seem like home.

"It's the truth. No matter how we get caught up in TV or magazine ad versions of what a home looks like, decorating wise or yard wise or number of rooms wise, or how much I like doing all that stuff, what really makes a home *home* is the people or pets you fill it with." Katelyn darted a look at him, then lowered her eyes and laughed self-consciously. "Whoa, sorry. Self-help lecture ended. I think I needed to remind myself of that. Really, home's probably something a bit different for everyone."

Brian nodded. "Maybe." He was suddenly light-headed and hollow-stomached, like he'd been hitting

EV BISHOP

gin and tonic early or something. "But I like your version of it."

She noticed the rectangle of paper in front of him and the red paint he held. "Are you going to paint?"

"I was thinking of it."

Sawyer's head flew up and he grinned. Lacey looked excited too. "I'm no Picasso," Brian warned. "I won't be winning any great painting prizes or anything."

"Mom says that in art, and maybe in life, there is no mistake, no 'win' and no fail. There's only make."

Brian's eyebrows shot up. "Your mom has already taught you that? How old are you guys?"

"Seven," Lacey said archly, as if she was plenty old thank you very much.

Sawyer held up four fingers, then returned to his work.

"Okay, okay, my little savants. Stop showing off. And I didn't make up that saying, the artist Sister Mary Corita Kent did. It just came up when we were talking one day."

Brian squirted a huge blob of red paint smack in the center of his page. "Well, I'm impressed, and you know what? You should meet my mother."

"I'd love to meet your mother!" Katelyn said without a second's hesitation. Their eyes met and a current passed between them, shocking—and shaking—them both. At least he wasn't the only one feeling this weird vibration between them today.

"Okay," Katelyn practically stuttered. "How about you create your masterpiece, and I'll . . . go unpack some more. Do you mind?"

"Not a bit."

He listened to Katelyn's soft puttering overhead while he painted—keeping it all red, much to the amusement of the kids—taking small breaks to snack and/or to admire their fifty or so (hardly exaggerating!) works of art. When the reminder he'd set on his phone buzzed, he was startled. Where had the time gone? He needed to go back to the main house for dinner with Jo and Callum.

Katelyn was nowhere to be seen. "Hey," he called. "I've gotta run."

She bounced down the winding staircase, holding a picture frame. "Already? Too bad."

"It was really fun."

Her head bobbed in agreement. "It was—and thank you. Having you here was a huge help. The kids had a blast, and I think I'm all done."

She placed the frame down on the end table by the loveseat as if to emphasize her words.

Brian glanced down, expecting a photo of her and the kids or something, but it wasn't actually a picture. Instead it was a quote written across a stormy sky. "Bravery is not the absence of fear. It is doing what you need to do or what is right despite any fear."

She caught him looking and misread his expression.

"See?" she exclaimed. "Now you know why I needed the kids to paint. I need some real art in the house, not just inspirational goop."

He shook his head. "I was thinking that I liked it."

When she didn't respond to that, he added, "Still on for movies tonight?"

Katelyn chewed her bottom lip and looked pensive, but then her expression brightened, like she'd forcibly pushed off whatever was worrying her. "Absolutely," she said. "Yeah. Sure."

He noticed that she shook her head, like she was disagreeing with her own words while she spoke. What's that about? he wondered, but didn't get a chance to ask because Lacey and Sawyer had launched themselves off their chairs to say their own good-byes.

While he'd been indoors with Katelyn and the kids, the earlier drizzle had turned to a downpour. He held his jacket over his head and jogged across the yard. He was almost at Callum and Jo's door when he realized he'd left his paint-doodle behind. Great, just great.

Chapter 15

KATELYN STOOD BY THE COFFEE maker, willing it to hurry, and stretched her head from side to side, trying to ease the crick that had formed during her restless night. It wasn't the first uneasy sleep she'd had since coming to River's Sigh, but this time it wasn't Steve who'd kept her tossing and turning with nagging unnamed worries. It was Brian.

"Mom, mom," Lacey said insistently, appearing beside her.

Sawyer tugged on Katelyn's nightie to add weight to his sister's plea.

"Can we watch cartoons with our breakfast?"

"Sure. Go ahead." It would be a nice distraction for them—and might hide how distracted she was.

"Please," Lacey wheedled, then her mouth dropped open. "Wait. We *can*?"

Katelyn laughed. "Well, do you want to or not?"

"Yeah!" Sawyer whisper-yelled, and he and Lacey sprinted to the couch.

Lacey turned on the TV and the Pokémon theme song filled the room. Katelyn brought them cheese cubes, fruit and homemade oatmeal bars, thinking that even if they did accidentally spill, everything would vacuum up easily. Then, trying not to sigh with audible relief, she settled herself, coffee in hand, at the little table in the kitchen and resumed staring at the cause of her jumbled emotions and concern: Brian's painting— if you could call it that. He'd painted each of their names, his, Katelyn's, and both kids', then added curlicue hearts and flowers and the big question, "What are we doing, K?" followed by another heart.

She had no idea if he'd left it behind intentionally or not. But the problem wasn't that he'd left it. Or even what it was. It was that it mimicked exactly what she had been wondering—and had been too scared to face directly.

She'd known from the first minute they met again by chance in the airport that she found Brian physically attractive. But she was off men, at least until her kids were grown, and maybe permanently. She'd been so sure that if they spent time together, she'd see all the ways he was wrong for her and even the physical attraction would wane. At best, they'd be friends. And at worst? There *was* no worst. If they didn't work as friends, it would almost be easier.

She hadn't even considered another possibility: that rather than ripping out stitches of lust, getting to know Brian a bit would only knit a desire to know him even better, would make her like and appreciate the actual man he was, not just his pretty face.

The awareness that she genuinely liked him had been scary enough, but she'd been confident—even while they ran together, even while they kept finding time to steal a conversation whenever and wherever their paths happened to cross, even while she was more and more eager for every hour they spent watching movies and chatting—that she could keep her silly crush under control.

Her first inkling that she was out of her depths had hit her before he'd even left after painting with the kids. When he'd asked if they were "still on" for movies later, all she'd wanted to do was beg him to stay right through, to eat dinner with them, to be part of the kids' bedtime stories and going to sleep rituals. The idea that she felt all was right in her world when Brian was there beside her, and that Lacey and Sawyer were benefiting from his calm, easy presence made her queasy. Literally. She'd ended up texting him and begging off their movie plans, claiming she wasn't up to it. Which was true, just not for the reasons she wanted it to be.

And now this. Now she couldn't pretend that the electricity that zipped between them was all in her head.

She traced one of the red curlicues Brian had decorated his paper with. If her feelings weren't one-sided, if he felt even remotely the same way she did, there was nothing safe about her infatuation, nothing harmless about her fantasies. She, *they*, had stumbled into a danger zone.

Now their attraction was something to be dealt with, figured out, put to sleep. And that was too bad. Really too bad. In another world, in a different place and time . . . if Greenridge could be anything except part of her past, a place she had to escape for the health and welfare of her little family, she would've loved to explore a possible future with Brian Archer—

She stood abruptly and downed the remains of her coffee in a final gulp. She could obsess to death about Brian later. When they met next, they'd have a quick conversation, sensibly agree that feelings were just feelings, nothing that couldn't be exorcised by rational facts—the key one being that nothing more could develop between them—and then they could continue on with their easy friendship. For now, he was out of sight and she needed to put him out of mind. It was time to get ready for her day and to get the kids ready for theirs. Specifically, she had to pack their overnight bags for their weekend with Steve. With that thought, bam, all silly notions of possible romance fled. She needed the complications of another man in her life like she needed a frontal lobotomy.

Chapter 16

THE COMBINATION OF WARM RAIN and fits and spurts of sun had turned the gray world green overnight, and despite a tedious call to his insurance broker to go over claim details, the fact he was due to see his mother tomorrow, and that this was his last weekend of freedom before starting work Monday, Brian was oddly cheerful. And he, curse it, knew why full well.

It had been forever since he and Katelyn had hung out alone, aside from running together almost every morning, that is. The finger painting with the kids day hardly counted, plus she'd canceled their last movie night. She'd logged a twelve-hour workday on Friday, eight in the shop, four or five sewing in her cabin. And who knew how long she'd worked today—but now it didn't matter. They had a whole evening in front of them, with plans to eat dinner together and binge on Netflix.

He rapped a silly pattern of knocks on the door and Katelyn opened right away, obviously fresh from the shower. A veil of citrus scented steam surrounded her, and her hair was held up in a towel. Her face was

125

flushed with the heat, and she was in flannel pajama shorts and a soft-with-age university sweatshirt. Brian's temperature spiked and his heart beat amped up. The thing he liked best about Katelyn—no, correction, just one of the many, *many* things he liked about her—was her casual, down to earth ways. Maybe it was because she had zero interest in him, but she always seemed to be who she really was with him. He'd dated girls that, throughout their whole relationship, he'd never seen without perfectly applied makeup and immaculately done hair. And the women he'd been more serious with always donned lingerie or silky robes for any sleepovers. But then again, as he'd just reminded himself, he and Katelyn weren't a couple like that. If they were, maybe she'd feel pressured to be more overtly sexy. Maybe those other women preferred to sleep in big shirts too. He'd never thought to ask.

"What?" Katelyn asked, breaking into his thoughts.

"What do you mean, what?"

"You're staring at me like a freak."

"I'm staring at you like you're a freak?" Brian was genuinely confused. He did think she was different, but "freak" was the furthest thing from his mind.

"No, you're staring at me like *you're* a freak." Katelyn balled up the damp towel from her hair and threw it at his head. He grabbed it, laughing—then caught sight of that stupid painting of his. She had, of all the crazy things, hung it on the fridge. And here, after she'd seemed so normal on their running days, he'd had the stupid notion—and extreme relief—that the kids had thrown it away or painted over it.

He read his silly, swirly words and felt himself go as red as the paint he'd used.

Katelyn saw him notice the painting and her nose wrinkled. "Yeah, about that. We should probably clear the air and talk about it, hey?"

Talking about it sounded like an awful idea, and maybe she thought so too, because despite bravely putting it out there, she opened the fridge and commenced rummaging, very effectively hiding from him.

"Maybe we should—or maybe not, if it will be too awkward. Do you want me to go?" he asked a minute later, when she still hadn't emerged from the fridge.

She turned with a plate of veggie sticks and a container of onion dip in hand. "I don't know. If you need to, sure. But I thought we could still watch TV or something, if you want to."

He did want to. Absolutely. But he was suddenly beyond uncomfortable. "Dammit," he muttered. "Damn it, damn it, damn it."

Katelyn's eyes widened. "Damn what?"

Brian covered his eyes with his hands and scrubbed at his face.

"*What?*" Katelyn repeated, sounding more alarmed.

"You're supposed to be my friend."

Katelyn stepped back and set the snack food on the counter behind her. "And, uh, I am."

127

"No. I mean I thought I was your friend."

One of Katelyn's eyebrows shot up.

Brian shook his head, then sighed. "I'm not articulating this very well. You and me, we're supposed to just be friends, but I'm not feeling very, um, *friendly* toward you."

Understanding dawned in Katelyn's face, lightening her slate gray irises to a soft charcoal. She nodded toward the painting again, looking pained. "I know." She jutted a hip, planted her hands on her chest and waggled her eyebrows coquettishly. "You think I'm gorgeous . . . You want to kiss me . . . You want to hug me . . . You want to looove me."

Yes, yes, he did. He wanted to do all those things. "I knew we never should've watched 'Miss Congeniality' together," he mumbled. "And don't hide behind lame jokes. That's my thing."

She laughed. "Well, heaven forbid anyone steal *your thing*." But then she dropped her hands and her expression, still soft, grew serious. "We spend a lot of time together and we're both single, both straight. It would be pretty weird if one or both of us didn't sometimes wonder what if."

Brian searched her eyes and found warmth and mutual fondness—but she was shaking her head as if denying his silent question. "But your life is here and mine is definitely not. I'm leaving Greenridge as soon as I can, for better or for worse. I have to. For my kids, but also for myself. You need to find someone who's

actually available, Brian. You're a great person. You
should let someone else see that, trust them with your
true self."

Suddenly uncomfortable, Brian sought levity, holding his hands up in a don't shoot position, then
winking. "I was just going to say that if you're sexual-
ly frustrated and looking for a friend with benefits, I'm
your guy."

His words did not get the grin he was aiming for.
Katelyn frowned and gave a curt shake of her chin.
"Don't do that. Not with me. I don't mind needing to
have an odd, slightly awkward chat about boundaries
now and again, or taking the risk of being hurt if we
find out we can't pull off being just friends and have to
stop seeing each other, but I don't like games. I like
people to say what they mean and mean what they
say."

"Maybe I said it like a joke, but I was actually serious."

"If I merely wanted sex, I could have it any day of
the week. I don't want that. Or not just that."

"I know that," Brian said quickly. And he did. He
also realized that what made him uncomfortable with
Katelyn was not the confusing, changing nature of his
feelings for her, but how her extreme honesty chal-
lenged him. She made him want to be honest, however
painful, too. He closed his eyes. "I think I was hoping
if we had sex, I'd be able to get over you that way, and
happily return to feeling purely platonic."

Katelyn burst out laughing. "Okay, that's not how it works—or, at least, that's not how it *should* work."

"No," Brian agreed. "But that's how it's always been for me in the past."

Katelyn removed the cling wrap from the veggie plate, passed him a carrot stick, and took one for herself. Her crunching was loud in the small room. "That's really sad."

He shrugged. "I never used to think so."

"So . . ." she said after a long minute and a couple of veggie sticks. "Are you staying or going?"

"For the movie or in the friendship?"

Her smile, so big and genuine, made his stomach flip. "See, that's what I mean. It's feels good to be clear, to ask what you really want to know, doesn't it?"

He shook his head. "Kind of."

"It's up to you. We might get hurt, aiming for friendship, but flirting with more—or we might end up being lifelong bosom buddies."

"I'd like to try," Brian said finally, "but if it gets too difficult, we might have to be the kind of friends who never see each other or talk to each other."

"Wow, that sounds like a close friendship," Katelyn said, eyes crinkling, but she nodded.

"Also, never refer to me as your bosom buddy again. I do have *some* testosterone you know."

Katelyn's laughter tinkled like a soft breeze moving through a glass chime. "I think that all sounds really good," she said. "And I reserve the right to say we need to distance ourselves too."

Brian's pounding heartbeat slowly calmed. He still had his friend. He hadn't ruined everything. It was definitely the most bizarre relationship he'd ever had with a woman—and he was starting to feel like maybe it was his first real one. Did other men find themselves wanting to tell the woman in their life every single nuance of their soul? He'd have to ask Callum. No, on second thought, he'd take the very idea to his grave.

He settled onto the couch with his plate of vegetables (so weirdly satisfying!) and Katelyn curled up in the big armchair.

"So what'll it be?" she asked.

"Surprise me," Brian said, but she didn't get a chance to. The cabin's landline rang and as he watched her answer it, he could tell by the crease that appeared on her forehead that something was off.

"Ah, yeah, he's here. Just a minute."

"Who is it?" he asked as she handed him the receiver.

She shrugged, but still looked like she was struggling to put pieces together that should fit but didn't quite.

"Hello?" Brian said. "Hello?"

He heard the click of the line disconnecting, but tried again regardless. "This is Brian. Who's this?"

There was, of course, no answer.

"No!" The word was a yelp, and Katelyn dropped the celery stick she'd been munching. She left it where it lay. "That was a friend of Steve's. It had to be. Now he knows. He *knows*."

That there really wasn't anything to know, a fact their conversation had just reaffirmed, did nothing to ease the alarm slamming through Brian. He knew what Katelyn meant. That Steve knew he, Brian, was here in the cabin with her alone. And that was a bad thing. Maybe a terrible thing. He could see it in every one of Katelyn's tensed for flight muscles. In her instantly bloodless face. In her eyes, which darted left and right, as if scanning for and logging possible escape routes.

Brian was suddenly hit with a crippling bullet of remorse. He should've stayed away. Even by being Katelyn's friend, he was hurting her. Putting her in danger.

Chapter 17

THE FIRST TIME STEVE TOLD Katelyn he thought a man (of note: that's how he said it, *a man*, not a person) was completely justified in doing "whatever it took, using whatever force necessary," to protect what was his, she'd thought he was joking, exaggerating, trying to impress her with his strength or make her feel safe. And she thought he meant like his stereo or his car or his house or something.

She'd been so naïve. It never occurred to her that some people (oh sorry, Steve, some *men*) considered their wives and children to be possessions. His words had never been intended as a reassurance. They had always been a warning—one that, over time, she started to heed. At first because it was easier. Dealing with him, his insecurity, his jealousy, was . . . exhausting. It was better to avoid situations and people that brought it on. Later because she was afraid. His temper, and what triggered it, was unpredictable to say the very least. But eventually, despite the fear—or maybe because of it—she'd realized she had no control over what caused his rages and they were only going to continue to get worse, more intense. And so she'd left. A decision she knew was right, but that carried its own danger too; she was always waiting for the repercussions of her choice.

Spring cabin had always seemed cozy and secure, cloistered away as it was. Now it felt like a trap—a tiny, remote place in the middle of nowhere that hardly anyone knew about. A place where Steve, if he timed his actions carefully, could find her alone and unprepared. No. She refused to go down that road. She stood up gingerly, like she'd aged a hundred years, like perhaps her bones could no longer support the huge weight she carried: fear, anger, impotence.

She glanced at Brian. She could read him like a book—read him exactly how she'd learned the hard, hard way to read Steve. Oh, what different stories they were though. How terribly, cruelly different. Why had she learned to read so late?

"This is not your fault." She waved her hand to speak to the whole big mess. "It's not you or that you're here. It could've been Callum, just for owning River's Sigh. It could've been a gas clerk for filling up my tank. It could've been *anything*."

"But it's not Callum or some other random man. It's not anything. It's me. Here."

She shook her head. "No, it's nothing. It's always nothing. Don't make me feel like I have to comfort you or something. Please. It makes it even worse. Just take my word for it and let yourself off the hook."

Brian set his food down on the coffee table, looked at her steadily, then nodded. "So what happens next? What do you do? What does he do?"

It was interesting to her in an academic way that Brian seemed to understand that this was nothing new. That he sensed it was an old dance between her and her ex-husband, one with familiar steps—and only the knowledge that one day she might falter, might forget a rule, or that Steve might decide to try a new routine kept her moving to its ugly music, kept her terrified, no matter how she sought to be independent of him.

"I can't believe that guy has unsupervised visits," Brian said under his breath, but he didn't appear to be talking to her, so she addressed his earlier comment instead.

"He'll call my cell in a minute, sounding like sweetness and light itself, and try to convince me to meet him for coffee. When that doesn't work, he'll say the kids want to see me, that they need me, so why don't we all do something together for a few hours."

Brian didn't meet her eyes. Instead he gazed intently at the floor as if reading some unseen note for advice or something. He tightened his hands into fists, then stretched his fingers as far as they would extend, and repeated the motion several times.

Finally he spoke. "And does that work?"

"Does what work?"

"Telling you the kids need you. Does it get you to go to him?"

Katelyn's whole body drooped. "It has. In the past. Yeah."

"And then? After he convinces you to see him, what happens?"

"It depends. Sometimes he can continue his good guy act for days or weeks afterwards. He uses that one or two hours of calm as proof he's 'changed.' Other times just seeing me triggers one of his tirades."

"Does he hit you?"

Katelyn unconsciously fingered the tiny crescent scar by her eye. "Not anymore. I captured video evidence of one of the "kerfuffles"—Steve's word— when he came to pick up the kids one day. I turned it over to my lawyer, who submitted the clip at our last hearing."

Brian made an angry huffing sound. "And he still managed to weasel unsupervised access."

"Yeah. Steve's lawyer had already presented the notion that some "things" had happened that Steve was very distressed by and was seeking help for. Said it was just that Steve was so upset by the idea of losing his family and everything. The judge bought the story, but did say if there were any similar incidences going forward, he'd revisit it."

Brian shook his head, but Katelyn didn't take it personally. He didn't say it was unbelievable. But he wouldn't say that, of course. He worked in the courts. He knew anything was possible.

"Has he ever physically abused the kids?"

Katelyn hesitated, then shook her head.

"But you think he might."

Her stomach dropped. It was something she fought to not think about—fought hard—but she nodded. "They're the one thing he knows for sure he still has over me."

Brian muttered a string of low, venomous curses. "And if you stand your ground, refuse to meet him, and make him keep the kids without your intervention or help for his full weekend?"

She couldn't look at Brian. She hated the shame that roiled in her guts. She had nothing to feel ashamed of; it was just an oily residue left over from all those years of being with Steve.

"Have you ever managed to?" Brian prodded again in a gentle voice.

"Yeah . . ."

"But?"

"But it makes the following weeks brutal. He calls constantly, files bogus complaints against me to his lawyer, who then contacts my lawyer . . . and it's all money I don't have, you know?"

Brian nodded. "Well, it's your life, and I guess you know him better than anyone."

"But?"

Brian looked down.

"Tell me what you think."

"But I've seen too many cases like this to not have a bit of advice—only if you want it."

Katelyn nodded. "Sure. What?"

"He doesn't have you the way he wants you, in his house, as his wife, but he still has an incredible amount of power over you. He basically says jump and you jump—"

"To protect my kids!"

Brian's face held no judgment, just sadness, and because of that, and because Katelyn had gleaned a bit of Archer family history over the past months, she heard his words as genuinely intended help, not criticism. "But maybe what would really protect them in the long term is to see their mother truly escape their abusive maniac of a father, not to see her continuing to accept his control just in a different way. To see that, no, a person cannot continue to rule over another person indefinitely. To learn that, no, a person does not have to continue to let someone treat them badly forever, or endure them being a part of their life forever. To believe that no one is *entitled* to access to another person."

"But what if . . . what if . . . " Katelyn could hardly squeeze out the words. She had no air and no room in her lungs to draw in any. The swelling pain in her heart, the dread, took all the space in her chest. "What if he hurts them, what then? What if we become just another 'intimate partner' or family violence statistic?"

Brian's voice was ragged, like he too was on the verge of tears. "I don't know. There are no easy answers. None. But you've come this far, and while he hasn't liked it at all, in some ways he has learned to take no for an answer, does respect some boundaries."

He put his hands on her shoulders and pulled her into a gentle hug. She let herself sag into the strength of him. "You can do this, Katelyn. You can be free. Let him take care of his children, make him learn to be a single parent, show him that you are not a part of his world in the ways you used to be—in any way, shape, or form."

She uttered a stifled choking sound and Brian spoke even more softly. "And either he'll learn it and you'll be free, or he'll do something that the courts can't ignore."

"But my kids . . . "

"Are already damaged by him, *are still* being damaged by him."

That hurt—and angered—her, but she couldn't deny it was true. Lacey was too old, too watchful for her years. Sawyer, though slowly coming out of his shell, was still too quiet.

Katelyn's phone rang, making them both jump. She stepped out of Brian's embrace quickly, feeling like she'd been caught doing something indecent. And maybe she had been. Maybe the emotional closeness and safety she felt with him was more intimate than any physical act they could participate in.

The phone continued its incessant buzzing. Katelyn stared out the living room window and considered not answering. The trees and greenery, the mountains, the sky—the whole reality of the world beyond her—was nothing but a blur, a fuzzy idea almost blotted entirely from view by the gathering darkness and weeping clouds.

There were a few seconds of silence. Then the phone sounded again.

Katelyn looked at Brian. He held her gaze the same way he had held her just moments earlier: calm and steady. She nodded at him once, then picked up her cell and hit Talk.

"Steve?"

The verbal assault was instant and predictable, pretty much word for word what she'd told Brian it would be. She listened for a moment, then took a deep breath. "Well, I can talk to them on the phone for a minute if you need me to, but it's your weekend and you're their father. You know what they like. I'm working and can't come."

Again, his next level of response was no surprise. She shook her head, feeling surprisingly resolute. Her eye caught her framed quote about bravery, and she even found a smile—a genuine one—to put in her voice. "Yes, Brian is here. He's my friend, and just a friend, but you're going to have to adjust to this next phase of our lives. You and I are not together anymore and we never will be again."

"You don't know that."

"I do know that, and I think you do too." She took a long, shuddery breath. "Not because I'm interested in anyone else, but because you and I aren't good together. I know it's hard and sad for you that I feel this way—but you have all the tools you need, or you can get them, to be okay with it."

For maybe the first time ever in all their conversations and entanglements, she seemed to have rendered Steve speechless. He recovered quickly though.

"You cold, unfeeling bitch. You have no idea what you're putting me through—and you don't even care."

"I am sorry you feel that—"

"Don't give me your crap sorrys. You're not sorry. I always knew you were an unfaithful whore—but I never thought you were a bad mother until now."

Katelyn figured it was useless to point out that his last line was false, that he always made similar accusations. She just hoped above hope that the kids were busy watching TV or playing outside in the yard, not sitting anywhere nearby, listening in.

Finally he snorted, "The kids don't want you anyway. I was trying to be nice and make you feel needed. Now you'll have to wait until tomorrow to see them—until *you're allowed* to have them back."

The connection ended.

She hugged her Steve-free phone to her chest for a moment and glanced through the window again. The view, though still blurry, was lighter than it had been even a few minutes earlier. The clouds' tears had almost stopped and a few stars peeked through the darkness here and there.

"You okay?" Brian asked softly.

She gave a one-shouldered shrug. "You know . . . I think I am. And, even more shockingly, he seemed to take it . . . not too badly."

Brian smiled, but concern still etched fine lines beside his eyes. "Well, good—and look, I know we already discussed this, but I get it, I really do. If our being friends isn't worth it to you because it causes you too much trouble, I'll understand. Your situation is already complicated enough."

"Yeah, 'it's complicated' should be my perpetual online status." She paced the small room, feeling the nubby area rug, then cold hardwood flooring beneath her feet. She ran both hands through her hair, massaging her scalp as if she could rub some wisdom or insight into her head.

"I want to say screw him, like I did before. I want to reiterate that Steve doesn't call the shots for me, but . . . " Her voice petered out and she sighed again. "I'm sorry I'm such an emotional nightmare."

"You're the furthest thing from an emotional nightmare."

How she wished that was true. "That's nice of you to say."

"I mean it."

Katelyn's sinuses were salty and full to capacity, ready to rush down her face in an embarrassing flood that she feared might never stop if she let it out at all. Why did kindness sometimes trigger a need to weep even more than meanness did? She tried to joke, but feared her voice was half-strangled, revealing she wasn't jesting at all. "Can we play it by ear? Can I have a free to be a wimp card, just in case I need to call off our friendship sometime?"

Brian laughed a little, like she'd hoped he would— but it didn't touch his eyes, which remained somber, or his forehead, which remained furrowed.

"Whatever you need. I mean it."

"Sometimes I just get . . . tired, you know? Sometimes I just want the path of least resistance."

Brian nodded. "Let's amend our earlier agreement. We'll expand the terms, so it's understood that either one of us, at any time, for any reason, no hard feelings, can bail on being friends and go our own separate way. Sound good?"

"All right . . . I guess. But now that we've covered not being friends or only being friends under what circumstances two or three times already, let's never speak of when, ifs, buts and whats again."

"Excellent plan. Agreed." Brian retrieved the celery stick she'd dropped earlier and popped it in his mouth.

Katelyn shook her head.

"What? It's the fifteen minute rule."

"Gross. That's not a thing."

"I just invented it, so there. Now put the movie on already. We're getting old here." Brian's grin seemed to wrap her whole body in a hug, not unlike the one he'd given her earlier.

"Okay, okay, and hey, if you're still hungry, there are scraps in the garbage bin. They've only been there like half an hour or so. Does that work for you?"

"Har, har, har." He settled into the couch and tugged her down beside him. "It's easier to share popcorn when you're not jumping around the room," he explained.

It was. And it was also somehow cozier and more comfortable in general.

Before Brian left later that evening, he paused in the doorway. "Hey, are you and the kids going to the Spring Fling in town this weekend?"

"Yes, we are. I made us party clothes and everything. Why?"

"I don't know. I was planning to steer clear, but—" He shrugged cutely and Katelyn knew he'd been planning anything but. It made her smile. "—if you're going to be there, maybe I'll check it out."

"Well, if it works for you, it would be very nice to have a friend there to dance with, etcetera, etcetera."

"Etcetera, etcetera, hey?" He winked. "Sounds enticing."

She blushed. "That's not what I meant."

"I know," he said softly, suddenly serious. "Have a good evening, Katelyn."

He headed into the inky night, then, as was becoming their habit, he turned to wave before he got out of sight. She waved back, closed the door, and leaned against it, trying her best—and utterly failing—to ignore the almost manic happiness washing through her. She had stood up for herself to Steve, finally and firmly. She had not allowed him to use the kids to manipulate her—and it had been all right. And Brian Archer, lovely, lovely Brian Archer was still her friend. Her really good, wonderful friend.

Chapter 18

BRIAN WAS GRATEFUL FOR THE lengthy drive into Greenridge from River's Sigh, though he was suspicious that the twenty or thirty minutes would be nowhere near long enough to make sense of his jumbled thoughts and conflicting emotions.

He hated that he wouldn't be anywhere near Spring cabin when Steve dropped the kids off to Katelyn. What if she needed him? But maybe that was stupid thinking on his part. This was her life, her battle—and she'd managed thus far without his wannabe white-knighting. (Wow, Callum had really called him on that!) But he also couldn't deny feeling relieved that he wouldn't be there to witness or cause a scene.

He was worried his friendship with Katelyn was adding fuel to the fire of her already troubled relationship with Steve. Wasn't it completely selfish for him to keep hanging out with her? But then again, wasn't it completely egotistical, sexist even, for him to feel he had any right or responsibility to think such things when she'd told him not to?

Brian downshifted to a stuttering halt at the four-way stop before the bridges, one to his right, one straight ahead, that led into Greenridge via alternate routes over the river. Yikes, he was practically in town already, but he couldn't remember a thing he'd driven past if you'd paid him to. He was tempted to turn left and head to the next nearest small town—or, better yet, pull a U-turn and head back to River's Sigh. He could hole up in a snug corner of Jo and Callum's, where, yes, fine, okay, he'd admit it . . . he'd be on hand should Katelyn need him.

He shook his head and waved apologetically out his window as a big black Suburban honked. It was his turn to proceed through the intersection. What was his glitch anyway? Get it together, man. Get it together!

The inner command, muttered in his father's voice, almost worked. Or it brought him back to his immediate problems, a.k.a. his mom and dad, anyway. And just in time, he thought wryly, rolling up in front of his destination: his parents' house—or was it just his mother's now?

He strode up the immaculate walkway that curved from the pristinely maintained driveway—a driveway big enough for six cars to park with ample room in front of the three bay garage.

Even in this blah time of year when it was too early for most people to be out doing much in their yards, the lawn was obviously tended, already thatched and well on its way to being a lush carpet of green. Expensive ornamental shrubs and plants, whose names alluded Brian, though his mind's eye could see the color of various blooms and leaves, were free of the burlap they'd been wrapped in for protection over the winter and looked freshly clipped and pruned.

Everything was in its place and there was a place for everything. Obviously his father's yard mainte-nance team was still employed. This front entrance was intentionally planned to dictate a very specific first impression of the Archer family home: wealthy but tasteful, well assembled and held together, big, power-ful and moneyed. It all yelled his father, Duncan Archer, in a not to be ignored way. Everything was arranged just so for maximum positive impression.

If Brian walked around the back, however, through the archway into his mother's realm, it would be a different landscape all together. Caren loved plants and growing things the way some people loved and overin-dulged children. Even now, with winter barely gone, it would be a jungle, featuring vines that should've been clipped back, heritage lilac bushes that were more like trees, and a myriad of shoots and stalks pushing their way up through the ground, spreading at random wherever they chose.

The juxtaposition of his parents' individual spaces, which continued from the yard and into the house, and how clear a difference it showed in their personalities, made Brian smile as he rang the bell, even though he felt sad. Just a glance at their yard showed anyone with half a brain how unsuited they were to each other.

A pitter-patter of happy dog feet sounded behind the big double door.

"Who's there, Trixie? Who's there?" Trixie, his mother's purebred Sheltie, did something that sounded like a tap dance in delight at the question. Then his mother opened the door and looked up at Brian with something almost like surprise, though she'd been the one to pick the time and day and place for lunch.

Brian looked at his watch, then down at his mother again. "You were expecting me, right? If not, I can come back."

Caren shook her head. "Don't be silly. You're always welcome. I'm just . . . distracted. I knew you were coming, but I got busy in my studio and lost track of time."

She hadn't moved to let him into the house yet.

"Would it be easier for you if we headed down the hill into town? We could have lunch out."

Caren finally opened the door wider. "No, I've been excited about your visit. Looking forward to it. I made everything ahead yesterday."

And Brian knew her words, that she was excited, had been looking forward to visiting him, were true. She was just in the unsettling, not quite with you state that always accompanied her working. In a few minutes, she'd be more present.

As usual, she moved through the big foyer, the great room, the living room and the formal dining room as if they weren't even there, were merely the pathway to the real house—and in a way that was exactly true. In the kitchen, a clean but cluttered space, she slowed down and graced him with another smile. This one was brighter and more engaged. She was already more solidly back in the realm of here and now.

"It's been forever. Have we ever gone this long without seeing each other before?"

"I don't know. Probably. Maybe when I was in school?"

"Maybe," she conceded. "But either way, it's been too long. Do you have a hug for your old mother?"

He laughed. No matter what anyone thought of Caren, and despite the fact she was his mother and thus should seem somewhat old, at least to him, *old* was not an adjective she conjured. With her slight, bordering on skinny build, unlined face and shoulder-length blond hair, often worn, as it was now, pulled back in a loose ponytail, she was ageless. She looked and acted like the exact same woman he had adored as a child and still adored now, despite how remote and somehow unreachable she often was.

She was wearing what Brian's father had always called—affectionately, it had seemed to Brian—her "artist costume," a man's oversized white button down shirt, the long sleeves rolled almost to her elbows, leggings and ballet flats. Was it weird that he always noticed things about his mother in such minute detail? He and Callum had talked about that, both wondering, because Callum did it too. They had decided it was normal, a side effect of growing up in a home where reading their parents' barometers was a survival tool. Not that Caren would ever harm any of them specifically; she would just disappear sometimes—or you would—regardless of her physical presence in a room or proximity to you. But their father had been a more volatile housemate. By watching Caren, they were cued to his mood and could be on alert.

"*What?*" Caren shot Brian a concerned look and laughed self-consciously. The musical sound broke into Brian's thoughts like sun through clouds—another thing that was uniquely heartbreaking to his relationship with his mother: how he longed, even now, pathetically, to be seen by her. "You're staring at me."

He tried to shake his loony thoughts and leaned in to hug her as bidden. "Well, like you said, it's been a while, that's all. How are you?"

"I've been better," she admitted. "Now come and eat."

He moved toward the heavy wooden table that was painted fire engine red, and settled into a royal blue chair. Caren perched on the edge of a green one. The yellow and orange chairs were occupied too, with towering stacks of magazines. Caren followed his gaze. "For another project. Sometime. Maybe."

She filled two clunky gold rimmed glasses with homemade iced tea. Then, over a lavish spread of assorted deli meats, cheeses, pickles, olives and rye bread, they made small talk about his trip, neither of them tackling the awkward reality that it had been more a case of him fleeing his family than a true fun seeking holiday.

Trixie lay at Brian's feet, the picture of canine obedience, but Brian knew it was only because she suspected he'd be a softer touch than Caren, more likely to sneak her pieces of salami or Havarti.

Caren had the metabolism of a hummingbird, and like the petite flier, she needed a crazy amount of food daily. When she finally finished consuming what seemed like her bodyweight in cheese, the moment Brian had been hoping to put off indefinitely was upon him. Awkward truth telling, say how he felt time.

Caren held up a hand to stave him off, however. "I know," she said. "It's okay."

Well, that was fine and good and all, but it wasn't like he could just take her vague word for it, much as he'd like to. "Sorry, what do you know exactly?"

"What you said on the phone—that you don't want to represent me if I divorce your father. Don't worry. I'm not hurt or offended in the slightest. I completely understand. In fact, I apologize. It was a terrible thing to ask of you."

Wait a minute, what? *If* she divorced his father? The food Brian had enjoyed turned to writhing maggots in his gut. Of course, *if*. He couldn't believe he'd wasted time and energy worrying that she might feel he wasn't supporting her.

"I'm not sure we'll be divorcing, after all," she confirmed, as if her earlier "if" wouldn't have caught him like a sharp barb and told him all he needed to know.

He studied the crumbs on his plate. When he finally looked up she was watching him sympathetically. "Please don't take this badly. It's just I'm not sure. We built a life together. We have a lot invested."

Brian didn't respond, just propped his elbows on the table and rested his face in his hands, feeling about eight—a feeling that intensified when Caren pushed a plate of sweets toward him, like chocolate chip cookies could make everything okay. Oddly, he felt saddest for Cade. This news would hit him the hardest. And then he stole a line from his eldest brother's vocab too. "Sure, Ma. Whatever you say."

She nodded, gave him a happy, approving smile, then jumped to her feet and motioned toward the back of the house and a sunroom that served as her studio. "I knew you'd understand. Now let me show you something I've been working on."

Despite the low burning disappointment and confusion blistering through him, a small flame of interest flared in Brian. A few years back, when Callum had just re-met Jo, hadn't even gotten back together with her yet, he had told Brian and Cade that Caren was working on something different from the landscapes she was known for. But none of them had seen so much as a square inch of the mystery canvases.

Caren's hand was white-knuckled on the glass knob of the antique French door leading to her studio. Just as Brian tuned into her stress, she turned to him, frowning. "I'm sorry." Her face pinched in sorrow. "I thought I could show you, I thought I was ready, but I'm not. But I will be . . . soon." She pulled a shiny postcard from the shirt pocket on her chest. It was an announcement for a gallery showing, featuring the collective works of Caren Oliveria Queen, who was his mother, or the artist side of her, anyway. It was scheduled, not for the upcoming summer, but for the one after that, a full year and a bit out. He was speechless.

"I just think . . . maybe it's better if you guys see my new stuff the same time everybody else does. Is that okay?"

Was it okay? Sure. It was her art, her choice. But it was also . . . bizarre. She could handle a gallery show, but couldn't bear revealing her paintings to her own children? Had his dad seen them?

Then again, in some ways strangers were less terrifying than people who knew you best. Strangers didn't have any preconceived notions about who you were or weren't that shaped you and affected you, possibly limited you, even when you wished they didn't. And you didn't crave their high opinion in the same way either. So, come to think of it, maybe he did understand her reticence. "Whatever you need, Mom. Seriously."

The anxious tension melted from Caren's face. She

reached up and patted his shoulder. "Thank you."

"Are you going to the Spring Fling?" Brian asked on his way out the door.

"No, no, not this year. I'm going to stay home and work."

Brian nodded and they made lunch plans for late the following week.

Brian was long gone from the Archer driveway, down the hill and back in the city center, in fact, before he realized that Caren hadn't revisited the fact that he'd lost his home and everything he owned in a fire. And he hadn't said a word either. But he guessed it made sense. She had a lot on her plate.

Chapter 19

IT WASN'T RAINING EXACTLY, BUT it also wasn't *not* raining. The clouds were so dark and heavy they seemed to touch the earth in places, and the mist was so thick, it felt as if you were walking through a cloud. It made everything damp and depressing to Brian's mind, but from the buzz of conversation and laughter streaming all around him, it was clear he was probably the only one in the crowd who held that opinion.

For the tenth time in the last half an hour he wondered why he'd even come to the Spring Fling. What a dumb idea, especially so early in the year. It didn't feel like spring, and it was definitely too cold for all the bright summery clothes everyone was sporting. There was a mile long line up by the hot chocolate vendor, and not because people were craving the sweet beverage, but because they wanted something warm to hold in their frigid hands.

He circled the library park one more time, though "circled" was too optimistic a description. "Inched fruitlessly" was better. Or "got bumped into, had to stop for the hundredth time." Or "was an idiot for even trying to wade through the crowd." And he was the only single guy. Everyone else was part of a couple or a larger group. Normally adept in social events, Brian was totally out of his element. He didn't belong here, even if he wanted to. He should be home in his condo, saying yes to some last-minute dinner invite and making plans to go to the pub. Or he should be on a date with some cute girl who'd smiled at him in the grocery checkout.

He sighed heavily. Even if his house hadn't burned down, he was well aware that neither of those plans fit him well anymore. What was wrong with him?

Then a familiar laugh sounded nearby. Brian's insides leapt, a smile jumped to his face—and he knew exactly what was wrong with him. Shoot. He'd been a big whiny baby because he hadn't found Katelyn and the kids yet. And now that he was sure they were there? Well, his mood was one hundred percent altered. How totally lame.

Another laugh. Brian followed the sound, maneuvering around a lady with five children each carrying multiple helium balloons, then sidestepping a kid who was dressed as a clown and pulling a wagon. He looked right, then left, sure he'd lost her—but no, there she was, weaving her way through the crowd with Lacey and Sawyer in tow. Both kids were grinning ear to ear, had balloons tied to their wrists, and clutched big bags of candy corn. A moment later Aisha appeared from behind a big man with a beard.

"We're in, let's go, let's go." She winked at Katelyn and whisked the kids away.

"I want to be a dragon, I want to be a dragon!" Lacey cheered as they departed.

"Me too!" agreed Sawyer.

Brian had no idea what they were talking about and had a weird twinge seeing them go. He'd envisioned himself wowing them at the dart throw and winning them each a stuffed animal or something, but then Katelyn turned, saw him, and flashed a smile that made him forget whatever he'd been thinking about.

"You came!" she said happily.

"I did. It's great."

She gave him a side-eyed look.

"Okay, okay—until I finally found you, which took forever—I was wondering what on earth I was doing here."

"Testing, Testing," a loud male voice hollered over a mic from the main stage, cutting off whatever Katelyn was about to say in reply. There was a screech of speakers, some kind of adjustment, and then another blaring yell, "And here's the band that needs no introduction—*No Introduction.*"

There was a ripple of polite laughter at the weak joke, then someone got busy on the drums. The crowd's cheering grew louder and more sincere.

"I haven't danced in forever!" Katelyn did a little spin—and Brian's heart did too.

"That's a great dress," he said.

"What?" she hollered over the music.

He shook his head. "Nothing."

Then the kids were back and Lacey, wearing a dress that matched her mama's to a T, was indeed a dragon. The appointment they'd rushed off to must have been for face painting.

Brian screamed and pointed at Lacey.

Five faces—Katelyn, Lacey, Sawyer, Aisha and Mo—all stared at him in alarm.

"Dragon," he yelled. "*Dragon!*"

Sawyer shot a wide-eyed glance at Brian, then at his sister, then back at Brian. "No, no, don't be afraid. That's Lacey. She's only *pretending.*"

Brian put his hand to his heart. "Phew!"

Lacey giggled and so did Aisha—as she rolled her eyes.

Katelyn shook her head. "You, Brian Archer . . . "

"Me, what?"

She didn't get a chance to finish her sentence. The kids pulled her into a circle to dance, then pulled Brian in too. He ended up holding a whiskered, black-nosed Mo by her slightly sticky little hand.

"I kitty cat," she said proudly.

He nodded. "Meow," he said agreeably.

"No, *me*," she insisted with a pout, pointing a chubby thumb toward her chest.

Aisha laughed. "She's definitely my kid, what can I say?"

Brian noted that Aisha wore a heavy metal T-shirt

cut into a makeshift vest over her pretty cherry print dress—and she was sporting black and white canvas high tops.

"I like your vest."

"Thanks." She laughed again, then pointed at herself with her thumb the same way Mo had. "I weirdo."

If someone had told Brian, even six months earlier, that he'd be dancing in a circle with a bunch of face-painted kids and their babysitter, not even touching the woman he was crushing on, and loving it, he would've said they were nuts. But he really was, bizarrely, having the best time.

After a couple of raucous songs, the band moved into a love ballad. The kids immediately stopped bopping around, clearly not as into the slower music.

"We should go get hotdogs for the kids, or something more substantial than popcorn anyway," Katelyn remarked.

"I'll do it, and I'll take the kids," Aisha said quickly.

"No, that's okay—"

"Please? It'll be fun!" Maintaining their hand-held chain, Aisha rushed away with the kids, leaving a confused Katelyn looking after her. "That was weird. It's not like she's babysitting—"

"I think she thought we might like to dance this one," Brian said.

Katelyn's cheeks flamed. "Oh," she said. "*Oh*!"

She looked so cute that Brian wanted to . . . well, a

lot of things. But he settled for placing one hand on her waist. She lifted her hand, about to rest it on his shoulder, but Brian was suddenly jostled. Hard. He stumbled a little.

"Hey, watch it," he mumbled halfheartedly, expecting the oaf who'd body slammed him to be long gone already—but no such luck.

The band's lead singer crooned something about love never dying, just as Brian realized Katelyn was more than six feet away from him, her wrist held in a death grip by an irate looking Steve. The creep was practically frothing.

"You look ridiculous. *Ridiculous.*"

The song was feverishly soft now, unfortunately, and Steve's voice turned heads.

"Dancing around like a slut, like you're not some stupid used up cow—"

Brian grabbed Steve's free hand, his brain working overtime. Something worse than fear shone from Katelyn's eyes—complete and utter humiliation. How dare this fucking asshat—Brian stopped the furious thought cold. Stooping to this guy's level, pouring anger and aggression back on him would only blow everything up bigger and hurt Katelyn more—but what could he do?

He took a deep breath, then made a big show of shaking Steve's hand like he was some long-lost friend he hadn't seen in years. "Buddy," he said warmly.

It worked. Steve looked at Brian, gobsmacked. The

small distraction was all Katelyn needed. She wrenched herself free of Steve and moved behind Brian.

"Come on, man, your kids are here," Brian said. "Don't let them see you like this."

Steve recovered from his surprise at Brian's approach to things, and his eyes narrowed. "What the hell's my family to you anyway?"

Oh, how Brian wanted to tell Steve exactly what "his" family was to him—and what he wanted them to be—but poking the bear was probably a bad idea right now. He'd call the police and report Steve's behavior later, though fat lot of good it would probably do. Right now he just wanted to spare Katelyn more grief.

He held his hands up in a conciliatory way. "I'm just a friend of the family—"

"Bullshit! You're always sniffing around her like she's some bitch in heat."

White-hot rage blurred Brian's vision. His hand clenched into a rock-like fist and his arm rocketed back. It was like he wasn't attached to his body, was just watching a guy who looked a lot like him getting ready to punch an asshole.

His own words filled his head.

Your kids are here. They weren't his, of course, but the message brought him up short regardless. Lacey and Sawyer could not witness him hitting their father. Absolutely not. They'd seen enough violence in their short lives.

He dropped his hand and took a step back, shaking with the effort it took to do so.

Steve sneered and his eyes glinted like he'd won some victory. "That's what I thought, pretty boy. That's what I thought."

Brian didn't bite, and after a second, Steve spit on the ground. "This isn't over. Not even close."

Steve stormed away, disappearing through the throngs of people who were roaming toward food trucks and the various vendor tents now that the band was on break. Brian watched long enough to make sure he was really leaving, and to ensure he was headed the opposite direction of the kids and Aisha—then he turned to Katelyn.

She had moved a few paces away and was standing motionless by the trunk of a huge maple tree, staring down at her pretty red slingbacks.

"There's mud all over the heels. They're ruined," she said, without looking up.

Brian gently raised her chin and stared into her eyes, which were bigger and grayer than usual. He shook his head. "They're fantastic," he said. "Perfect, in fact. A bit of mud's nothing. Mud can always be washed off. And damage? I don't see any, but even if there is some, damage can be repaired."

She didn't say anything and although she didn't shake his hand away, she turned her head slightly, so she didn't have to look at him anymore—or so that he couldn't look at her so directly.

"Come on, Katelyn . . . please. Don't let that guy wreck one more thing for you, ever. Not one more moment."

He smudged away a solitary tear that escaped her suddenly brimming eyes, catching it softly as it crowned the tiny scar that few people ever noticed, preventing it from sneaking any further. "You're lovely. In every way. Inside and out."

She chewed her lip, shaking her head.

"You are. I mean it."

"Thank you," she whispered finally. The din of canned music they were now pumping through the speakers ceased to exist for Brian.

"For what?" he said, forcing a small laugh. "Not being a total douche? You're welcome."

She shook her head. "No, for being so nice to me. For taking care of me—being careful *with* me. I really appreciate it. You're a good friend."

He wanted, desperately, to make some off the cuff comment or silly remark. He wanted to say something casually dismissive or corny like, "De nada," or "My pleasure, little lady," but he found that he couldn't. *Taking care of her. Being careful with her.* Was that what he was doing? He'd always shuddered when he heard women say their men took care of them and grimaced when women went on about husbands who were like having an extra child, who couldn't fend for themselves or take care of their own needs. Yet now, in a way, he could see what Katelyn meant. He did try to help her out—but really, no more than she did the same for him, including him when he was lonely, making him snacks because like his mom, he needed food every couple hours, and letting him talk or *not talk* as he felt compelled. Was that what it meant when people spoke of leaning on their partner, of "needing" them?

Maybe depending on someone, or wanting someone to depend on you, wasn't weakness or codependency or a trap. Maybe it was a deeper, more complex—even sweeter—level of real friendship. Huh.

"Brian?" He felt her hand on his forearm, heard concern in her voice. "Are you all right? You look about a hundred miles away."

"What? Oh, sorry, yes. I'm fine. Just thinking."

"About?"

He shrugged and discovered his ability to duck and run for cover was alive and well, after all, despite all his weird longings and fantasies. "Cotton candy—and maybe a beer."

She paused, looking up at him with those serious gray eyes of hers, and suddenly the band was playing again, and the noise of the evening was back in full flood, filling his ears. She noticed the change too and glanced over her shoulder. Whatever moment might have been his to grab had sailed on.

"Sounds good," she said lightly. "Get me a bag of blue and a bag of pink. No beer though."

"Two colors?"

"Yep, I'm special."

She was suddenly swished away by the crowd, already dancing again. An older gentleman, smiling like he'd just won the lottery, caught her hand as she passed and twirled her like they were at an old-fashioned ball.

She'd been joking, of course, but she *was* special. Brian knew it. And he knew it was only a matter of time before she realized that other people—other good, deserving guys, the kind of guys who would cherish her—thought so too. And just like she danced away now, she'd dance away again, permanently. The question was: what, if anything, was Brian prepared to do about it?

"Hey," he hollered, loud enough to be heard above the crowd.

She looked back at him, momentarily stilled, her expression quizzical.

He strode a couple feet toward her—close enough to no longer yell, but not close enough to touch her. "You *are* special. I mean it. What am I going to do when some other guy realizes how great you are and tries to steal you from me?"

She laughed, her somber eyes suddenly twinkling—oh, how he loved that shift in her. How instant and immediate it was. How he could cause it.

"Oh yeah, that's a real fear."

"It is."

"Well," she started moving again, but not in

dance—in feigned swordplay. "Then I guess you'll have to fight for me."

He laughed and a couple intercepted them, blocked her from his view. "Now get me my cotton candy," she called.

He nodded, though she couldn't see him, then wound his way through the crowd toward the food vendors. There, he'd told her. She hadn't believed him, but at least he'd sort of put how he felt out there.

BRIAN'S JEEP HUMMED ALONG THE quiet highway into town. The low cloud cover, light rain, and thick mist rising off the river created the sensation that he was driving out of a dream. And maybe he was. After so many weeks of holidays, followed by his slightly surreal time at River's Sigh B & B with Katelyn, it was hard to get his head around the idea that minus his condo, of course, he was returning to "real" life. Going back to the grind after so much time away was the furthest thing from his thoughts, however. His mind was full of Katelyn.

He didn't like that he was counting in hours how long it had been since he'd last seen her. And he really didn't like that he was consumed with questions about how long it might be until their paths crossed again—especially since it had only been a few days since the Spring Fling. How could that feel so long ago? She'd been busy sewing all day Saturday for some last-minute wedding. It hadn't worked for them to go running on Sunday morning either. When she'd returned after picking up the kids from Steve, he figured she'd appreciate some alone time with them. Plus he'd needed to iron a week's worth of newly acquired work clothes. And that was the weekend, gone.

Now it was Monday and he had a full day ahead of him—probably more than full, trying to play catch-up after being gone for so long. With Katelyn's regular hours at the shop and her piece sewing on the side, they'd practically never see each other. Which wasn't even normal for friends, let alone *friends*. The thought made him scowl and confront the real issue bugging him. He wanted to be way more than friends. And she, for very sane reasons, did not. He was a jerk for being unable to control his emotions. Or he was a jerk for not going all out and fighting for her, asking her to at least give them a chance. Either way, the truth was unavoidable: he was a jerk.

Brian's circular thoughts kept his brain busy right up until he pulled into his reserved parking spot behind Archer and Sons, a flawed name now that Callum had deserted the business. But then again "Archer and Son," though accurate, would sound odd.

It was early and the damp street was empty. He let himself in through the side door, rather than the front entrance, and wasn't surprised in the slightest to see light from his dad's big office flooding the end of the dark hallway. (No sense in lighting the whole office, spending dollars needlessly, until it was open for business.) Brian had never in his life beaten his dad to work—and he was a chronic early bird himself. What *was* slightly surprising was the fact that his father's big double oak doors were open. The light poured forth from the doorway, not just from a crack beneath the door.

Brian's footfalls made no sound on the lush carpet installed in this part of the building to mute noise and increase privacy, but his arrival didn't go unnoticed. Just as he neared the hallway that would take him to his own workspace, his father's big doors swung shut and latched with a dull thud. Brian turned the corner toward his own office, again unsurprised. Extended leave of absence or no, what would've been shocking was if Duncan interrupted his precious early morning routine to do something as mundane as welcome him back. But he hadn't called his old man upon his return to town either, so he couldn't really fault him.

He sank into the deep chair behind his leather-topped desk and swiveled in a slow circle. His secretary—bless her—had obviously kept track of his return date. There were fresh flowers by his window and the coffee pot in his coffee station had been set to brew by timer. The aroma of a rich espresso blend he especially enjoyed filled the room. He might never have been gone at all. Then a sheet of yellow legal pad paper caught his eye, and he had his first surprise since returning to work. A bona fide note from his dad. Wow.

It read, in full:

Let's do lunch.

– Archer

P.S. I can lend you whatever you need to get set up again while you're waiting on those insurance losers to send you a check. Three percent interest. That's better than the bank.

Brian snorted and reread the note. It practically made a guy need a minute to get over the sentimentality . . . but it was a gesture, an acknowledgement of his loss at least, and Brian did appreciate it. The "Archer" bit cracked him up though, like it would kill the guy to refer to himself, or be referred to, as Dad in the workplace.

Brian powered up his Mac and sent an equally tender response. "One o'clock, Don's. Got it covered, thanks." Then he got down to work. He had about two hours before the place would be buzzing like a madhouse; he'd power through his eye-bleed of an inbox and get himself up to date as much as he could before then.

The little restaurant was jam-packed, and it took Brian a moment to locate Duncan.

"Hey," Brian said, sliding into a seat across from his dad.

"Hey yourself, sons," Duncan said, and Brian half smiled at the old joke. When Callum left the firm, leaving only Duncan and him—one son—working there, Duncan had started calling Brian "sons" as a nickname.

"What looks good?" Brian asked, turning his head to peruse the menu written in chalk across one wall.

"I'm having ribs."

Brian nodded and requested the same when their server delivered a complimentary basket of artisan bread and whipped butter.

Duncan, to Brian's shock, was interested in where Brian had traveled and what he'd seen—because he was thinking of going on a trip himself.

"All work and no play makes Jack a dull boy," Duncan said when he saw Brian's surprise, then reached for a piece of dark rye bread.

"So they say, but I'm not sure I believe it," Brian said. "I like to work."

Duncan grunted his agreement and changed subjects abruptly. "So you've seen your mother, I take it?"

"Yes."

"And?"

Brian fiddled with the paper sugar packets on the table, even though he took his coffee unsweetened and hadn't ordered one. "And . . . I don't know. She seems well."

"You're really going to make me ask?"

"She's going with a better lawyer after all."

Duncan dropped his chunk of rye and stared. "So she's . . ."

Brian narrowed his eyes. "What exactly do you know, Dad? Were you aware that while I've been agonizing over what I should do, she's been rethinking things?"

"She said that?" Duncan retrieved the fallen rye and buttered it vigorously.

Another server arrived and deposited large plates of delectable smelling roasted meat, but Brian's appetite had waned. He scrubbed at his face with his hands.

"I don't get you guys. Has this all been some kind of weird game or power play or something?"

Duncan took a mouthful of the garlic mashed yams that accompanied their meals, waggled his fork like he was about to give a lesson, then swallowed. "Relation-ships are always a game, sons. Always. And the number one rule in the marriage game is that women say one thing and always mean another."

"That's . . . " Brian shook his head and lowered his own potato burdened fork without tasting it. He recognized the relationship game comment. He'd made it himself more than once, but hearing it out of Dun-can's mouth it sounded ridiculous. Jo and Callum didn't play games. Cade and Noelle had learned not to. Even his mom . . . it wasn't fair to say Caren played games. She just didn't always do or say what you expected. She thought differently than other people.

"You don't agree?"

Brian shook his head again. "I don't actually." And he was as surprised by that as Duncan seemed to be.

"Well, it just goes to show a man's gotta have four kids to get one smart one."

"And you had three. Good one."

Duncan washed a mouthful of ribs down with a big swallow of iced tea. "So your mom said she's taking me back?"

"No . . . she said she's thinking of not divorcing you. I don't know what that means."

"Will you ask her?"

"No, I won't ask her. Ask her yourself."

"You're better at talking to her than I am."

Heaven help them all, that was probably true—and it didn't say very much. At all. Brian sighed, then recalled something Katelyn said and sat up straighter. "Mom's your wife, for better or for worse, until she isn't, and that makes your relationship—talking about it, fixing it, demolishing it—your job, not mine. I'm the kid."

Duncan looked up from ripping two rib bones apart. "Is that so?"

"Yeah, that's so."

Duncan shrugged. "And what about the Wilkerson contract? Is *that* your job?"

Brian had to smile, but it wasn't without sadness. The old man was the game he always accused everyone else of being—and Brian could suddenly see he

173

was losing. He wanted his wife back, but didn't have the guts to tell her himself or to do the work. "Yes, that's my job."

And just like that the conversation moved to work stuff, and Brian was pleased to find his appetite returned. Before he headed back to the office, he ordered a peanut butter pie to take home to Katelyn and the kids. She might not have a lot of time to see him right now, but that didn't mean he couldn't drop off treats.

Chapter 20

RECENT RAIN HAD LEFT THE air smelling sweet and heady with hints of pine and earth and water. The soft duff trails on the forest floor were dry, however, protected by the heavy canopy of cedar, hemlock and various other conifers. Katelyn, panting slightly, slowed to a walk and pressed a hand to her ribcage to ward off a stitch. "That's enough for me today."

Brian slowed immediately, falling into step with her.

"No, no, you don't have to stop. I'll walk back."

"Not a chance. Being with you is the highlight of my day." He shook his head. "I mean . . . well, no, that is what I mean. I'm really glad we're going to keep running together even though we're back to work."

Katelyn's cheeks were warm from more than just the workout. She actually believed he meant his words. "Ditto."

"Ditto?" he repeated, then laughed. "How heart-warming."

She smiled and tugged at his long-sleeve T-shirt—the closest thing to physical contact with him she'd allow herself now, the most touch she could trust herself with. "You know what I mean."

Brian's eyes crinkled. "Yep, I do."

They walked on in easy silence. "So how are things with your mom?" she asked eventually. "And the first days back at work with your dad?"

He shrugged. "Surprisingly good. I took your advice."

"I gave you advice?"

"Words of wisdom, actually."

Katelyn laughed hard. "Okay, now I know you're teasing."

Brian grinned too. "No, seriously. I used your 'I'm a kid, your relationship is not my job' line with both my parents at different times. It worked like a charm."

"You know, I always wonder about that . . . Does stating that kind of truth change the person who hears it or does recognizing it and putting it out there just somehow change us?"

"Good question, but I have no idea." Brian shrugged. "Maybe it doesn't matter which?"

"Yeah, it probably doesn't."

They were comfortably silent for a breath or two, then Brian asked, "How was the kids' weekend?"

"Fine, I guess. Dropping them off and picking them up was a simpler process than usual, but because I'm a freak, that has me more on edge than if there'd been a small blow up."

"You think it's just a calm before a storm."

She nodded. "I was, I *am*, a bit worried about fallout from the Spring Fling."

Brian's stride lengthened, though consciously or unconsciously she wasn't sure. "Makes sense you'd feel that way."

They were almost back at River's Sigh. The newest cabins at the back of the property, in various states of construction and renovation, were still out of sight, but Katelyn knew they were there, just beyond the next curve in the trail. Brian stopped walking abruptly, as if he too realized their run was coming to an end and he, like her, wanted to extend it.

"Tell me the truth?" he asked.

"Of course. About what?"

"Are you going to get back together with Steve? Go back to him?"

It was so far from whatever she'd expected, it took a moment for her to register what he was asking. When she finally answered, her voice was so shrill she didn't sound like herself. "How can you even ask that? It's like the one thing, the only thing, I do know. I'm not going back to Steve. Ever. *Ever.*"

Brian raised his eyebrows, but nodded. Then he plunked down on a huge fallen log near the edge of the trail. He held his water bottle out to Katelyn. She took the bottle, but didn't drink from it.

Instead, she sat down beside him, straddling the log so she could watch his face while they talked. "Sorry if I sounded mad. I wasn't—just . . . shocked."

Brian took his water back and chugged it, squinting into the unseen distance. She nudged his forearm softly and tried to ignore the fact that she was counting how many times she'd touched him today. He started at the gentle pressure, looked down at her hand, then into her face. It was a rare moment: for once she had absolutely no clue what he was thinking.

"It's just . . . I don't know. Lots of women repeatedly leave their husbands, abusive or not, only to end up going back, not seeing their decision through. It's sort of a classic move actually."

Katelyn warred against the indignation surging through her. She was not "lots of women," but she suspected this wasn't really about her. Or she hoped it wasn't. "Um, I'm not sure what you're getting at, but trust me, if I was ever going back to Steve, it would've been in the early days when it was so hard. Not now when I'm so close . . . when I know I can make it. Know I can be free."

"That's what I thought, or maybe hoped is a better word, but I see it all the time at work. Women—and men—leaving the courthouse hand in hand with the same loser that minutes earlier received a restraining order from the judge. And my mom's no different. I thought I didn't want to represent her in the divorce because I didn't want to be stuck in the center between my parents, but now I don't know. Maybe it was really because I knew she'd backpedal again, that no matter how serious she'd seemed or how public she'd made her last decision to leave him, it was too good to be true."

It was quite a speech and it made Katelyn wonder all the more about the real Brian Archer. She was so used to this thoughtful, quiet, puzzling side of him that she almost couldn't reconcile it with side of him she'd known all those years ago and that Callum and Jo still seemed to identify with: Brian as a playboy, Brian as a shallow, womanizing boy-man.

"I know how it must look, or I can imagine, when you see the same case, different face, time after time . . . and I don't know tons about your parents or their marriage or whatever, but all I can say is despite whatever similarities you might see, I'm not them. If you can't separate me and my life and my decisions from case studies and what you see at work or in your family of origin, we're going to have a problem."

He didn't respond right away, which made her tight with anxious, irritated energy. She sprang to her feet and started walking again.

Brian caught up with her in one leap. "Case studies and family of origin. You sound like a textbook."

She kept moving. "Well, I've read enough stupid books on how to do this that I could probably write one."

He reached out and touched her shoulder, and she faltered and came to a standstill. "I'm sorry if my question hurt you. I wasn't trying to say you would go back to him, or that I thought you were any kind of specific person. I just . . . I just needed to know."

All Katelyn could feel was the heat of Brian's

hand, the strength of it, on her shoulder. It was a weight that somehow lightened all the things she carried around with her. Suddenly she wanted, more than anything, to repeat herself, to stress her words.

She wanted Brian to truly, deeply, positively *know* that she wasn't going back to Steve, not just because he was a friend who cared, but because whether she liked it or not, her feelings for Brian were growing, were changing . . . or maybe they weren't, maybe they'd always been romantic. Either way, she couldn't just ignore them anymore.

It was on the tip of her tongue to ask Brian why he needed to know she wasn't going to back to Steve, what the answer meant to him, and she opened her mouth to speak. Then closed it again. She knew full well why he wanted to know.

The only true question, or the only one worth pursuing, was what, if anything, she could do to slam this door? She had to protect them both from a complication they absolutely didn't need.

She shifted uneasily. "We . . . I . . . should get going." Before the words were fully out of her mouth, she shifted into a dead run. And this time she didn't make it a silly game. She pumped her arms and legs like her life depended on it. If the change in her demeanor struck Brian as odd, he didn't say it. He just followed her lead, keeping close, but maintaining a distance as if he was not only running with her, he was also guarding her back.

Chapter 21

KATELYN WAS BEYOND GRATEFUL FOR their early morning running dates, but at the same time, they made her all too aware that seeing Brian every other day for thirty to forty minutes was not enough for her. Not even close. She missed him with a hollow dull ache in her center that felt like hunger. But she was back to working full-time at the shop now, and she coveted the two hours or so between getting off shift and putting the kids to bed to spend quality time with them. Then she spent a few hours at her sewing machine on piece work before falling into bed herself.

Brian, likewise, seemed busy readapting to a regular work schedule again. He left for work, as far as she could tell, pretty much the minute he took his runners off—maybe he even showered and dressed at the office—and was never back until after she'd returned from work.

She wondered though, busy or not, if there was more behind Brian's decreased visits than just a hectic work schedule. Maybe he too was hyperconscious of their hours apart, feeling the lack, counting the days, and missing being together so acutely that it was terrifying. Maybe he, like she, was hoping a bit of distance would, well, create some distance. Or maybe he didn't feel anything remotely like that at all. She honestly couldn't tell which she hoped was the case. And she still didn't know if she'd been right or wrong to quell her impulse to tell him how much he was starting to mean to her when they had their awkward "are you going back to Steve" chat.

Then late Friday night, just as she was stretching her arms and rotating her stiff neck, thinking she should call sewing quits for the night, he texted. "It has been too long. What are you doing tomorrow?"

It made her a total geek, but she loved that he used proper punctuation and grammar even when he texted. "No plans. S has the kids." She inserted a frowning face. "Doing something sounds great!" She added a smiley.

A second later her phone rang.

"Hey," she said a bit too breathlessly. She could've kicked herself for being so obviously thrilled to hear from him.

"Hey yourself." The smile in his voice made her realize he was as happy to be talking to her as she was to be talking to him. She forgot about feeling self-conscious, and went warm and melty inside instead.

"So what's your idea of a perfect date night?" he added before she could say anything else.

"Um . . ."

"Sorry, let me rephrase. I mean if you were dating, hypothetically—what's your dream date? Like, not with me."

Except she was afraid her dream date *was* to have one with him. Damn it. She might have to use her free to be a wimp card after all. "Why?"

"Well, it's been a long while since I planned a big night and I may want to date sometime again in my life. I don't want to get too rusty."

Katelyn inhaled sharply, unsure whether it was relief or disappointment that made her breath hitch. "Well, okay, as long as it's for charity."

He laughed, giving her the stalling time she'd been aiming for.

"My dream date would be . . ." She trailed off. It was so embarrassingly mundane, but ah, heck, why not tell him? She told him everything else—but first she needed a promise. "You can't laugh."

"Of course, I won't. Why would I?" He sounded mildly offended. "How can anybody possibly criticize another person's dream date?"

"It's just that it's really plain. To go on an old-fashioned picnic, like with a blanket and a basket and everything, maybe near water or a lake, and eat food the guy had prepared or purchased, specially thinking of me. And to just talk and joke—or not even talk, but just be comfortable being quiet together."

When Brian didn't say anything immediately, she groaned. "See? You do think it's lame."

"I do not. Not at all. I think . . . it's sweet and low-key and, well, pretty cool."

She nodded, then felt stupid. They were talking on the phone. He couldn't see her.

"So seven?" he asked like she hadn't just paused awkwardly in the middle of their conversation.

"Sorry?"

"Does seven tomorrow night work to hang out?"

"Sure . . ." She paused, hating to have to ask, but not wanting to assume anything. "So, uh, should I eat dinner ahead of time or are we actually having this practice picnic or whatever?"

"A practice—? Oh, right. Yes, I'm sure we'll eat something. Definitely save your appetite."

After Katelyn said good-bye and ended the call, she held her phone to her chest for a second. Then she rolled her eyes at herself and grinned.

She considered sewing a bit longer, but it was already after ten and it had been a long day. She had earned a treat. She turned off her serger, made cocoa, and found her book.

Saturday passed in a blur of satin and tulle—and mostly satisfactory progress. Usually Katelyn loved alterations but sometimes, especially when it came to formal gowns, she preferred to start fresh. In this current job, a sequined prom dress, changing the neckline was proving to be a real challenge. Nonetheless, fretting over stitches beat worrying about Sawyer and Lacey, and the day passed quickly. Even so, she found herself with time on her hands that evening, after she forced herself out of her pajamas, or her workplace casual, as she liked to call them.

After showering, then spending too much time deciding what to wear before finally choosing a simple white cotton dress, she found herself bent over her machine again, so engrossed in her work that when Brian knocked on the door, she jumped.

She couldn't keep herself from beaming when she opened the door. "Hey."

Brian grinned too. "Hey yourself." His gaze drifted from her head to her feet, then quickly rose, the tips of his ears reddening just a bit. Katelyn glanced down at her feet too. What had he seen that made him blush?

"You dressed up," he said softly. "No sleep pants tonight, hey? You have legs."

It was true that it was the first time she'd dressed up specifically *for* him. She hoped she hadn't made the night weird. It wasn't a date, but . . .

"Yep, two legs, in fact—and for several years now."

He laughed and she took in the huge wicker basket at his feet and the rolled blanket tucked under his arm.

"You really did pack a picnic!"

His face lit up at her enthusiasm, and his eyes were so warm, so soft, that her breath caught. How sad was it that the first time in her life that a man asked her what her dream date was and tried to make it happen, he wasn't even a person she was actually dating.

Brian's happy expression faded a little. "A picnic, yes—except we have a problem." He jerked his thumb, motioning behind him.

Beyond the porch overhang, the sky was letting loose in torrents, as if some giant stood over them sloshing out buckets. How on earth had she not noticed until now? How had she only seen Brian?

"There's a possible workaround. I just hope it doesn't ruin it for you."

"No way," Katelyn said. "Nothing could ruin it. It's the thought that counts, right?"

"I don't know. Technique and execution are pretty important too." He waggled his eyebrows in case she'd missed his double entendre—which she hadn't.

Katelyn shook her head at him, which made him grin all the broader. "You know, I'd let my brain go in the gutter occasionally, except you're always there first, taking up all the room."

Brian pointed at her like she'd made a particularly astute observation. "Heh, good one." Then he looked past her. "It won't be quite what you described, but if we spread my blanket on your floor and count the rain, there's water nearby."

"I love it." She opened the door wide and reached for the fabric bundle he handed to her.

Brian opened all the windows, so it would be, in his words, as close to sitting outside in the fresh air as possible. The screens effectively kept any early season mosquitos at bay and let in the delicious evening air.

Katelyn asked if he wanted music, but he shrugged. "Nah, the rain sounds good to me."

It sounded good to her too, heavy and primal somehow—yet dreamy. Looking out at the heavy bank of charcoal clouds and the fog that hid even the closest trees from view, it was easy to imagine that nothing else existed, just them.

"Ready?"

Katelyn turned at Brian's voice and realized she'd lost a minute or two, staring out the window. He had spread the blanket, which was a beautifully faded patchwork quilt, its cotton squares so smoothed and softened by time and life that it called out to be touched. The huge walnut brown basket with curved bowl-like sides beckoned within easy reach. Like the quilt, it was a thing of beauty. But Brian's home had burned down, along with everything in it. Where had he—

Reading her mind in the way he was so disconcertingly good at, Brian answered her unvoiced question. "My mom donated to the cause when she heard I was planning a picnic. The antique basket and the blanket are hers—well, the blanket was all of ours, our family's I mean, when I was a kid."

"They're gorgeous."

There was a breath of a pause and Brian's gaze felt heavy on Katelyn's skin.

"What?" she asked.

His voice was rough. "I'm out of practice. My line

187

back there should have been, 'No, *you're* gorgeous.'"

Katelyn twisted her hair around her thumb, then flipped it over her shoulder. "Even for practice or whatever, you don't need to feed me lines."

Brian shook his head, but didn't argue. He reached into the basket and withdrew an unscented candle in a big jar, which he set on the coffee table and lit. Next he pulled out three pottery bowls: a blue one filled with jewel-red strawberries, a deep yellow one bearing blueberries, and a jade green one loaded with cubed cantaloupe.

It was so pretty that Katelyn gasped. Then she frowned at herself. Seriously, the way her breathing was affected by Brian, she was starting to think she had a breathing disorder.

"You're always telling Lacey and Sawyer that fruit is the best sweet treat there is," he said.

"Well, sure—and cheesecake."

Brian grinned and pulled out a foil-wrapped plate.

"No way."

He flourished his hand like a magician and uncovered the plate to reveal a creamy work of baked art. Katelyn lowered her face to the plate and inhaled deeply. "Chocolate mocha? Be still my beating heart!"

He reached into the basket again and she shook her head. "There's more? You've got to be kidding. It's too much. You've already outdone yourself."

But he didn't listen, just kept retrieving small dishes. Soon all her favorites lay spread out before her—

gourmet cheeses, morsels of smoked salmon, and tiny skewers of tomato, olives and cucumber. He'd also packed a thermos of espresso, miniature ceramic mugs, and two bottles of wine, one white, one red, along with beautiful crystal goblets.

"How did you even . . . ? This is nuts. You're—"

"Unnaturally insightful and amazing? I know."

She shook her head, but couldn't really disagree with him or find his cocky grin and crinkled eyes anything except adorable.

Time slid away as they snacked and chatted about this, that and everything under the sun, including how their work weeks had gone. Mostly, though, they focused on fun stuff, like dream vacations, favorite books, and what time period they'd live in if they couldn't be in the here and now.

It was after nine when Katelyn put her hands on her stomach. "I can't eat another bite."

"But could you do another glass of wine?"

She shrugged—then giggled. "Who am I kidding? Yes, absolutely."

Brian poured obligingly, but then set his and her stemmed glasses aside. She looked at him questioningly as he got to his feet, reached for her free hand and pulled her up to join him. Looking up into his face, feeling her hand in his, Katelyn felt every mouthful of wine she'd indulged in.

"So, uh, why are we standing up when I can barely stand?" She giggled again and almost felt embarrassed, then realized she was too tipsy to care.

"Well, half the fun of picnicking near water is going in the water, right?"

"I guess, but—"

"Come on, it'll be fun. Don't pretend you'll melt. We run in worse."

"You're serious?"

He nodded, still holding her hand.

"Okay, let's do this!" She pulled him toward the door, then shook her head vehemently when he paused to put on shoes. "No shoes. You can't wade in shoes!"

"Why, Miss Katelyn Kellerman—are you drunk?" he asked, smiling.

"Yep!"

"Lightweight."

"Absolutely. You don't even know."

His grin lit a fire inside her and she felt silly with excitement. He pulled off his socks.

Outside on the deck, the rain was drumming to beat the band, and the wooden planks were cold and wet beneath her bare soles. In mutual, silent agreement, they headed down the porch steps and into the small yard. Katelyn held her arms out and spun in a wide arc. "I'm singing in the rain! I'm singing in the—"

Brian laughed and caught her, then clasped his hand over her mouth. "How about you dance in the rain instead?" he whispered. "The singing might attract a crowd."

Katelyn leaned into him. The air was fresh and he

smelled good. Like line dried sheets and cologne and man. She giggled. Yikes, she was giggling a lot. Like a lot, *a lot.* She giggled yet again.

"What?"

His question—and maybe the cool night air—sobered her a little. She was never going to tell him that thought. Never. Except—

"Just you smell sooo good. When you go on real dates, you should always smell this good." Wow, so much for *never.* Perhaps she should try a new never, as in never ever drink with Brian again.

He laughed. "Come on, lightweight."

They walked on, close but no longer holding hands, through the soaking grass to a bench perched beneath a huge cedar. The tree acted like a massive umbrella and they sat for a spell, not talking, just listening to the night breathe and deepen as water dripped and streamed around them.

Eventually though, soaked to the skin from their dance through the rain, Katelyn shivered, which stirred Brian immediately. He stood. "We should go in before you catch your death."

Back in the cabin, Katelyn headed to the bathroom to grab towels. She was only gone a minute or two, but when she descended back into the living room, towel drying her hair, Brian was grinning and holding something up.

The book she'd been reading last night. Shoot!

"I never in a million years would've taken you for

a bodice ripper fan," he said.

"Where did you get that?" She threw the towel she'd gotten for him at his head.

He caught it one-handed, draped it around his neck like a scarf, and wasn't distracted from the book one bit. She noticed his thumb holding a spot near her bookmark and lunged.

He leaped onto a chair, laughing and holding the book out of reach. Then he read from his marked spot in a low growl, "His narrow hips pressed against her and through the thin muslin of her gown, every part of her female softness felt his hardness. She wanted him, but she didn't. Or she shouldn't. He was so bad for her, but so good—" Brian looked down and made eye contact.

Katelyn's stupid body, completely unrelated to the chill from her damp dress, chose that dumb moment to shiver again and Brian's expression changed. His eyes darkened and he hopped down from the chair. When he spoke next, the teasing had left his voice, replaced by something like surprise. "Wait a minute, you really *do* like this stuff."

Katelyn sagged against the wall. Brian dropped the book with a thud and caught her with both hands. The wine in her system was still traipsing through her, keeping complete embarrassment at bay—or mostly at bay anyway. "Stupid, I know . . ." She trailed off, wrong again. Even the wine wasn't keeping the flood of heat from her face. "Steve thinks novels like that are disgusting. Calls them smut."

"Steve's a complete idiot, so of course he doesn't like them. He probably finds storylines where women have their needs met and end up happy and self-sufficient threatening." Brian shook his head. "I get the attraction. I once dated a Women's Studies major, who wrote a paper called 'Feminist Romance; an oxymoron?' She argued that the romance industry and the genre itself is radically feminist."

Leave it to Brian, Katelyn thought. Was there any subject that didn't interest him or that he hadn't learned something about?

His arms were still around her, still supporting her, still keeping her steady—yet she was falling all the same. For him. She was suddenly, in a way that was too much like the passage from the book for comfort, hyper aware of the proximity of his limbs to hers, the differences in their builds—his maleness, her femaleness. She tried to make a joke. "Of course you've dated a Women's Studies major. Is there any type of woman you *haven't* dated?"

"Well, one for sure." His eyes held hers, and she knew her attempt to move things to a lighter, more comfortable terrain had failed.

"Will you answer a question for me?" he asked.

"Maybe. What?"

"If this, if tonight, was a real date, and the evening, just as it was, *as it is*, was coming to a close, would you want me to kiss you right now?"

Katelyn often thought of Brian's gaze as warm, but now it was searing—a tidal wave of blue heat that made her dizzy and hot and liquid-centered. She nodded.

He shook his head. "You need to say it."

And it wasn't the wine in her bloodstream that gave her voice. "Yes," she whispered. "If this was you and me on a real date, I'd want you to kiss me."

His hands moved from her hips and slowly slid up the curves of her body. She was suddenly extremely conscious of how her thin cotton dress, soaked from the rain, clung like a second skin. She shivered, but not with a chill. It was as if his delicate touch caressed her bare flesh.

Brian paused when he reached her face. Then his fingers traced her jaw and cheekbones, smoothed her hair behind her ears, and moved back to her chin. He gently lifted it and bent in to kiss her. Katelyn's stomach whooshed and her legs turned to jelly. Instead of meeting her upturned mouth, however, he sought the hollow at the base of her throat. She felt her heart pulse wildly against his mouth. But then he stopped. Stepped back.

"And if this was a real date, would you kiss me?"

"Yes," she whispered.

He cocked a challenging eyebrow. "Show me."

She clasped her hands around his neck and stretched up on tiptoe, then paused, trying to memorize every second of the moment to savor later: The feel of him responding to her, the pressure of his hips. The grip of his hands on her lower back, rocking her closer. His scent, limes and rain and *him*. The first soft rub of his barely-there stubble before she pressed her closed mouth to his.

The chasteness of their kiss lasted only a breath, the same amount of time it takes for the lick of a flame to make paper ignite. Then his hands moved south and cupped her buttocks. In one fluid movement, he lifted her—and opened her mouth with his tongue.

As he carried her toward the kitchen counter, Katelyn's legs clenched around his hips like she'd been anticipating this moment forever and maybe she had been. She let his teasing, insistent tongue probe her mouth—then responded in kind, kissing him back deeply, tasting him, getting lost in him.

She was sitting on the counter now and its surface was cool, almost cold, against her heated skin. Her skirt had rucked up and she could feel the button of Brian's Dockers, his reinforced fly, and the firmness of his erection against the cotton gusset of her panties. The strength and immediateness of her physical response to that mildest of stimuli tightened her belly and made her moan in surprise.

Brian echoed her impromptu sound with a low groan that sounded just as involuntary. Her eyes flew open and when she found him staring back, a current of electricity ran through her so hard it almost hurt. Her lower parts clenched and she shuddered against him. His eyes fluttered shut and he made another soft guttural sound. "Holy shit," he whispered.

She wasn't one for cursing, but agreed with his sentiment all right. This was a . . . kiss?

Brian's fingers, still on her bottom, found the edge of her underpinnings and played along the elastic at her thighs, getting closer and closer to—

Almost unconsciously, her legs fell open wider . . . but then she stopped the movement, scissoring them shut against his hips again. She unlocked the grip she had on his neck and pulled her mouth from his. Bracing her hands on his chest, she pushed lightly. Brian took a step back but remained between her trembling knees.

Katelyn bowed her head in frustration and leaned her forehead lightly against his chest. "I said I'd kiss you, not . . ."

He lifted her chin and she fell into his gaze again. "I know," he said, voice ragged. "I hear you."

They disentangled fully but were slow to move apart, mutually reluctant to be separated. Katelyn smoothed her skirt back down, and Brian followed the movement with hungry eyes. Then he shook his head ruefully, held out his hands, and helped her off the counter.

Chapter 22

THE CANDLE FROM THEIR PICNIC was still glowing, and, perhaps happy to hide a little in the shadows, they didn't bother to turn on lights. They sat on the couch together, turned slightly so they could face each other. Katelyn pulled the patchwork quilt onto her lap and carefully avoided touching Brian. He knew her restraint was smart, but all he wanted to do was continue where they'd left off. He couldn't resist reaching out and twining a strand of her hair around his finger. It shone softly in the dim candlelight.

"So that was some practice date, hey?" she said when the silence stretched too long.

He shook his head. "I'd been wanting to do something special for you, but when I arranged everything, I sincerely thought it was going to be a casual night of feasting as good friends. But now . . . "

"Now what?"

"Now I'm wondering if I haven't been lying to myself ever since we met. Maybe every time we hung out was a 'real date'—from my side anyway."

Katelyn sighed. "I know. I've been worrying about

that exact same thing. For me, I mean."

Brian put his arm over her shoulder and she leaned in, took his hand, and laced her fingers through his. They were quiet for a long time, then Brian said, "Why does this feel more like some kind of sad good-bye than a hooray, we've found each other?"

Katelyn studied his face, then touched his bottom lip with her pointer finger. Her expression was anything but happy and it made his heart clench.

Before she could say anything, he spoke quickly, "You know earlier, when you asked if there was a kind of woman I hadn't dated, and I said, at least one, but I didn't elaborate?"

"Yeah?" Her whisper was as soft as lace brushing cotton.

"I've never dated anyone who convinced me two people could really be meant to tackle life together, or who made me wonder if some people are stronger together than apart. But when I'm with you—"

Katelyn winced and she pulled her hand from his. "You don't know how simultaneously happy and destroyed that makes me feel. There's a part of me, such a huge part of me, that wishes we could see where this goes, but . . ."

"But it's too complicated, right?"

Katelyn's eyes filled, and she nodded. "I'm sorry though, I really am. And I want to thank you so much."

Brian shook his head.

"For being such a good guy, such a fun guy—and

for reminding me that I'm not dead yet. Because of you, I can almost believe that someday I might have someone to really share my life with, someone I can be myself with, talk for hours to—and want to tear the clothes off of."

Brian wanted to argue his case, to say it couldn't be a fluke that they'd fallen for each other so strongly when they'd both been the furthest thing from interested in pursuing a serious relationship when they first met. They *had* to be meant for each other, or at least meant to spend some time together finding out if they were. But his gaze touched on an eight by ten frame directly across from the bravery quote. Katelyn, Lacey and Sawyer grinned out at him, dressed in outlandish clown costumes, arms wrapped around each other. And this time, he was the one who winced. He had to make life easier for Katelyn, not harder. She had enough on her plate, and he did really, really like her. Cared for her. Unfairly and paradoxically, he realized that meant he could only do one thing: back off.

He took a deep breath and forced a jocular tone he didn't feel. "It's probably for the best, though I admit you make relationships not seem like the next best thing to root canals. But then again, dentists always go on about 'painless dentistry' nowadays—and that's a myth too."

Katelyn smiled wistfully and shrugged, but he was sure she saw right through his stupid joking. Just like at the Spring Fling, he experienced a weird plummeting sensation in his gut as he imagined Katelyn laughing and holding hands with some faceless future man, in some time and place when things were different and her life wasn't so volatile. But why did it matter so much? So they'd shared a kiss—albeit a hotter one than he'd ever known, but still *just a kiss*. And they talked a lot. So what? He could talk to someone else. He'd branch out a little. They were running buddies, and that's where they'd leave it. He could let her go, because there was hardly anything to let go of. He was Mr. Happy to be Single Guy, right? He'd never wanted the complications and shackles of a committed romantic relationship before, so why start now? It was probably the combination of losing his home and staying with Jo and Callum, a.k.a. Mr. and Mrs. Lovefest. It was messing with his head, but he could get back to normal. Absolutely he could.

On the coffee table in front of them, the candle that had burned so brightly all throughout their picnic and the rest of the evening flickered and went out.

Chapter 23

A KNOCK SOUNDED ON SPRING'S front door, but Katelyn knew who it was, so her heart only raced a little bit harder—out of reflex, not true fear.

"Come in," Katelyn hollered from upstairs. In the living room beneath her, Sawyer and Lacey echoed her, "Come in, come in," and Monster yipped.

Moving quickly, Katelyn laced her ivory jumps—similar to stays, but tied up the front, not the back, and not as tight, which was helpful for working and breathing, to say the least—over a square-necked peasant blouse. Then she tugged on faded skinny jeans and finished the outfit with vintage drop earrings and kelly green flats.

After she'd wrapped her braided hair into a coronet on the back of her skull and pulled a few tendrils loose to frame her face, she headed down.

Aisha stood chatting with Lacey and Sawyer, little Mo propped on her hip. She eyeballed Katelyn's outfit and whistled. "Okay, it's official. I no longer want to be paid for childcare. I want you to sew for me. Every single thing you wear is always so weird and cool."

Katelyn laughed. "That's quite the compliment." And it was. Wearing whatever her imagination conjured or her mood dictated felt fantastic. It had taken months of separation from Steve to feel comfortable doing her own thing, or to be unconventional if she chose to. Even now, two years later, she still occasionally heard his criticism in her head: *You look like a slut. You dress like a kid, not a wife. Why are you always trying to attract other men? You look like a crazy person.*

When she'd unpacked in her first new place, fresh from leaving him, it had appalled her to realize that all her clothes were sedate neutrals, two sizes too big. She'd vowed then that she'd return to wearing whatever she wanted, whenever she wanted.

"Sorry, pardon?" she asked, realizing Aisha was saying something again.

"Oh, nothing really. I just asked if work was going well."

"It is, thanks. Very well, in fact. Sometimes I wish I had more time to sew for fun and maybe to sell, like you suggested, but mostly I'm just grateful they took me back."

Aisha gave a derisive snort. "Whatever. More like they're lucky to have you."

Katelyn laughed. "Well, thanks."

"How do you afford it?"

"Well, it's not easy, but I'm managing. Jo's giving me a real break on the rent because of my sewing, and at least paying you to watch the kids means we're both benefitting—"

"No, not how do you afford childcare, though I do feel bad. I know paying me eats into your paycheck. I meant how do you afford to dress so well and buy all the fabric you need for all the things you make?"

Katelyn winked. "I'll never tell."

"Witch," Aisha exclaimed with feigned outrage.

"Yep, the worst witch ever," Katelyn agreed, cackling happily. It was pure delight to have a friend with a kindred passion for making something new or better from something old and discarded. "I repurpose everything. This outfit cost me about three bucks. The fabric is from a beautiful old top sheet that I picked up for a buck at a thrift store."

"Wow." Aisha shook her head, as if a bit awed. "Nicely done. And is free sewing time the only thing you miss now that you're back at work?"

"What do you mean?"

"Oh, I kinda thought you might be missing spending all your surplus time with Mr. Lawyer-slash-hot-body."

Katelyn giggled, then shot a concerned look at her kids, but she needn't have worried. For once they were oblivious to her. They were sitting under blankets they'd pillaged from their beds and draped over the couch to make a fort, sing-bellowing the ABC's to Mo, who was shrieking with joy and trying to copy them.

"Well, I do kind of miss Brian," Katelyn admitted.

"But I don't know. Maybe the enforced time apart is actually good."

"I get it. Way easier, hey?"

"You said it. Speaking of which. Have you heard any more from—" Katelyn had been about to ask after Mo's father, "the sperm donor" as Aisha called him, but her phone's alarm dinged. It was time to get moving.

"Ah, saved by the bell," Aisha announced. "But yeah, we'll talk. Later."

Katelyn climbed into the fort, kissed each of the kids good-bye, including Mo, then clambered back out and grinned at Aisha. "Bring me a sheet you like. I'll get you into jumps in no time."

"Awesome—and I mean it about paying for your time with babysitting."

"Okay, okay."

"I'm serious! Also, if, I mean, *when*, I open my shop, I want you to sew things to sell in it."

"I wish." And Katelyn did wish, but not with any sense that it could ever be a reality, more like it was a nice daydream. Right now, and for the next foreseeable years, she'd feel blessed beyond measure to just keep making ends meet.

The car took a few tries before it started, and every time the engine turned over without grumbling to life, Katelyn's stomach flipped too. She couldn't afford car problems right now—but then it was purring, and she was off. She couldn't help but notice that Brian's jeep was, as ever, long gone before she was. And on that note . . . she had done pretty well and managed not to spend all morning mooning over him, but now, with the kids in Aisha's capable care and a long commute ahead of her, she was free to think of nothing but Brian. His smile. His kindness. The way he seemed to like spending time with her, genuinely, not merely as some means to some end. As she thought about him, a peaceful sense of happiness flowed through her, holding her anxiety about their relationship at bay—at least for a little while.

Since their not-a-date date, his suggestion that she might be someone who convinced him two people could be meant to tackle life together, could be stronger together than apart, had rattled around in her head constantly. And she had come to a conclusion. He was right. Except that he was that person for her. The one who made her wonder if she could have real love. Made her want to. Made her think the potential gain might be worth the risk.

And even though meeting some man and forming a new relationship had been the furthest thing from Katelyn's plans, a person couldn't control everything and shouldn't even try. It was, perhaps, the only lesson she'd learned from her years with Steve that she appreciated. *You couldn't—and shouldn't—control everything.*

In fact, now she was not only wondering if she should take the scary leap into exploring a deeper relationship with Brian, she was starting to believe she'd have permanent regrets if she let Steve keep her from doing so.

Facing those truths made something else clear too. She was going to get a divorce. Whether or not she and Brian had a future together as anything more than friends, it was time to make it crystal clear to Steve that he and she did not. They were over and she was going to gather the courage to make that final.

With a good fifteen minutes to spare before her shift started, Katelyn sat in her car in the employee-only parking lot behind the fabric shop, called her lawyer, and started the divorce ball rolling.

Chapter 24

INSTEAD OF THE CALM SENSE of control and belonging his pristine office usually fostered, Brian felt jittery and out of place. He paced the perimeter of the room, then stopped at the coffee maker and poured another ill-advised cup of coffee. He set the mug on his desk and sank into his office chair. Then he hopped to his feet again, leaving the beverage untouched, and paced some more.

If he was doing the right thing, why did he feel so unsettled? *Because you're selfish*, an inner voice—his mother's—prodded. *Men never think of things from the perspective of the women in their lives. They can't. And in this case, you just want to find some loophole that will allow you keep pursuing what you want, to hell with the consequences.*

Well, maybe the voice was right, but for Pete's sake, he was certainly trying to consider Katelyn's feelings. He'd thought of practically nothing else since the night of that stupid picnic. He'd known then he needed to back off. And why. And he knew it now. And he even knew the easiest way to go about building space between them, so why was he still hesitating weeks later? If he didn't stop waffling, he'd not only lose out on the opportunity that had arisen out of the blue, he would make things that much more difficult for Katelyn and himself. That painful fact jarred him into action. He strode back to his desk, picked up the phone, pressed nine for an outside line, then dialed before he could change his mind.

"Brian? Hello, long time no talk. Is that really you?" The cooing enthusiasm pouring from the other end of the connection almost undid Brian's resolve. Curse call display. Of course, the office's name and number had shown. And of course, Naomi put two and two together and got six.

"Hey, Naomi. Yes, it's me—and yes, it's been a long time."

"Too long. Extremely too long!"

Brian cringed. "Listen, I was wondering if we could get together and—"

"I'd love to. *Love to.*" Her voice dropped, became throaty. "If you only knew how much I'd been hoping you'd call."

And talk, he'd been going to say, *get together and talk.* He shrugged. If Naomi was that happy to hear from him, who was he to crush her? Besides, he needed a place to stay that wasn't River's Sigh—or, more importantly, wasn't right beside Katelyn and the kids. In a perfectly timed coincidence, he'd heard that the tiny suite above Naomi's garage was available. He wasn't going to kill his chance to rent it by telling her she'd misunderstood his reason for calling—or not over the phone, at least. And who knew? Naomi was pretty and sporty and fun. Maybe when they met in person again, he'd be able to stir up some of the feelings she so obviously hoped he still had.

You're a shit, Brian. The words were so sharp they were nearly audible, and for half a second he thought someone had joined the call to tell him off. But it was just his brain. And his brain was right. He could be pretty shitty sometimes, but he didn't mean to be. He sighed.

"It'll be great to see you and catch up, Gnome," he said, using his old nickname for her out of habit, "but I have to be honest. Nothing's changed since I left. The reason I'm calling is I heard you have a place to rent and I'm desperate."

Naomi inhaled and when she spoke again, her voice, though still friendly, was definitely dampened. "I should've known. Well, at least no one can ever accuse you of stringing a girl along."

"I'm—"

"No, don't be sorry." Brian could almost see her shaking her head. "It's all right—and of course you can check out the suite. I told a girl at work that I'd hold it for her until next week though, so I can't promise it's yours."

"Fair enough."

"Where are you staying right now?"

"With Callum and Jo at River's Sigh."

"Sweet. Do they still do that amazing Saturday brunch that's open to the public?"

"Yeah—"

"Great! I'll come by Saturday, we can eat and catch up and then you can come see the place."

"Oh . . . okay. Tomorrow doesn't work?"

"No, I'm on graveyards and need to sleep. I'm wiped. You're lucky, caught me before I went to bed for the day."

There was a beat of silence, then Naomi chuckled lightly. "Not even a small joke about joining me? Damn, I guess we really are over."

"I'm—"

"Nu-uh. No sorrys, I said. It's fine. I'll see you Saturday. Tell Jo to make extra coffee. I'll need it."

After the call ended, Brian tried to tell himself it had gone well and that he was relieved. He had no doubt that in person he'd be able to talk Naomi into renting to him instead of the other nurse. And, as he'd established and reiterated enough times in his head to drive himself crazy, getting away from River's Sigh B & B, away from Katelyn, was best for everybody. So why did he feel so bad?

Chapter 25

FOR MAYBE THE FIRST TIME ever, Katelyn wasn't desperately unhappy that the kids were with Steve. She was on a mission that she wouldn't have tackled with them in tow. She skipped down the porch stairs, inhaling deeply as a stomach rumble inducing aroma of pumpkin pancakes, fresh bacon and espresso kissed her senses. It was as if River's Sigh's dining hall itself was trying to lure her to breakfast. Like she needed another lure! She practically sprinted down the trail.

When she opened the hall's heavy door, she hesitated. It was full of chatting, laughing bodies. Katelyn recognized a few guests from the other cabins, but lots of people had come from town too, as was the Saturday custom. She steeled herself. It didn't matter. If it was too loud, they could sneak outside. Katelyn felt like a bouncing ball of happy nerves as she walked into the crowded room. It had been weeks since she'd taken part in one of the breakfasts—Jo and Callum were giving her and the kids a good enough deal as it was without feeding them too—but she'd noticed Brian's jeep, miraculously still present in the parking area. She couldn't wait another minute to talk to him. She was desperate to say that if he wanted to start officially seeing each other, to see where things might lead, she was in—and that she had asked for a divorce to prove it. Marilee would have the documents prepared by Monday, and Steve would be served his copy early the next week. Her glee ratcheted up a notch to something closer to anxiety—

No, she commanded herself. Worry about how Steve will react when the time comes. For now, just be happy. Focus on the moment.

She spotted Brian by the coffee island. As if feeling the heat of her gaze, he turned and broke into a welcoming grin. But wait. What the—? The happy ball of emotions playing through Katelyn hit a wall.

Who was the cute, athletic blonde standing close to Brian, one hand possessively on his arm? Wow . . . that hadn't taken him long at all.

What did you expect? she asked herself. You told him flat out that you guys could never be a thing. He respected that and he's moving on. You can't fault him.

Still, she was hurt he'd shown up *here* with a date. And so soon.

Brian's smile faltered and his expression changed from welcoming to questioning. She shoved her stupid disappointment away and pasted a smile back in place.

Brian leaned in and whispered something to the woman on his arm. She darted a look Katelyn's way, then chuckled lightly and released her hold on him.

A second later, Brian was by Katelyn's side, two mugs in hand now, one of which he passed to her. Unfortunately, the blonde had come with him.

"Um, thanks," Katelyn said, and for the first time in ages, she felt a bit shy with Brian. Thank goodness she hadn't texted him the "exciting" news. This was bad enough. How awkward that would have been!

"So how are you? How was your week?" he asked.

"Great, great. And yours?" She groaned inwardly the minute the words left her suddenly dry mouth. Really? This was what they were going to become? Acquaintances who sucked at small talk? She wished she hadn't accepted the coffee. Now she'd have to drink it or it would be obvious she was fleeing. If she hadn't taken it, she could have made an excuse, said she'd come to talk to Jo or something, and left right away.

"Yeah, mine too. Great."

Well, at least he was doing no better with small talk than she was. At a loss for anything else to say, but desperately needing to do something, Katelyn extended her hand to Brian's friend. "Hi, I'm Katelyn."

The woman smiled and, of all the slightly weird ways to respond, nodded before she shook Katelyn's proffered hand. Then, seeming to realize Katelyn was out of the loop, she added, "Oh, I'm sorry. I'm Naomi. I've heard so much about you, I just assumed Brian told you about me too, especially since he's moving in."

What? Katelyn's head reeled and she tried to hide the hurt shock ripping through her by taking a big gulp of coffee. It was scalding hot and burned all the way down, but she kind of relished the pain. It gave her an excuse for the tears that sprang to her eyes. "Ouch, sorry," she coughed. "That was stupidly hot."

"Are you all right?" Brian rested a concerned hand on her shoulder.

Katelyn pushed him away. "I'm fine. *Fine*." She coughed again. "Just surprised." Shocked was more like it though. How could he move in with someone a mere week after telling her she was the first person to make him believe two people could be meant for each other? Was it just a line he used? Maybe she'd misread him from the get-go. Maybe she was the queen of not being able to tell a good guy from a bad one. She closed her eyes. No, Brian was a good guy. Just one she had rejected and who was moving on.

When she opened her eyes, Brian was staring at her pensively. "Well, it's not a sure thing yet—"

"No, Brian. Don't worry," Naomi interrupted. "We have a history and I want to make this work. Just let me settle a few things."

Jo took that moment to burst through the swinging kitchen doors with fresh cinnamon buns. Katelyn could've kissed her.

"Oh, I want one of those!" Katelyn pivoted toward the kitchen, eager to escape. "Nice to meet you,

Naomi," she chirped over her shoulder. "I'll talk to you later, Brian."

He caught her arm and she looked down at his fingers on her flesh, trying to ignore her racing pulse. "What?"

His face was full of something intense, but he shook his head and his next words were out of sync with the raw emotion burning in his eyes. "Nothing, not really. I just wanted to know . . . are we still on to run together tomorrow morning before you get the kids back?"

Katelyn's gaze crept to Naomi, standing a few paces behind Brian, and she shook her head. "I'm sorry. I don't know. I don't think it's a good idea."

Brian followed her look, and one of his eyebrows lifted in confusion—then smoothed as he apparently arrived at a moment of clarity. He nodded. "Yeah, you're probably right."

Katelyn wanted to reach out and clasp his freshly shaved jaw in both hands. She wanted to plant a kiss on him that would loosen all the tight, disappointed, frightened places in both of them. She wanted him to read her mind, pull her body to his, then lift her up and swing her around in joy-filled excitement. She wanted—

But then Jo was greeting a new family of guests who were just entering the hall, Brian was reaching for a cinnamon roll, and Naomi was chattering about how "amazing" the coffee was and how she was "dying" for a refill—and Katelyn was slammed by just how alone she really was.

She leaned toward Brian, head bowed, and whispered, "Are you really thinking of moving in with her?"

"Yeah, but it's not—"

Katelyn raised her hand to stave of explanations. He didn't owe her any and she couldn't bear to hear them. A burning lump threatened to close off her throat and it was work, hard work, to swallow it.

"That's great," she said weakly. "You've been looking for a new place to call home and now you've found it. I'm happy for you."

She turned and dashed away before he could utter a word of the regrets she saw so clearly in his eyes.

Maybe he'd been about to follow her because she heard Callum stop him. "Brian, wait up. I've been trying to catch you all week. There's something Jo and I think might interest you."

It's for the best, she told herself sternly. You can't stay in Greenridge, and Brian loves it. His whole life is here. Why shoot for something you can't keep?

So why'd you even bother with divorce papers then? a little voice nagged.

Katelyn slammed the dining room door harder than she intended. Jo's wiry mutt, asleep in a patch of sunshine on the porch, lifted his graying muzzle and gave her a very odd look.

Chapter 26

BRIAN RAN FIFTY FEET OF the gravel trail in front of Spring cabin, turned and ran back the same fifty feet, then repeated the loop yet again. The circles he was sprinting in front of Katelyn's abode were ridiculous and embarrassing—and mimicked the circles of his racing thoughts, which always and forever seemed to roll back to her.

It had only been a few days since his very public breakfast meeting with Naomi, where the plans regarding his move had been so clumsily spilled—and so completely misinterpreted by Katelyn—but it felt like ten years. He missed her. Their runs. Their talks. Their time with the kids doing weird crafts, reading stories, and going for walks. Their movie nights and laze about, do nothing times. He missed everything to do with her. Even her strange little rat-dog, Monster.

He still agonized about his decision to stop and talk to Callum instead of clearing things up with Katelyn right away. The minute he realized she had jumped to the erroneous conclusion that he and Naomi were a couple, he'd started going back and forth, back and forth, much like he was jogging now. Should he tell her that Naomi was just his potential landlord? No, he should let her think he'd moved on. No, he should tell her right away. No, it was best to let her think he'd moved on. . . .

When Callum interrupted him, he'd taken it as a sign he should let her leave, let her think he'd taken up with Naomi, let her focus on whatever she needed to do to put her life together. After all, hadn't she made it clear to him that was what she wanted? And hadn't he been actively seeking a way to build a wall and give her the space she asked for? Just living further apart was an easy problem to circumvent. They both had vehicles. But him having a girlfriend that he'd moved in with? Well, that would close the door. It just would.

So why the hell was he running loops in front of her cabin like a lunatic? Because he hated lying to her, that's why. And omitting known facts, letting a false interpretation stand, was still a lie, no matter how he tried to rationalize it. And it was disrespectful. He wouldn't treat her like she was incapable of doing what she needed to do, or imply she was too weak to stand by her resolve by holding things back from her or manipulating her with half-truths.

And also, the thought replayed yet again, like the refrain to a song you can't get out of your head, *he missed her.*

On that note, he increased his stride, took her stairs in one bounding leap, and knocked loudly on her door before he could overthink it or chicken out.

There was a flutter of movement as the curtain that shielded a window by the door shifted. Weird. She was peeking out to see who was there? The door opened a crack, and Katelyn appeared, wedged in the small opening. "Oh, it's just you," she said, sounding weirdly relieved, though not exactly pleased.

"Yeah," he said. "Just me. Disappointed?"

Their eyes met and held. Katelyn inhaled a slightly shaky breath, then reached out and pressed her hand to his chest. "Not in the slightest. Thrilled, actually."

"Thrilled, hey?" Brian laughed in relief—and at her use of such an exuberant word when her body language suggested anything but. He removed her hand from his chest and rubbed it between his palms. She was cold or upset or something. Would she let him in?

"I'm sorry. It's probably a bad time, and I know things are awkward between us, but, well, I missed you."

She sighed, gave a sad smile and nodded. "Ditto." Then she stepped back, shook her head, and stretched like she was trying to wake up and shake off a bad dream. "Do you want to come in?"

"Do I."

"*Ditto. Do I.* Those are the exact same things we said the first time you ever dropped by to see me."

Brian grinned too broadly for the small joke, but he felt so . . . ridiculously happy. "Yep, we're wordsmiths all right."

Katelyn closed and locked the cabin door the instant he entered, and Lacey and Sawyer's elfin faces popped over the banister above his head.

"It's just Brian," Katelyn said. "Come on down. I'll make us a snack."

The kids tumbled over themselves to get to the fridge first, wanting to help, and once Katelyn had them busy—Sawyer stirring a dip for carrot and celery sticks, Lacy taking the waxy wrappers off mini round cheeses—Brian lowered his mouth to Katelyn's ear. "*Just Brian* again? I have to say the word 'just' used in relation to me twice in such close succession is hurtful."

Yes, it was a lame attempt to be funny. He couldn't help it. He was off his game because he was wishing so hard that she'd step into his arms, so he could hug her and press his face into her hair—

Oh yeah, this whole creating and maintaining distance thing was working fantastically. He shook his head at himself.

Katelyn turned—and because he'd moved close to whisper to her, she was deliciously near. "I promise you . . . I meant nothing mean or dismissive with that word." Then she spoke again and the warm feeling her nearness always triggered in Brian froze and cracked. "I thought you were Steve."

Ice moved through his veins. So it hadn't been his imagination at the door. She was acting strangely.

What had happened? *Something*, obviously. He opened his mouth, but she pressed a finger to her lips and tilted her head in the direction of the kids. He nodded and didn't say a word.

"Hey, guys."

Lacey and Sawyer looked up from their food prep.

"I'm going outside to talk to Brian for a minute. You can start eating, okay?"

"Can we have two cheeses each?" Lacey asked.

"I don't know. You two don't even like cheese that much," Katelyn teased, but there was still something off about her vibe, something Brian couldn't quite place.

"Yes, we do. We love it," Sawyer said in a serious tone.

Katelyn smiled at him fondly. "Yes, you guys may have two cheeses each, but that's it, no more. And lots of yummy veggies, right?"

"Right!" they cheered and returned their attention to their snack, more interested in the acquisition of cheese than any boring conversation their mom was set on having.

Out on the porch, Katelyn motioned for Brian to take the large rocking chair. Then she pushed the door shut firmly and leaned against it.

"Nothing has happened, but . . ."

"But?" he prodded.

She closed her eyes and spoke in a tense whisper. "I've asked Steve for a divorce—and Marilee called just as I was getting off work earlier. He was served with the papers today and didn't handle it well. The bailiff recommended she warn me, and he called the cops about it too."

"Shit."

"Yeah," she agreed, pounding her clenched fist lightly against her mouth.

It was hard to think. "So what now?"

She shrugged and took a deep breath. When she spoke, her voice was too calm. "We wait, I mean, *I* wait. It might blow over, might be nothing."

"And if it's not?"

"Then I cross that bridge when I come to it."

Brian shook his head. "No, you were right the first time."

Katelyn bit her lip and one of her eyebrows arched.

"Not 'I.' You're not alone. We. You and me. Us. Whatever happens between us or doesn't, we're friends. You aren't alone."

Katelyn pressed a hand over her eye. Brian stood up and opened his arms to her. She walked into them. She didn't sob or wail or even make a sound, but his sweatshirt grew damp beneath her cheek. He rubbed her back in small circles and wondered how many times she, not wanting to alarm her children, had wept silently or kept herself rigidly under control. Please be okay, he begged in his head, be okay, be okay, be okay.

Katelyn seemed to have a child awareness chip inserted in her heart that cued her to how long she had until she was needed, even when distraught. After a long moment—but not so long, Brian knew, that the kids would start to question—she pulled back and looked up at him.

"Better?" he asked.

She wrapped her arms around herself. "Maybe. A bit." Then she added, "Do you want to stay for dinner?"

"I'd love to. Want to take the kids for a walk first? Burn off their snack and some energy before bed?"

She smiled and nodded, but looked deeply, deeply sad.

"What?" he asked.

"Nothing," she said.

As she pulled the door open and they moved to go back inside, Brian heard a car start up and rev hard. He jogged to a break in the trees to see who the jerk was, but only caught the rear end of a blue hatchback disappearing at Mach speed around the first bend in the driveway. No doubt one of Jo and Callum's constantly coming and going guests. He'd have to suggest that they post a "Slow" sign in the parking area, just in case. There were always kids around, not just Sawyer and Lacey, and it wasn't merely a liability issue. It would be horrific if anyone got injured at River's Sigh.

Chapter 27

THE AIR WAS WARM AND sweet with the fragrance of blooming lilacs, and despite the approaching evening, the sun was still strong and bright, promising long, full of light days and shorter nights soon. Soft rays filtered through the newly greened cottonwood trees, decorating Sawyer and Lacey with dappled shadows and making the deep green conifer branches shine jewel-bright.

Katelyn was lost in thought, and she and Brian walked mostly in silence, while the kids pranced ahead, laughing and pretending they were deer. It was all too easy to pretend everything was perfect and right in her world—and even easier to play make-believe that the four of them were a family. Every so often, however, a breeze kicked up, whispering a warning that rustled through the bushes and touched Katelyn's bare legs with a shivery chill. They weren't out of the woods yet. Literally or figuratively. While it seemed that spring had arrived and was shifting into summer early this year, there could still be storms ahead.

Brian noticed her tremble, but misinterpreted it. Or

maybe he didn't. He unzipped his sweatshirt and wrapped it over her shoulders.

"Won't you be cold?" she protested.

"Nope."

As they continued on, the forest and the quiet deepened. Then Katelyn spotted a fork in the path. "That's far enough, guys. Let us catch up," she called. Both kids stopped like she'd pulled a cord and busied themselves lifting rocks, hoping to find salamanders.

When she and Brian caught up, Brian joined in the reptile search. A bumpy fist-sized toad was discovered, and if anyone had witnessed the scene, they'd have thought someone struck gold by the amount of cheering and sheer delight.

"This place is the best," Lacey enthused as they left the toad to his wanderings and recommenced their own.

"It really is," Katelyn agreed, but her happiness in seeing her children enjoy themselves so fully was bittersweet. A throbbing sadness, thick as blood, pulsed through her. River's Sigh B & B, quirky Spring cabin, and this crazily beautiful property were such a wonderful place to raise kids—but it was all as fleeting as mist. Soon they'd be wedged into some low rent apartment, surrounded by concrete and close neighbors. That was all she'd be able to afford in a bigger city.

There was no help for it. She couldn't stay here indefinitely. Even staying into the fall was iffy. Lacey needed to return to school in September, so they had to be settled somewhere by then. And there was the issue about the reliability of her car. If she was worried about it on summer roads, there was no way she could trust it in bad weather conditions. And last but not least, there was Steve—her ultimate, insurmountable problem, as always. Yes, he was quiet now, but he wouldn't remain so for long. He never did. And now she had pushed him by asking for a divorce . . . Her eye twitched and she fought off a fresh jolt of nerves. She needed to break free of him, once and for all. She—*they*—needed a fresh, safe start. Far away. Soon.

"Turn here," Brian said, directing them to the right, interrupting her morose thoughts.

"Are we actually headed somewhere specific?" she asked.

"You'll see," Brian said, grinning.

The kids galloped away on the straight stretch again. Then suddenly they stopped, staring at something invisible from Katelyn's vantage point.

"Holy cow!" Lacey yelled, and they both tore off again—then vanished.

"Hey, wait up," Katelyn called, but this time they didn't comply. She and Brian jogged to catch up and a second later, she saw what had brought her kids to a standstill and tempted them into ignoring her.

"Oh my goodness . . ." Her whisper trailed off. "It's . . . beautiful." But beautiful seemed inadequate. It was mystical. Otherworldly. Magical. Awe-inspiring.

Beside her, Brian inhaled like he was gathering strength for something. "I know, right?"

A meadow of yellow, pink, and purple wildflowers stretched as far as the eye could see, flanked by protective walls of vivid green forest and navy mountains. In the foreground, a lazy creek danced and frothed over massive flat rocks and craggy stones. In the far distance, a weathering house beckoned to her. Deserted before it was finished, it stood silver and proud and somehow expectant in the tangerine glow of the setting sun.

Brian took Katelyn's hand to help her down a rock strewn four-foot drop—the reason you couldn't see the meadow from the trail until you were almost on top of it. For a second Katelyn was completely distracted from the view by their skin-to-skin contact. Her pulse thudded.

They followed the crushed grass footpath Sawyer and Lacey had created, and a soft burbling sound like suppressed laughter grew louder.

"Mom, *look*," Lacey said, wonderstruck. "There's even a bridge."

And there was. A faded boardwalk spanned the creek in a gentle arc, complete with a sturdy, protective railing on either side constructed of gnarled branches. It was both rustic and enchanting, perfect for this forest-fringed fairyland in the middle of nowhere.

As the four of them clomped over the bridge, Sawyer muttered, "Trip, trop, trip, trop," happily under his breath, obviously relating the bridge to his favorite fairy tale, "The Three Billy Goats Gruff," but equally obviously from his grin, not thinking of the ogre at all.

The bittersweet feeling clamped Katelyn's heart all the harder. This moment was beyond special. It felt, impossibly and surreally, like some sort of homecoming as the four of them marched together toward this previously abandoned house that waited to be made into the home someone had envisioned once upon a time.

"This land belonged to one of the area's earliest homesteads," Brian said. "The site was chosen because of its access to the river and the train tracks that run along it. The original cabin, and later, a larger house, were destroyed by house fires."

Katelyn gasped at the coincidence—that Brian would find this spot after his own loss.

He shrugged as if hearing but no longer needing her unvoiced sympathy, clearly enjoying his tale. "Then, twenty or so years ago, some distant relation of the original family decided to live here and built this house—but he stopped mid-project and never came back. No one knows why."

As Brian spoke, Katelyn noticed details that supported his story. Here and there were stumpy remains of burned out fruit trees, black char marks still visible if you looked closely. Beyond them was a pile of river rock and the crumbling remains of a chimney, still standing after all these years.

Lacey bent over something nearby in the long grass. Further digging, prodding and wiping revealed a pretty piece of brass rimmed porcelain—the decorative front plate of a wood cook stove. She held up her prize triumphantly and Brian high fived her with enthusiasm.

"We're standing in what was once the kitchen," he explained. "You can still find bits of the old foundation too."

"It looks like they had a whole orchard," Katelyn said as she recognized what might have been rows of trees at one time.

"Yep, and there's a massive patch of strawberry plants and mint that have gone wild too."

As they got closer to the abandoned building, Katelyn's awe grew. The house was a classic farmhouse shape and style, which sort of embodied what she'd describe as her dream house if ever asked. It was two stories tall with a bay window off the front of the main floor and two dormer windows on the top floor. Remarkably, all the glass was still intact.

A wide staircase led to a wraparound veranda. Katelyn could practically see a collection of brightly painted rocking chairs lined up for the four of them. She pictured a porch swing in the corner too, like Jo and Callum had, always filled with a cozy quilt to snuggle in while they watched stars light up the evening sky.

Brian shook his head. "It's such a shame, hey? Imagine building a whole house, complete with glass, doors and a shingled roof—and then just walking away. Callum can't believe the waste. He figures the builder ran out of money, or had some family tragedy or something."

Katelyn prodded the first step with one foot, testing it for sturdiness.

"Everything's still solid," Brian reassured.

She climbed a few more steps. "Someone has to know the story of this place. Greenridge is a small town."

"Yeah," Brian agreed. "Callum just hasn't found out yet. He didn't even know it was here. A realtor cold-called him, thinking he and Jo might be interested."

Katelyn stepped onto the verandah and put her hand on the front door's knob. It turned easily under her hand, but she released it like she was burned and stepped back.

"What?" Brian asked, alarmed.

"Nothing." She shook her head, not having the foggiest idea how to articulate the tumult of emotions colliding through her.

"Can we go in?" Sawyer asked eagerly. Katelyn scooped him up and buried her face in his sweet little boy neck. The pain in her heart was spreading through her limbs, poisoning the whole evening. Brian would live and build a home here. She knew it. That was why he was showing it to her, not to gloat, but because he was excited. Maybe he was even thinking of it as a project for him and Naomi—

She cut that thought off. It didn't matter. It would never be her home with him.

"Yes, shall we?" Brian said.

"No," she said. "I can't." She knew she was being confusing and weird, to her kids and to Brian, but it was unavoidable. She couldn't cross that threshold with Brian, couldn't go room to room with him and the kids, imagining them, their things . . .

"Please," Lacey wheedled.

"I said no." Katelyn carried Sawyer down the stairs, in a hurry to retrace their steps and retreat the way they'd come.

Brian's hand on her shoulder stopped her. She turned reluctantly to face him.

He lifted Sawyer from her and placed him on the ground. "Why don't you guys see if you can find a few strawberries? It's early yet, but there might be one or two ripe ones."

"Can we, Mom?" Lacey asked.

She nodded wordlessly and the kids sprinted away, excited and eager. Watching them, her heart ached and her throat burned. There was so much she wanted to give them—and so much she'd probably never manage to.

The light was starting to fail, and Katelyn was skeptical about the possibility of them finding any berries. It was merely a ploy to keep them busy, so Brian could talk to her alone. She crossed her arms over her chest and Brian's brow creased.

"Will you please tell me what's wrong?" he asked softly.

"Just . . . everything." She uncrossed an arm long enough to wave at the property as a whole, then wrapped it tightly around herself again.

"I don't understand."

She shrugged.

"Talk to me. That's our thing. What we do." In the deepening dusk, Brian looked as miserable as she felt. He reached out and traced her jaw with his fingers. "Are you upset about Naomi? If so, I need to clarify something. We're not dating, let alone going to live together. She only meant I was moving in with her as a renter. When you got the wrong idea, I thought it might be—"

"Easier for us to maintain some distance if I thought you had a girlfriend out of the blue?" Katelyn finished the sentence for him and knew she was right. It was immediately obvious to her, and equally clear that she'd only jumped to conclusions in the first place because she was as desperate as he was to try to put something, *anything*, between them.

Brian nodded.

"Our efforts to keep away from each other and our attempts to let our feelings die down don't work very well for us, do they?"

Brian shook his head exaggeratedly, which made her smile. She motioned toward the house once more. "It wasn't misunderstanding about Naomi that made me twitchy back there—or if it was, it was only part of it. Why did you want to show me this place?"

Brian shifted his weight from foot to foot. "It was supposed to be me running it past you, like asking if I'm nuts to even be considering buying it, fixing it up—but," he shook his head, "now that we're here, I realize exactly what's freaking you out."

"Oh, yeah?"

"Yeah," he said matter-of-factly. "What I was really doing is showing you *our* house, the place we're supposed to make a home. Together."

"But we've already established this so many times: I can't, Brian. I *can't.*"

He nodded. "And I wouldn't have dragged you here, except I didn't consciously realize what I was doing. Then we arrived and I saw the longing in your face as you looked around, and I realized what I was hoping for."

"Mom!" Lacey's indignant shriek pierced the quiet. "Sawyer's picking green berries."

"That's okay—"

"No, it's not! That means there won't be any red ones later and that's not fair!"

Katelyn sighed and shot Brian an apologetic look. He smiled, but his eyes were pensive. "We should get them home anyway. To be continued?"

Katelyn nodded, but she felt afraid. She knew where she wanted the conversation to go. She knew where—and what—she wanted to be continued. But was it fair to Brian to lead him on when she couldn't stay? It was clearer than ever that he saw himself in Greenridge long term. No matter how they felt about each other, they had no future.

But you asked Steve for a divorce precisely for this reason, to start clearing a way for you and Brian to be together, her inner voice lectured as Brian lifted Lacey to his shoulders, distracting her from her outrage at her brother.

And look what that's gotten me! a different part shrilled back. *Steve is furious. I should never have entertained the daydream. It's too dangerous. For me. For Sawyer and Lacey. And for Brian.*

Chapter 28

AMAZINGLY AND MERCIFULLY, THE KIDS went to bed without complaint, done in by the long walk, a simple but good meal of vegetarian chili and buttery rolls, and three bedtime stories, one read by her, two read by Brian. The observation pained Katelyn: Brian would be a sweet, involved father someday—just not to her kids.

She lit a couple candles and poured them each a mug of chamomile tea. Lord knew, she needed the calming effect.

"Is it to be continued time?" Brian asked. She nodded.

They sat thigh to thigh on the couch, and it was impossible for Katelyn's whole body not to remember their not-a-date date. The feelings it had forced her to admit would not go away, apparently, no matter how stupid, ill-timed and impossible they were.

She sipped her tea, enjoying the solid presence of Brian beside her even though she knew she shouldn't.

"I'm sorry." Her whisper split the comfortable seam of silence.

"No, *I'm* sorry. I really like you, Katelyn, maybe even, I don't know, could love you, like really love you."

It was the first time he'd spoken the L-word to her; she wished he'd just curse or swear instead.

"And I'm selfish," he continued. "I keep promising myself I'll leave you alone, but then I miss you so much that I convince myself I can handle it, that we can pull off just being friends. I mean I have other women friends. It's seriously not that hard—"

"Just with me it is."

His laugh was sad. "Yeah, you get it. As usual."

"I feel the same way and worse, like I'm leading you on, saying one thing, but doing another or acting in a way that makes a liar out of me."

"No, I get it. The things you want and are striving for are smart and necessary—but your heart just happens to be as stupid and illogical as mine."

Now it was Katelyn's turn to laugh. And it was sad too. "I guess it's like the old saying, the heart wants what it wants."

Brian sighed. "Exactly."

They each took large mouthfuls of tea, as if seeking to fortify themselves.

"So where does that leave us?"

Katelyn groaned. "I don't know? Tortured? Suffering cruel and unusual punishment?"

Brian chuckled. "Well, I guess there's some comfort in the fact that it's not one-sided agony." He clapped his hand on her knee.

It was a simple, companionable gesture. It shouldn't have felt sexual in any way, but Katelyn shuddered and clenched her mug in both hands, struggling against a wave of arousal. Why did his nearness, let alone the merest physical contact with him, always trigger this over the top reaction? What was wrong with her? Why was a touch between them never just a touch?

"No, never fear that," she agreed.

He grinned, but his eyes were rueful in the candle's glow. "This back and forth, hot and cold, stay, no go . . . it's killing me."

"Me too. It will be better once I move away."

"What if you can't move?"

"What do you mean?" Katelyn had been feeling relaxed, meltingly so even, but now her backbone solidified again and all her muscles tightened.

Brian sighed. "Steve is a grade A, all caps total douche bag, for sure . . . but it's a very rare judge that will permit a parent to relocate a family for no other reason than to punish the spouse."

"It's not to *punish* him!"

"I know that and you know that, but it's not like you're being forced to relocate for work or better opportunities. If anything, it's a sounder financial decision to stay here, and it's less disruptive to the kids. Plus, the new trend in the courts is to go with 'the best interest of the children,' and for some reason that has been translated into having contact with their biological parents, pretty much regardless of what one parent has done to the other parent or even to the children. The judge will frown on a move just for a move's sake."

He was right and she knew it—just like, in her darker moments, she knew she would be tied to Steve for the rest of her days, divorced or not, shared geography or not, because they had kids together.

"I've been calling about rentals in town for the fall," she admitted.

He nodded. Their cups were almost empty.

"So where does that leave us?" he repeated. "If you're living here . . . "

Katelyn took a deep, wobbly breath. "For weeks now, for months even, I've been wanting to say we should go for it. That's the whole reason I decided to finally get divorced, so we could . . . explore what's between us."

The happiness her words sparked in Brian's eyes brought a lump to Katelyn's throat, so sharp it was like she'd swallowed glass. He must've been able to read her expression as easily as she read his, however, and his countenance fell.

His voice was soft. "But you also keep wanting to play it safe, to focus on building a life for you and Sawyer and Lacey without bringing down any more of Steve's ire than is absolutely unavoidable."

She nodded miserably. "And I can't ask you to

wait for me to sort myself out. It's not fair."

"I don't even know what I'd be waiting for," he agreed. "I've never seen myself as a long-term commitment guy, but it's like I said, I can't stop seeing us together, no matter how much my brain yells, what are you thinking? Are you nuts?"

Katelyn slammed her empty mug down on the end table. "I know. *Exactly*. Why, since we both want nothing more than friendship, can't we just turn off the bloody romance and fireworks machine?"

"You should go," she said a moment later. Brian nodded and moved to comply, but then she placed her hand on his arm and he stayed put. Next, despite every line of logic ripping through her brain and every rational reason why she shouldn't do what she was about to, she added, "but first, if you want, if it won't make everything worse, you should kiss me good-bye."

Brian reached across her body to place his empty tea mug beside hers, then settled back to sitting—but with a greater space between them than had existed seconds before. He looked at her for a long time, staring first into her eyes, then dropping his gaze to her mouth, then meeting her eyes again.

"Kiss you good-bye until we meet up next, or kiss you good-bye as in we're going to stop seeing each other, going to stop . . . whatever this is?"

She had no good answer, and after a second's pause he shrugged.

He pressed a finger to the plumpest part of her lower lip, and her mouth fell open involuntarily. His eyes, staring into hers so intensely, darkened. Her insides thrilled.

He cupped her cheek with one palm, tilted her chin and angled her mouth to receive his. She stretched up to meet him, her whole body longing for whatever short, stolen, quick before they came to their senses moment this would be—

But he didn't kiss her. Or not her mouth, anyway. Instead he brushed his lips across her temple, then bent in and gently rested his forehead against hers.

"I want to, but I can't," he finally said. "Or I won't. I don't know what's gotten into me, but until I know exactly what you're offering—until you know what you want, I'm not in. I just . . . can't. I think you'll hurt me."

He thought she could hurt *him*. She pulled back, breathing hard, dizzy with unfulfilled want, humiliation . . . and anger. She was furious with herself. He was right. Again. She was being terribly unfair. And weak. She had to stop this emotional pendulum of want, want not, want, want not. It was exhausting. And maddening. And beyond frustrating.

"If we can't be more, I would like us to remain friends. But that means we need set in stone boundaries."

She nodded. It made sense. Perfect sense. And it was wise. She even appreciated him for stating it. But it sucked. It totally and in every way *sucked*.

The trail they'd walked with the kids earlier—and the fork in the path—flashed into her mind. She had reached another fork and couldn't stall forever. She needed to decide whether she truly lived by her motto in the framed picture or not. She couldn't keep taking one step forward, three back. If she did, she would eventually hurt Brian to a point where they couldn't even be friends.

She was bereft but no more enlightened when the cabin's door opened, then shut, and Brian was gone.

Chapter 29

KATELYN WAS TEN MINUTES LATE for work—and that was according to the spool-shaped clock hanging in Got The Notion, which always ran a bit slow. Tardiness was completely unusual for her. She considered not arriving ten minutes *early* as being late. It wasn't her fault exactly, well, it was, but it was the lesser of two evils.

Steve had called and she had tried—unsuccessfully, she worried—to calm him down. No, that wasn't quite right. He was calm. Icy, steely calm as he outlined every single way he perceived she had wronged him, was wronging him, had hurt him, was hurting him, and had damaged, was damaging the kids. There was nothing new in his tirade of complaints; the divorce papers had just amped him up. But a chilly, flat toned list of her failings was always a worse sign of danger than one of his hot-tempered flare-ups.

She noticed she was twisting her hands, and, with effort, stilled the anxious tell and smoothed her fifties' style pencil skirt instead.

"Cute shoes. New?" Jayda asked, appearing from

behind a hanging display of upholstery.

Katelyn looked down at her yellow Mary Janes. They were cute and they suited her retro outfit, but that was pure luck. She could've arrived barefoot or even shirtless for all the mental energy she'd given to thinking about her wardrobe that morning. "I'm sorry I'm late."

Jayda shrugged, barely glancing up from a basket of bright-patterned Fat Quarters she was putting together for a door crasher sale. "It's your first time *ever*. It's fine. Are you okay though?"

"Um, yes. I think so. Why?"

"You're as white as your blouse."

Katelyn looked down again. Sleeveless. Boat-necked. Ecru. Good choice, but Heaven help her if she was really that bloodless. "It's just stuff with Steve. Sorry. Nothing to take to work."

Jayda, never idle, had finished her basket stuffing and was straightening a counter display of eclectic buttons and fasteners. She paused now, however, and gave Katelyn a steady look. "Just another thing I love about you. If every employee understood there should be a work-home life divide the way you do, I'd never have a moment's stress."

Jayda meant it as a compliment, but it was easy to hear the unspoken command too: don't start sharing your troubles or ask for a stress day. Katelyn smiled, bobbed her head in a nod, and headed to the flannel section. Fall and winter prints had arrived over the weekend—seasons always ran about six months early in the shop to give crafters time to get inspired and to get projects done in time—and she needed to make room for them. She'd been looking forward to the task because handling new fabric always kindled ideas for her own sewing, but her heart wasn't in it now.

She couldn't shake the sense of foreboding Marilee's warning had triggered, a feeling that had only intensified since Steve's phone call. The lovely evening of respite from her fears, walking with Brian and the kids, checking out the beautiful abandoned property, might as well have never happened. It felt like the distant past, irrelevant now. The fact that she and Brian would most likely never enjoy a similar ease or visit again, and the pain that knowledge should have caused, was overshadowed by a low simmering dread. She was only numbly aware that the loss was going to hurt like the dickens when she was able to process things again.

"It's just a feeling," she muttered, pulling out a bolt of cotton candy pink flannel. "Stop being crazy." But she wasn't convinced. If anything, more than Marilee's words of caution, more than Steve's cold scariness during the call, the "mere feeling" was what had her on high alert. She'd learned long ago how much her safety and wellness, and Lacey and Sawyer's, depended on her respecting her gut intuition.

But the morning passed without incident. She checked in with Aisha on her break, and the kids were doing great. It was unusually warm for May and they were having a blast running through the sprinkler and making homemade popsicles for later. Then a local quilter came into the shop with eight adult students she was doing a sixteen-week course for, all new to sewing, all in need of materials for their first projects. The rest of the morning evaporated.

At lunchtime, she called Aisha again and was reassured everyone was still fine.

"Is everything okay? You never call this much," Aisha said before they hung up.

Katelyn hesitated. She didn't want to be a drama queen, especially if there was nothing . . . but then again, what if Steve did show up?

"I should've told you this before. It's probably nothing, but Steve and I had a bit of a row. He's not happy about the divorce papers. If he shows up . . ."

If he showed up, what? Should Aisha panic and run the kids into the house? No, that probably wasn't warranted and could be traumatizing. Should she call Jo or Callum? Or would that set Steve off?

She was saved from further deliberations by Aisha's dry voice. "Exes, hey? Can't live with them. Can't kill them."

Katelyn's laugh was more like a croak. "Exactly."

"Listen, it's no problem and you don't need to worry. We just finished lunch, Mo is wiped and ready for a nap, and I've already prepared Lacey and Sawyer for a quiet afternoon. They're going to color while I read to them, and when Mo wakes up, we'll do puzzles. We'll stay inside, door locked, until you're back."

The surge of relief that rushed through Katelyn was almost painful, like blood rushing into a limb that has had its circulation cut off. She was almost nauseous with it. Which also scared her. What was she picking up? What?

She checked her messages after they said goodbye, then ate on the fly while running errands. She returned library books, picked up a few groceries, and hit a cash machine. The car was cranky leaving the bank. She finally got it going, but it limped down the road like it was having a hard time staying powered. Her gas tank was half full. Rats! She so didn't need this. But then again, maybe it was car trouble her brain was intuiting. Maybe the bad feeling had nothing to do with Steve. Wouldn't that be nice?

As she pulled back into the staff parking area, however, a sloppily parked vehicle taking up two spots made her heart thud. But why? It was just a little blue car. There were thousands of hatchbacks exactly like it on the road. In fact, there was one like it at River's Sigh just the other day—the thought froze her in her seat.

"It's a coincidence, just a coincidence," she whispered, forcing her inert foot to accelerate lightly and her stiff hands to guide the wheel and turn in. "It's a guest's car, a *guest's*."

But then, before her brain could catch up with *why*,

she killed the engine, threw off her seat belt, grabbed her phone from the dash and crashed out of her car. She sprinted to the back entrance, without bothering to grab her keys from the ignition or even to shut the driver side's door.

Because what River's Sigh guest would ever choose—would ever even know about—these inconvenient alley parking spaces? They wouldn't. They'd park in the customer lot out front.

Inside the long narrow hallway that opened from the back entrance and functioned as an overflow storage room, Katelyn removed her noisy click-clacking shoes, and forced herself to walk at a snail's pace. Finally she was in the store front, sneaking around a ladder display of fuzzy fleece and her previously unsubstantiated fears took on shape and form: Steve's shape. Steve's muscular form.

His rage-gripped face, so terrifyingly familiar to her, was focused on someone else though. He hadn't noticed her yet. It took Katelyn a beat or two to register what she was seeing. Then her whole body started to shake. Her limbs felt dangerously light while her center filled with lead, like all the blood from her extremities was pooling in her stomach.

"She is *my wife*." The words scraped through gritted teeth. "*Mine*. You have no right to keep her from me."

The side of Jayda's face was flattened against the checkout counter, held fast by her long black hair, gripped punishingly in Steve's left hand. His right hand white-knuckled a knife. Katelyn's gorge rose and bile burned in her throat and nose. She forced herself to swallow against her gag reflex and prayed that the whining shriek making her ears bleed was only in her mind. You need to be quiet, stay very quiet, she cautioned herself. And be still. Very still.

Steve pressed the blade to the curve of Jayda's smooth brown jaw, which glistened with perspiration, tears or both.

Jayda's hazel eyes were wild and rolling. They fixed on Katelyn for a moment, but Katelyn didn't know if she really saw her.

"That bitch is not worth it. I promise you. Just tell me where she is and you can go back to destroying families. Just. Not. Mine."

In a series of steps that seemed to take years, Katelyn dragged her finger across the face of her phone to bring it to life. Then she pressed nine-one-one and hit Talk.

A yelp so soft it was almost nothing more than an intake of breath yanked Katelyn's attention back to Jayda. A crimson line burst from a pinprick cut on her jawbone, followed the curve of her throat and raced toward her clavicle. Katelyn was so used to seeing Jayda working with trims and lace that for a moment her shocked brain registered the blood as ribbon and she almost admired the color against Jayda's rich flesh.

"This is nine-one-one. What is your emergency?"

Everything seemed to simultaneously slow down and speed up from then on out. Katelyn, though she'd have no recollection of what she'd said or hadn't said later, managed to get out the basics: ex-husband, knife, store name, address, hurry.

Steve's concentration on Jayda broke the instant he heard Katelyn's voice. He loosened his hold on her boss and turned to Katelyn, smiling with something that looked horribly like genuine joy.

"It's time to set a few things straight, Kiki," he said conversationally, starting toward her.

This was it. In the later years of their short marriage, she'd come to believe that while other women she knew might die tragically of cancer or shockingly in car accidents or even in some lovely way like from old age, she might die at the hands of her husband. Steve had seemed to sense—even enjoy—her fear, often murmuring, "Till death do us part, right?" when he kissed her hair or patted her shoulder after an "argument." After she'd left him, she'd felt she'd gained a reprieve but not a pardon, sure that sometime, someday, he'd snap and she'd be there when he did.

The fear Katelyn constantly lived with and managed, that she occasionally thought of as an enemy, but more often considered a friend, grew from the mouse-sized skittering thing she always felt in Steve's presence into a roaring beast.

She backed away fast, purposely upsetting fabric stands and shoving a rolling wooden box of cushions into his way. Steve kept coming, knife hand raised, but all rage in his expression long dissipated.

And then he was within an arm's reach of her and there was nowhere to go, just the dead-end storage hall. She had no room inside for anything except terror—not even her recent lunch. Just as Steve lunged, she vomited violently, spraying coffee and half-digested food onto the reclaimed barn wood floor.

The slick sickness of her fear was Steve's undoing. His foot slipped in the mess and he went down. He landed horrifically close to her. The dispatcher's voice carried from Katelyn's phone, asking her to hold on, saying there was a car on its way—and then Steve was up like a shot and out the door.

A swarm of police officers and ambulance attendants arrived, but Katelyn had lost her ability to distinguish individual faces. There could have been four uniformed people or forty. A cacophony of strident voices, all speaking with the practiced composure of emergency responders, battered her ears. She could still identify Jayda. Her boss. Still crying. Katelyn was addressed by her full legal name and told to stay put by someone with a calm, reassuring voice. Someone else was talking into a radio, trying to give directions about "the assailant" who'd left on foot.

"No, he . . . has a car, a blue car," Katelyn said, but she didn't make sense of much of the rest of the clamoring around her. She folded into a triangle, butt on floor, heels to butt, knees to chin, against the unpacked boxes of fall fabrics and dialed Aisha with trembling hands.

"Aisha, it's me. Are you and the kids . . . all right? Are you okay?"

Aisha voice was concerned even as it reassured her. "We're fine. We're good. Why?"

"Uh, just checking in," she managed to croak. "Keep the doors locked, please, and don't let Steve in for any reason. I'll be home soon, will explain then." She clicked End before Aisha could say another thing and rang Brian—eyes closed, tears streaming. She found no words at all when he answered, "Hey, this is a nice surprise on a rotten day. What's up?"

Chapter 30

BRIAN WANTED TO BE ANYWHERE but at his mother's. No, that was false. He didn't want to be *anywhere*. He wanted to be in one very specific place: Spring cabin with Katelyn—or, at the very furthest away, sitting in the main hall at River's Sigh B & B, so he was close by in case she needed him. He was still having a hard time processing Friday's events and even though it was Sunday now, it still felt more like a nightmare than reality. How could the cops still not have caught the guy? He couldn't imagine how Katelyn was coping, but somehow she was. She even seemed like her normal self, just a bit quieter than usual and adamant about not leaving the kids' sides. Which he totally understood. But Caren had called early in the morning, insisting she needed to see him about something "urgent." Katelyn had been equally insistent that she would be fine for a few hours. So here he was, drinking tea with his mom—who wasted no time in getting down to what she considered the big emergency.

"I've heard a rumor that I'm hoping you'll ease my mind about," Caren said. "Tell me you're not seeing the Kellerman woman."

The Kellerman woman. It took Brian a second to figure out whom his mother was speaking about in such a disdainful tone. Katelyn. She meant Katelyn. But what was it to Caren if he was "seeing" Katelyn. Why on earth would she have a problem with Katelyn?

"Callum's boarder, the one who makes her own clothes, has two kids?" Caren prodded.

Confused anger and defensiveness churned through Brian. How could Caren of all people fault a person for being creative? Or was it Katelyn's motherhood status Caren found offensive?

"Who gave you that idea?"

Caren's normally passive expression tightened and she ignored his question. "She's not for you. She has a troubled marriage."

Brian's jaw dropped and after he gaped for a moment or two, he hooted with laughter. "Oh dear," he said in a sarcastic, high-pitched voice, "not a 'troubled' marriage."

"This isn't a joking matter. It's serious. She's an abused wife."

Apparently the Greenridge grapevine had been at work with lightning speed. He wondered what exactly his mother had heard about Steve's visit to Got the Notion and about the rest of Katelyn's life in general—and from whom? Not that it mattered. When it came to gossip, no one was a reputable source. The nature of talking behind someone's back precluded it.

Brian cracked his knuckles and pushed his tea away, feeling like he'd fallen into an episode of the Twilight Zone. "Okay, well, not that it's any of your business, but Katelyn's no longer his wife. She's been legally separated for two years and has started divorce proceedings. And as for her being abused, I'm not sure why you sound like that's her fault or is something to condemn her for."

Caren frowned, clearly unmoved.

"And seriously," Brian continued, "isn't that a bit like the pot calling the kettle black?"

"What's that supposed to mean?"

"C'mon, Mom. Be real for once—you know, like you tried to be at that disastrous anniversary dinner when Cade and Noelle were visiting last summer. Channel *that* woman."

"Your father has never hit me," Caren hissed. "He would never hit me!"

"And that's your measure of a healthy, 'non-abusive' relationship? That one person doesn't hit another person?"

Caren's already pale face had gone the color of skim milk and the freckles she used to always cover up and now never did stood out in sharp rust-colored blotches. Brian had the surreal thought that in some ways he was older than her now.

"I just want you to be happy."

"No," Brian said. "You want me to be single and biddable. Your little bachelor mama's boy forever."

"That isn't fair." Caren's cornflower blue eyes filled. It was so rare, so unheard of, for his mother to cry, that Brian's own throat burned.

"I love you, Mom, and I'm sorry if my words hurt, but I'll date whoever I want to, and I won't have you of all people giving me relationship advice."

"So you *are* seeing her."

Brian shook his head. As ever, his mother seemed incapable of getting the point, incapable of getting *him*.

Caren rose to her feet slowly and, for the first time in Brian's whole life, she seemed every one of her years. "Maybe it's someone like me, your *mother*, the woman who loves you more than any other person in the world does, the person who, yes, has made mistakes and, yes, lives with regrets, who is *exactly* the person to give you relationship advice."

"But—" Brian started.

Caren made a slicing motion with her hand, silencing him. "I don't want to fight with you. I'm just, whether you believe it or not, concerned about you."

She took a deep breath, like she was going to say something more, but didn't. She squeezed lemon into each of their mugs, freshened their tea, and sank back into her chair.

A deep, familiar sadness—almost rage—coiled and uncoiled in Brian's guts. You are not your parents, he said sternly in his head. A person can break free of patterns. Look at Katelyn.

"Mom," he said softly. "Katelyn is a good person,

a strong person. You'll like her."

"You mean you think she's better than me, stronger, less complacent."

"Aw, come on. It's not a question of anyone being better or stronger—" He broke off suddenly, recalling a conversation he'd had with Katelyn.

"What do you get out of your relationship with Dad anyway?"

"What do you mean?"

"What's the payoff? You're *not* weak. You're not . . . complacent, as you said. You're passionate, disciplined, artistic—and you'd be able to support yourself quite nicely, or very nicely, depending on your settlement."

"I still don't—"

"It's not complicated. Everyone stays in a relationship for a reason. The reason may not make sense to anyone else, or it may be built on flawed logic, but it exists. Some women stay with abusers because they're afraid of the consequences of leaving. Some have financial realities to think of. They can't afford to break free, or, at least, they can't afford to raise their children without their husband's help. Some people get an ego rush from feeling superior to their abuser, others have religious convictions, or—"

Caren held up her hand again. "Okay, okay, I get it."

Brian bit his tongue as long as he could, then blurted, "So, *why*?"

"Your dad isn't the complete villain you all seem to think he is," Caren said slowly. "And I'm not the easiest person to be married to either. I love you boys, I really do—but I've always thought I'd have made a good single person, like you."

Anger and age old frustration thumped at Brian's temples. "I know you mean well," he said, "but you have to stop comparing me to you. I'm not you. I'm me. My whole life everyone has acted like I'd never be able to sustain a relationship, like I'm too shallow, too self-absorbed, too . . . I don't know. It never occurs to any of you that I might want a real relationship, a home, a family."

Caren's eyes widened. "*That's* what you think of me? And that's what you think people are saying, what *I'm* saying, when you're compared to me?"

Brian shrugged.

"Oh . . . " Caren's voice trailed off and her eyes fluttered shut. When she opened them, she had found her composure again. "So then you understand, at least partly, how your father has always felt—like he came second in my life, or, once you boys came along, further down the line than that even. And then, of course, he acted in ways that only created what he feared all along—that I would cease to love him or that I had never loved him."

Caren had always overshared with Brian. He still resented it like crazy, but now, as an adult, he at least understood it—the loneliness she must feel, the isolation, that would make her turn to her child and talk to him like a peer.

"So what? You're staying with him now, after making it public that you don't care for him, to what? Punish him?"

Caren laughed lightly, sorrowfully. "Relationships are complicated. No one understands what makes someone else's marriage work—not even the people who are married."

Brian shook his head. "I reject that." The vehemence and volume of his words shocked them both. Caren actually jumped a little. "Kindness, appreciation, respect . . . laughing together . . . those things go a long way in any relationship."

"Wow, you really do like this woman."

"I do, not that it matters. She, like you, thinks it's not worth pursuing, that she's too much trouble."

Caren sipped her tea and looked distant again. "That was the most surprising facet of all this to me. When I broke free of your Dad, when he moved out, I realized that all these years I'd been using my distance and preoccupation with my work as a tether, a way of controlling him. Once I decided to leave him, all I could see were the things I'd miss about him."

"Like what?"

"He's brilliantly smart, your dad. And a hard worker."

"And a womanizer, a bully, and a braggart."

"If you'd known your grandfather, your dad's dad,

you'd be more understanding."

Brian scrubbed his face with his hands. "This whole conversation is madness, Mom. Do what you want, but please stop involving me in it. I just . . . I can't. I love you. I love Dad too, actually—but you guys spent a lifetime being unhappy with each other, and I'm not going to pretend I'm jumping with joy that you're back together again."

"You know what you should do?"

Brian set his mug down too heavily. It sloshed and almost spilled. She really was going to ignore everything he'd said, like he hadn't spoken at all.

"Stop thinking about us, me, your dad, your brothers. Stop thinking about all the court cases you've seen and clients you've worked with."

"I'm sorry. I'm not following—"

"I'm not, *we're not*, the reason you've never pursued a serious relationship. It was fear—justifiable, smart, completely reasonable *fear.* You're analytical, you study things, you arrive at conclusions."

"Um . . . "

"So use that knowledge and your years of observations to do what your brothers have done: build the marriage you want, centered around love."

"Wait a minute. First you're all up in arms because I might be *seeing* Katelyn. Now you're practically commanding me to marry her?"

"Not at all." Caren stood up once more, showing that the conversation and their visit was almost done.

"I'm saying you're a grown man, with a good career and a solid head on your shoulders. It's time for you to forgive me and your dad for any ways we've failed you, any bad examples we've set. And it's past time to stop using us as your excuse for not trying, for not taking risks, for not seeking the relationship you obviously crave. We're just people trying to live the best we can, and sometimes, yes, I'm sorry, we fail."

Brian had followed Caren's lead, standing when she did, but now he plunked back into the chair and fiddled with a teaspoon. Was that what he'd been doing all these years? Not wisely steering clear of long-term relationships because monogamy and "true love" really were bunk, but because he immaturely thought so, based solely on his childhood home life?

How many times had he told young offenders he represented, when faced with their common as potatoes denials of responsibility for their actions, saying it was because of this or that in their past, that it didn't fly with him? That if you didn't recognize something had affected you, yes, you were off the hook, but the moment that you did realize you might do X because you'd experienced Y or lived through Z—then you were responsible for acting on that new information and choosing the better path, the higher road.

He sighed, set his teaspoon down, and looked up. Caren had already disappeared into her studio.

On his trek through the quiet memory laden house toward the door, a trio of odd thoughts occurred to

Brian. Maybe curing his disillusionment and self-imposed bachelorhood really was up to him, like his mom pointed out. Maybe happiness was just a matter of choosing to live and love differently than his parents. And maybe he'd already started to.

On the heels of everything with Steve, it suddenly seemed urgent that he and Katelyn not waste another day letting that bastard hold them back or keep them from each other. But was that selfish of him?

Chapter 31

STARING AT HER PHONE, WHICH she'd just thrown across the kitchen like it was a snake that had bit her, Katelyn pressed her clenched fists against her mouth and tried not to howl at the unfairness. She was vaguely aware of Lacey watching her with big worried eyes and of Sawyer, curled up on the couch, thumb in his mouth—but for once, she couldn't get her act together, couldn't calm down and pretend everything was okay, couldn't comfort and reassure them immediately.

She and the kids had been holed up at River's Sigh for three days, and there was no sign of their enforced captivity ending soon. There was still no word about Steve. A young constable checked in with her twice a day, saying he was pretty sure Steve wouldn't be a problem, that he'd probably left the province. Katelyn was equally sure that wasn't the case—but Steve wasn't even her primary worry at the moment.

This latest call threatened to be the last straw, the incident that made Katelyn throw in the towel and give up.

How could Jayda? How could she? Why, why,

why? And how dare she act like Katelyn should have been mollified by her stupid, lame offer to continue to "pass her name on," like it was some huge kindness?

Of course, that was only Katelyn's emotional response. The rational side of her thought it made perfect sense. Why on earth *would* Jayda keep on any employee that might lure a loose cannon like Steve back again?

You could fight it, a voice in her head muttered. There has to be a law against letting someone go just because their ex is a monster. But even as the thought formed and scuttled to the edges of her brain, she knew she wouldn't. Working in a place where your boss had been forced to keep you on or risk facing a wrongful dismissal suit would be hell. And Katelyn, not that it ever helped her, had her pride.

"Mommy? Are you okay?" Lacey's voice was small and uncertain, quite unlike her usual boisterous, slightly bossy tone.

Katelyn became aware of the ocean coursing down her cheeks. She sniffed loudly and choked a little on the mucus trying to drown her. Another wave of sorrow and desperation slapped her hard, and the undertow threatened to pull her into despair again. No, no, *no*. She fought hard to tread water, to get her head above the surface again. She forced a tremulous smile—which must have looked terrifyingly fake because Lacey took a step back.

You're all right, she tried to assure herself. The

voice in her head reminded her of how she spoke to her kids when they'd been awoken by nightmares—how fitting. *She* was in a nightmare. And she wanted to wake up. She wanted to wake up right now! Take a deep breath, she soothed. You're safe. You're safe.

But not for long. The keening gale force of despair inside her head threatened to dunk her again, but she focused on Lacey's worried face and reached for her hand. This time when she spoke, she was much more in control.

"I'm really sad," she admitted to Lacey. "I lost my job and I'm concerned about that, but things will work out. You let me worry about it, okay? You and Sawyer try not to."

At the sound of his name, Sawyer made eye contact and bobbed his head as if to say, yes, he'd try.

"Is it because of Daddy?" Lacey asked.

What do you say to that kind of question? Katelyn didn't want to lie. She also didn't want to embroil the kids in her adult problems any more than they already, so frustratingly and heartbreakingly, were.

She hated how quickly Lacey seemed to understand the dilemma, how she patted her mother's hand reassuringly. "Things aren't as bad as they seem," Lacey said, borrowing one of Katelyn's phrases again, making her cringe. "And one day, very soon, I'm going to be old enough to choose to never have to see Daddy again and then we can go far, far away."

Hearing the hope in Lacey's firm voice did something to Katelyn's insides and brought home a deep truth. It wasn't fair. She and the kids hadn't done anything wrong. They shouldn't have to live in fear, walking on eggshells because they didn't know what was going to happen next with Steve. They shouldn't be forced to leave the town where they'd built a life and had friends, or made to go to a strange place where they knew nobody just because Steve had some mental illness, at best, or was a psychopath, at worst.

With that, she rallied the dregs of her courage and hugged Lacey close, breathing in the sweet scent of the tearless shampoo she always used on the kids. "You are amazing, my girl. And you're right. Things aren't as bad as they seem."

And they weren't. A big shiny silver lining had just revealed itself to Katelyn's cloudy mind. Steve wanted to keep escalating and escalating and escalating? That was fine—awesome, in fact. In the past, the whole problem had been that it was so often his word against hers. He could talk such a good game, present so well and seem so healthy when he wanted to, making others, including the judge, think she was some unhinged hysterical woman blowing things out of proportion because she had a vendetta against him.

Now she had other witnesses—good ones, reliable ones: police officers *and* another victim, Jayda. She just had to survive until the police found Steve and arrested him. After that, freedom might well be within her grasp.

A knock sounded on the cabin door and Katelyn's heart raced with a confusing mixture of apprehension and hope. What if Steve had somehow made it onto the premises without anyone noticing? Or what if it was Brian? She was desperate to talk to Brian—to really talk.

It was neither. Instead, Aisha and Jo greeted her, smiling warmly and doing a pretty decent job of hiding most of their concern.

"Jo's hanging out with me and the kids today. She's taking us trout fishing, if that's okay with you?"

"Yes!" Lacey whisper-cheered behind her. "Let's get dressed, Sawyer." There was a flurry of quiet excitement as Lacey and Sawyer zipped from the room. Fresh sadness and guilt lodged itself in Katelyn's throat. Without her job at Got the Notion, Aisha's new job would cease to be, too.

"Um, about that," Katelyn started.

Aisha's eyes widened and her hand flew to her mouth before Katelyn managed to explain anything. "You need more days off, of course. When you said you were ready to start back today, I wondered—"

"I don't think that's it," Jo said quietly. "What's up, Katelyn? Has there been something more with Steve?"

Katelyn shook her head miserably. "I don't need you today, Aisha. And I'm sorry, but I probably won't be able to afford to have you babysit anymore in the future either. I got laid off because of—you know," she waved her hands around in the air, "*everything.*"

"What?" Aisha exploded. "She can't do that!"

There was a barrage of outraged comments from both Aisha and Jo, with Jo insisting Katelyn should get Brian to deal with it. Finally, though, they got to a place where they seemed to understand where Katelyn was coming from, how she didn't want to work at a place that only kept her on because they were forced to.

"Maybe it's not the worst thing," Aisha said after a beat or two of silence.

"Compared to what? Being murdered?"

Aisha, who could usually be counted on to find humor in any situation, no matter how dark, scowled. "Not funny."

Jo just looked anxious to the point of tears. "He won't. He can't . . . " Her voice cracked and died away. Katelyn completely got their inability to speak about it. There was nothing they could do, short of notifying the authorities if Steve called or showed up. It was a waiting game. A hideous waiting game. But would she have to live the rest of her life like this, always waiting for the axe to drop?

Aisha spoke again. "I just meant that maybe this will be the push you need, your chance to find a way to sew for a living or something."

Katelyn failed to keep her bitterness down. "Yeah, right."

Aisha gave a sad nod. "I'm sorry. It's probably too

soon for lame everything's going to be okay pep talks."

Katelyn shook her head. "No, *I'm* sorry. I just . . . " She couldn't go on.

Aisha patted her arm awkwardly, but managed to convey a whole lot of understanding. Jo, too, seemed at a rare loss for encouraging words.

"So, anyway, yeah . . . I can't pay you for today, but if you guys are willing to still take the kids fishing—and let me tag along—they would, *I would,* love it."

Aisha gave a small laugh that sounded heavy with relief.

"Absolutely," Jo said, like it eased a huge burden for her as well. "Brian took the day off too, and I already asked if he wanted to tag along. Is that all right?"

"Of course," Katelyn said. "It's great."

And it was. Or she hoped it would be. Brian had been wonderful in the aftermath of Steve's attack and escape. He'd brought her groceries and stayed late each night, playing with and distracting the kids, making sure Katelyn wasn't scared to stay alone, and outlining the safeguards Callum had put in place to keep Steve from getting onto the property unseen. But at the same time, they hadn't had much alone time. Katelyn couldn't decide if that was because Brian was still trying to respect her stupid boundaries (that he didn't know were smashed all to bits now), or if—and this was a possibility that made her heart ache—it was because recent events had shown Brian all too clearly, in a way he hadn't previously understood, what a nightmare being seriously involved with her would be.

She desperately wanted to believe that she hadn't lost her chance with Brian out of fear and her failure to be brave soon enough—but she wouldn't blame him if she had.

Chapter 32

BRIAN JOGGED OVER TO SPRING cabin empty handed, taking Jo at her word that she'd have whatever fishing doodads he needed. He spotted Katelyn before she noticed him and stood for a moment, watching her. Wearing faded jeans and an orange and blue flannel shirt knotted at her hip, she stood barefoot on the freshly clipped lawn, hanging crisp white sheets on a clothesline. With a huge tub of bright red geraniums nearby, she—and the whole picture—was so pretty, it made him pull in a breath. And was the smell of clean laundry being a turn on actually a thing?

She must've felt his eyes because she turned suddenly. "Oh!" Her hand flew up, but she was already smiling. "You startled me."

On the heels of her words, visions of the wildflower property and its patiently waiting house popped into his head. He knew it was time—past time. He'd go crazy if he didn't muster some emotional courage for once in his damn life. Katelyn very well might turn him down again, for real and in a final way, but at least he'd know once and for all. And at least he'd stop bailing on her, wanting to commit, wanting to try—then chickening out, using Steve as his excuse.

He had to know if they were moving forward as a unit, or if he somehow needed to get his act together without her and the kids in his life. His guts hurt at the thought and he wondered if loving her was giving him an ulcer.

The words stopped him in his tracks. Loving her. He couldn't tell if it was exhilaration or terror that amped up his heartbeat.

"We need to talk."

She smiled and nodded—but they didn't get their chance. Jo and Aisha piled out of the cabin, followed by Lacey, Sawyer, and a toddling Mo. Jo gathered up rod cases from the porch, handed one to Brian and one to Katelyn, then hefted a large tackle box.

"Okay guys, pick 'em up, put 'em down and follow me."

This was obviously a command they'd received from Jo before because both Sawyer and Lacey giggled and said, "Yes, ma'am!" then proceeded to march after her.

Katelyn looked at Brian. He looked at her. They both shrugged and fell into line too.

Jo took them down a short trail Brian never bothered with, thinking correctly that it led directly to the creek, which was a dead end for running, though, of course, perfect for fishing.

For once Brian was the low energy guy. The kids

chattered a mile a minute, Jo flitted back and forth explaining lures and baiting hooks, and he considered his options. He was resolute that he needed to tell Katelyn how he honestly felt. Where he wavered was in his previous notion that he should tell her as soon as possible, regardless of whether Steve was still on the loose or not. He wanted to be special to Katelyn, not another burden. But was his growing desire to stall once again really altruistic, or was it just same old same old—him being an emotional coward?

Katelyn was quiet too, but he suspected her thoughts ran parallel to his because whenever he glanced at her, she just happened to glance back. But maybe that was wishful thinking, maybe she was preoccupied with thoughts of Steve, and really, if she was, who could blame her?

He was yanked from his musings when Jo handed him a small neon blue fishing rod and asked if he'd help Sawyer.

"Absolutely. Come on, big guy. Let's bring home some dinner."

"You really know how?" Sawyer asked suspiciously.

"Yes, I really do," Brian said. "Scout's honor."

Sawyer looked at him blankly.

"I used to fish when I was a teenager, plus Jo has taught me a thing or two."

That apparently held some sway, and Sawyer walked with him to the water's edge. As Brian showed him how to cast his line into a shady green pool formed by a huge fallen tree, peace fell over him. He didn't have to rush anything. The right time to talk to Katelyn would come—and he would recognize it when it did.

The afternoon passed quickly, with enough nibbles to keep the kids interested, but no real bites until Jo called, "Fifteen minutes and we're going to call it a day, guys."

The words were barely out of her mouth when Lacey yelled, "I've got something. I've got something. I think it's a big one!" Her rod dipped and bounced like crazy as if to prove her claim.

Jo asked everyone else to reel in and rushed to Lacey's side, coaching her all the way. In no time at all a fat little Rainbow trout was in Jo's fish basket.

"Well," Jo said, her eyes twinkling, "should we go home now as planned, or should we keep fishing?"

"Keep fishing, keep fishing," Sawyer begged.

Jo nodded. "Oh, okay. Since you insist."

By the time another hour had passed, Lacey had two trout, Mo and Aisha had landed one, and Sawyer was heartbroken. "I knew I'd never catch one," he said softly. "I knew it."

"I'm sorry, buddy," Brian said, dropping to one knee. "There's always next time. Don't be too disappointed."

"Okay," said Sawyer glumly. "I'll try not to be."

The kid's constant willingness to try to do right

was beyond his years and somehow poignant to Brian.

"It's going to get dark soon," Jo said. "We should probably wrap things up."

"Do you mind if we try for just a few more minutes?" Brian asked.

"Go for it," Jo said.

"Nah, there's no point," Sawyer said in as close to a pout as Brian had ever seen him.

"There's always a point, even if it's just for the fun of it," Brian said. "And have you been having fun?"

Sawyer brightened like it had just occurred to him. "Yeah."

"So there you go. Success. And if you want to, you can try casting by yourself this time."

Sawyer gamely did as he was told, and though the sparkling wedding band landed too close to shore for Brian's liking, he didn't bother to correct it.

He felt the gentle pressure of a hand on his back and turned slightly. Katelyn. "You're so good with them," she said wistfully. Before he could reply, Sawyer squeaked, "Oh. *Oh!* I got something. I think. I think. Maybe."

Brian turned back just in time to see Sawyer's rod jerk hard. He grabbed it, supporting it before it was pulled out of the little boy's hands.

Jo was beside them right away. "I'd say you do. A *big* something."

She coached Sawyer the same way she had Lacey. Within minutes, the largest catch of the day was flipping and flapping on the rocky beach.

"Good job, Sawyer—and Brian—good job!"

"I couldn't hold on if Brian didn't help me," Sawyer confessed.

"Yeah, but I wouldn't have even known we had a fish on except for you," Brian said.

Sawyer's jaw dropped and he beamed. "That's . . . true."

"You did awesome," Jo agreed, hunkering down in front of Sawyer. "You were patient, the time was right, and you got her hook, line and sinker. It was meant to be."

"Yeah, meant to be," Sawyer echoed sagely.

Brian glanced at Katelyn and she looked over at him, the exact same instant—but Jo wrecked the moment by rounding them all up and getting them to help clean fish.

Back on the trail toward River's Sigh again, a rod case secured over his shoulder, Brian jostled for position in the line until he was hip to hip with Katelyn. He reached down and took her free hand. She gazed at their laced fingers, then up into his face.

"Hook, line and sinker," he said softly. "That's how you have me."

Katelyn shook her head, but she was smiling.

"Absolutely it is," Brian insisted, still whispering. "And it's like Jo said. Some things are meant to be."

"I think she was talking about fishing."

"I think you know it applies to us."

"But what about Steve and how and where—"

"We'll figure it out," Brian said. "Everything else is just details. This, *us*—you, me, the kids . . . It's right, Katelyn. *We're* right."

She opened her mouth as if to argue—but didn't. Instead she squeezed his hand and grinned. "You make it awfully hard for a girl to not just jump up and kiss you," she said.

"Well, lord, woman, don't let me stop you."

And on the trail, with everybody else walking only slightly ahead, Katelyn did just that, lifting up on tippy toes and giving him a quick, gentle peck on the lips.

"See, that's *almost* what I'm talking about," he purred. He dropped her hand and eased the rod case to the ground. She did the same. Then he gripped her slim waist and lowered his mouth to hers forcefully. She sagged against him and Brian felt her tremble, stirring something both protective and hungry within him.

When she broke away, they were each breathing hard. Brian lowered his hands to her hips and tugged her close, but not close enough. Never close enough. "Don't say we have to stop," he said. "Not now. Not again. Please."

Katelyn laughed, then joked with a prim accent, "It's not the time or place for more, sir. I'm sorry."

"But—" he started, then stopped. Her smile, soft and full of hope and something he realized he hadn't truly seen on her face until now—pure, radiant happiness—struck him mute with echoing emotions.

"Like you said," she whispered, "it's meant to be. We've been patient. *Too* patient. We'll have our chance. When all the mess is . . . not so messy."

He couldn't stop grinning. They retrieved the rod cases and straightened up just as Lacey, twenty paces ahead of them, pivoted on her heel, spotted them and yelled, "What's taking you guys so long?" It made him laugh out loud. Katelyn really did have a sixth sense when it came to knowing if her kids were going to chime in or need her for something.

A fat raindrop splatted on his face. Then another. And another.

"Hurry," Jo urged from ahead. "I think we're in for another downpour. Run!"

They all took her advice and ran, clumsy and awkward with the things they were carrying, but laughing too and hopeful—like there was actually a chance they might avoid the coming storm.

Chapter 33

THE KIDS WERE IN BED, Monster was fed and crashed out under the couch, and Katelyn felt boneless with pleasure. It was like she had been chained, almost crushed, by worry and concerns that were somehow miraculously disintegrating. Some far off part of her brain knew it was only a temporary break, but she'd take it. She'd take it! Right now, it was just her and Brian and—

"Are you sure?" Brian's voice was as soft as crushed velvet, and the throaty joy in his whisper, despite all the awfulness of the past few days, raised gooseflesh along her skin.

"Yes," she said. "More sure than I've ever been." She pressed her lips against his neck, his jaw, his mouth. . . . Her insides quaked when he kissed her back. His fingers laced through hers and he ran his thumb back and forth across her knuckles in an uncon-scious, constant loop. It was infinitely comforting, this soft, repeating reminder that he was with her. She marveled at it—and was completely conscious of the irony. If Steve hadn't flipped out and attacked Jayda, she might never have grabbed the courage to let herself completely go for Brian, heart, body and soul.

Brian had just reached beneath her shirt and ran his hands up and over her ribcage when the phone rang.

Katelyn closed her eyes and shuddered beneath the weight of Brian's still fully clothed body suspended over hers, but this tremor was not from desire. She knew deep in her blood, the same way you see lightning before you hear it strike, that the call would be anything but good.

"THIS IS A TERRIBLE IDEA," Brian said, his normally cheerful face one big scowl.

"It is," Katelyn agreed, already off the couch and at the door, shoving her feet into rubber boots. The night storm had intensified. A howling wind rattled the window panes and shrieked through the trees. Rain pounded the roof and ground in punishing sheets. "But I can't not try to help."

He frowned and didn't say anything.

She shoved her arms into the sleeves of her windbreaker. "Will you stay here and watch the kids for me?"

He still didn't say anything.

"I can call Aisha. It's all right."

"You don't want me to come with you?"

Katelyn reached up and stroked his cheek. "More than anything," she admitted. "I'm terrified—but I think it will only make things worse."

"I just . . . I mean, maybe it would be better if he did . . . " He trailed off miserably.

She shook her head, knowing exactly what he was thinking. "It might seem like that now," her voice broke with guilt, knowing she'd sometimes hoped for the same thing, "but it wouldn't be . . . not in the long run."

He nodded. "I'll stay with Lacey and Sawyer. Go—but come back safe, please."

Katelyn stepped out onto the porch. The wind kicked hard, slamming the door and separating her from Brian with a loud, final sounding bang.

Chapter 34

THE WIND TORE AT KATELYN'S jacket, wet worms of escaped hair plastered to her forehead, and water snaked in the side of her hood and slithered down her neck. And instead of just letting her do what she'd come to do, the officer standing by the yellow and black tape barricading the bridge wanted to argue.

"Yes, I'm his ex-wife, but I think I can help. Please let me try."

"How did you even know he was here? Did he notify you this evening? Did he tell you he was going to self-harm?"

Katelyn shook her head. A battery of voices surrounded her. Static crackled from radios on the hips and in the hands of a variety of uniforms. The darkness was cut by flashing red, white and blue lights. One wide, piercing beam sliced a straight line to a slump-shouldered man sitting on the railing of the bridge.

"I told you. A friend called me."

"And this friend, she told you your husband was—"

"She's not really my friend. She's my ex-boss. And she wasn't sure it was Steve. She just thought it might be—"

A heavy-set man strode toward them and stepped over the barricade. "Katelyn Kellerman?"

Katelyn nodded.

He introduced himself by name, reeled off something Katelyn didn't catch, and finished with, "You came to talk to your ex-husband?"

Katelyn nodded again, noting with dull interest that the officer had referred to Steve as her ex. Had Steve called himself that, or did the information come from somewhere else? She didn't have time to ponder it for long.

"He's been asking for you. Says he won't jump if he can talk to you—but I have to warn you, getting you out there to watch might be his whole plan. He might have it in his head that he can punish you, by—"

"By jumping to his death in front of me?" Katelyn whispered.

The officer nodded.

She stepped forward. "But . . . am I allowed to talk with him?"

The officer scrubbed his jaw with his fist, sighed, and gave a terse nod. "But you can't go within reach of him, okay? No closer than ten feet—and if I say move, you move—back here, fast as you can, got it?"

Katelyn nodded.

The middle of the bridge, despite the storm, seemed strangely quiet. The absence of cars, maybe—or . . . Katelyn was aware that her brain was trying to take her anyplace but here, trying to have her think about anything but . . . this.

The streetlights were yellow and dim, unable to do much to alleviate the smothering darkness, enhanced as it was by the driving rain and thick fog. Beneath them, Steve wasn't so much illuminated as he was blurred.

He turned when she was about fifteen feet away, though neither she nor the officer had said a word yet. It was as if he sensed her.

"Katelyn," he breathed. "*Katelyn*."

She hated the relief in his voice with every fiber of her being. What did he expect of her? What could she possibly have left to give him?

"Steve," she replied softly, then walked a cautious step or two closer, carefully maintaining the distance the officer accompanying her had insisted on. "What are you doing? Are you okay?"

Steve shook his head, then moved stiffly, swinging a leg over the rail so that he sat straddling it, able to look at her more directly. "I . . . almost hurt that woman. Jayda."

And that was what was horrifying to him? That he'd almost hurt a stranger, not her for all those years?

"I know."

He shook his head again. "I didn't mean to. I didn't. The knife . . . I only had it on me because I'd been cleaning out our camping trailer. It was my camping knife. For *camping*."

"She's all right, Steve. She's okay."

He nodded and gulped air like a drowning man, and Katelyn realized he'd been sobbing. She felt something leave her body like a physical presence—terror. He wasn't a threat to her right now. Not like this. Something had changed. In him? In her? She guessed it didn't really matter who—just that it had.

"I can tell you feel sorry," she said, "but you're sitting in a dangerous spot. Will you come down from there and we can talk some more?"

Steve continued, like he hadn't heard her. "And you won't come back to me because I scared you, right?"

She darted a look at the officer. He held her gaze, but shook his head once, like he didn't know what she should say either—but Steve didn't appear to need her words.

"I am not a bad man," he said vehemently. "I'm not."

"But you're sorry for any bad things you may have done, right? For any misunderstandings?" she said softly, falling into their old pattern and for once in her life, being grateful for it, grateful she knew the lines to say, the role to play.

"See? You *know*. You know *me*. I am sorry. So sorry. I know I lose it sometimes, but it's just because I love you. I love you so much."

Katelyn couldn't smell alcohol on his breath because he was too far away, but she recognized the bottle talking.

"I do know that, Steve. I do." She was hit by what might've been the saddest thing she'd ever thought: that in his own damaged beyond repair, delusional, no idea what real love was way, he did love her.

He rubbed his eyes and suddenly shifted his weight. It looked like he might swing his leg back and return to a ready to jump position again.

"You have a lot to live for, Steve. The kids love you. They need to know that while a person's alive, there's still hope."

"Ha!"

Katelyn froze at the explosive bitterness in Steve's voice like someone had just fired a gun. She couldn't help it.

He shook his head, his mood swinging as unpredictably and quickly as a branch caught in a river's current. "The kids don't love me. And they shouldn't. They're scared of me. They'd be better off without me. You'd all be better off without me. And that's what you want, right?"

Katelyn didn't hesitate. She threw the truth like a life preserver, praying Steve would grab onto it. "They would not be better off without you. If you hurt yourself, if you . . . die . . . it will be terrible for them."

Silence. Silence. Silence. Only the rain beating hard. And her heart beating harder.

Then finally, just when Katelyn feared she might scream with nerves, Steve spoke again. "But not for you. It would be good for you. You would be happy."

"No, it wouldn't. It would be terrible for me—terribly, terribly, terribly sad."

"If I . . ." Steve lifted his foot to the railing like he was going to try to stand—but slipped and came down heavily on his tailbone. Katelyn stifled a scream and rushed forward out of reflex. The officer beside her caught her wrist in a cement grip and restrained her.

"If I get help, if I promise to really, one hundred percent, get help, will you come back to me? Give me one more chance. Just one more. Please. I love you, Katelyn. I love you. I love you. I love you."

Katelyn realized she was crying and wondered if she had been ever since she stepped foot onto the bridge. "Oh, Steve . . . " Her nose was running back into her throat and her vision misted—but even so, she saw him shake his head and wrap his arms around himself, like he was trying to hold himself together.

"You won't. And I knew it. It's all over. And it's my fault. *My* fault." And just like that, without another word or sound, Steve jerked his body hard and pitched forward, falling with a wet smacking thud onto the surface of the bridge. It wasn't far to fall and he didn't appear badly hurt. He curled into a fetal position in the pooling rain and lay still.

The officer was instantly gone from Katelyn's side, joined by two others she hadn't even been aware were on the bridge. Steve didn't resist as the officers patted him down, checking for injuries and weapons. He didn't resist being handcuffed either.

When he was on his feet again, in what was probably a minute but seemed like years, he looked Katelyn's way once more. "I really am sorry," he said.

She nodded. "I know."

"Good-bye, Kiki."

It was hard to believe, but she actually smiled. "Good-bye, Steve. I hope . . . you get the help you need."

And then it was over. Steve was gone, shuffled away in the bleak night to the backseat of a waiting squad car.

Chapter 35

THE RAIN HAD LET UP and the sun was peeking out shyly from behind white fluffy clouds in a sky that looked like it had never been dark or ominous in its life. The grass was still very wet though and the kids were in slickers and boots, exploring the backyard and searching for earthworms. This was a new hobby that Katelyn had Jo to thank for. They were looking for bait.

Brian appeared around the curve in the trail. The smile fell from Katelyn's lips and her stomach flipped again. She was queasy with nerves now, not the happy butterflies that had danced through her just minutes earlier at the prospect of seeing him again.

After she'd gotten back to River's Sigh in the wee hours of the previous morning and explained everything that had gone on, they'd both agreed that he should sleep in his room at Jo and Callum's place. Despite their longing to be together, they didn't want to have to explain his overnight presence to the kids. They were going to have enough to adjust to in the upcoming months.

But Brian looked so . . . serious. Had something else gone wrong? Could their fledgling relationship, so rocky from the very beginning through no fault of their own, survive having yet one more thing thrown at it?

Maybe her eyes revealed her insecurity because as soon as Brian was near enough to do so, he reached out and stroked her cheek. "Don't panic. It's a good thing, I promise. Or I hope it is."

Katelyn bit her lip. "Should we sit down?"

"Yes, I think so. Definitely." They headed for the weathered bench swing in the shady part of yard. When they were settled, Brian took both her hands in his. It was a gesture of either really, really good news—or really, really bad news.

Katelyn tried not to stare at him in alarm *or* in desperate hope. Maybe she should interrupt him, get her words, her request, out first. Maybe it would lead the conversation to go the way she wanted it to, to talk of their future together, with no more wimpy fear-based excuses from either of them. But then again, if Brian really thought it was best for them to stop before they got started, she would let him go this time. You couldn't force a man to love you no matter how much you loved him.

Loved him. That did indeed sum it up—and had for some time, she realized, now that she was letting herself feel everything and hope for everything. She loved him!

She took a deep breath, inhaling the earthy scent of

warm, recently drenched, growing things all around her, and forced herself to meet Brian's eyes. They were a sun kissed sea blue today, and they shone with . . . the same emotions she was suddenly radiating. Her next breath came easier and she rubbed her thumbs along his. It was going to be okay. No, it was going to be wonderful. She should've known they'd arrive at the same place at the same time. Somehow they always did.

His words still managed to shock her though.

"So," he started. "I was up all night, thinking and thinking, and hoping and hoping. I must've told myself a dozen times what you said, to have patience, that it was enough for now to know that we were on the same page about wanting to be together, but I can't put it off anymore. I want to buy that property and build a life and a home there, but I realized I can't."

"You can't . . . " Wait, what? Maybe she was delusional after all—

Brian's hands tightened on hers, and he shook his head. "No, no. That came out all wrong. Why can I hardly talk around you sometimes? I'm usually an eloquent speaker. I mean, crap, it's what I do for a living."

Katelyn let him babble, a river of warm assurance running through her. She'd been right the first time. They *were* at the same place.

"What I meant to say is, I love you. I'm not joking or flirting or talking hypothetically. And I love Sawyer and Lacey. I knew there was something special about that property and house, but I didn't realize what it was exactly until you and I were there together. It's our home. Our safe place. And, if you'll let me, I will choose to love you all of my days. Together we'll make a life filled with peace and joy and fun, as much as we have any power to, for as long as we live."

Katelyn swallowed hard. She had words, oh so many of them, but they were lost in the tidal wave of joy overtaking her.

Brian smudged away one of her happy tears, then rubbed his salty thumb over her bottom lip and bent to kiss her. She closed her eyes—

"Mom? *Mom*? Where are you?" Lacey's voice came from the porch on the other side of the cabin.

"No," Katelyn moaned. "Usually I love to see them, but seriously?"

"They do have impeccable timing," Brian agreed, pulling back with equal reluctance, "a lot like me, perhaps—but I need to get it all out, here and now."

There was more?

He reached into his pocket. "I know we've only been friends for five months or so, and we never *officially* made our relationship anything more until very recently, but now that we know what we want, I don't want to wait another second."

A simple silver band lay in his palm, glowing in a golden ray of sun that danced through the veil of branches overhead.

"Mom?" Sawyer's voice this time.

"*Mom*!" Lacey again—but at least, from the sounds of it, they were both still on the porch. It was possibly the silliest and least romantic backdrop for a proposal in the world. Katelyn adored it.

"Yes, Brian, *yes*. And thank you."

He laughed. "Thank you?"

She could only nod mistily. That's how Brian Archer always made her feel: so thankful, so grateful. Because he existed. Because he was *hers*.

And then he was cupping her face, pressing his lips to hers, and—

"Oh, gross! Are you guys kissing?" The horror in Lacey's voice made Katelyn chuckle, even as she groaned.

The kids couldn't have been too put off by the public display of affection, however, because they scrambled onto the swing, wedging themselves in on either side of Brian and Katelyn.

"To be continued then?" Brian whispered against Katelyn's hair, always such a good sport.

"You know it," Katelyn whispered back.

"Continue what?" Lacey asked.

Brian pushed the ground with one of his long legs and the swing swayed to life, fast enough to be fun, smooth enough to not be scary. "Continue . . . everything!" he said.

For some reason his silly answer delighted Sawyer and Lacey as much as it did Katelyn. She and her—

their—kids giggled and cheered, and Katelyn wondered, half seriously, if a person's heart could explode with joy.

Epilogue

KATELYN STEPPED OUT OF SPRING cabin, leaving the door ajar so she would hear Sawyer and Lacey if they stirred. She looked up at the skinny building that had been her sanctuary for all these months, her own lighthouse. Then she strolled the narrow deck, inhaling fully, deeply.

The air was already warm, despite the early hour, and the sky was the kind of blue that made you feel like only good things were possible. And though Katelyn knew she was only minutes away from the other cabins, she still felt like the sole inhabitant of an enchanted world.

Spring was long, long gone and summer was in its full glory. Everywhere she looked there were bright, beautiful blooms and verdant testaments to life, growth, and change.

From the wooden bench beside her cabin's door, overflowing with the kids' damp, stinky sneakers and fishing rods they'd cajoled her to buy, to the waxy leafed, red berried holly bushes beside the porch, to the fairy carpet of impossible to keep down pansies, everything whispered that life was beautiful—or could be.

Katelyn descended the three steps from the porch to the ground, savoring the warm sunshine on her bare limbs. It felt full of the promise that no matter what happened, how cold a winter was or how much rain poured down, eventually the sun would reign in full force again.

A now familiar feeling welled up in her. Hope. She walked a few more steps, still in awe of the massive cedar trees nearby, standing tall and strong, as if bearing witness to her new life. She was going to miss this place, and she was beyond excited that her, *their*, new home was just a meandering trail away.

Knowing she was safe from view, she dropped the notebook she had jotted her most recent checklist into, lifted her arms and spun in a slow joyous circle.

Steve wasn't her direct problem anymore; he had received significant jail time. Her car, not that it was as big a worry now anyway, had merely needed to have its injectors cleaned. Since Callum had kindly helped Brian do that, she'd had no more problems starting it or keeping it going. Jayda had apologized, saying she overreacted because of the fright and knew full well that Steve's attack wasn't Katelyn's fault. She'd pleaded for her to return to work, and Katelyn had agreed, but only to part-time. She wanted to do her own sewing and have lots of time to nest. She would keep persevering. But best of all, so best of all she could hardly take it in sometimes, she, Brian, Sawyer, and Lacey would be a family. Together they'd create a safe, joy filled home, a place to live and grow and love—

Two muscular arms wrapped around her from behind and pulled her against a firm chest.

Katelyn shrieked. "You're not supposed to see me yet! It's bad luck."

Brian nuzzled her neck. "I had to. I couldn't wait until the ceremony. It's hours away. And I promise there will be no bad luck, only fun and adventure and trails we tackle together."

Katelyn turned into Brian's embrace, so she could look him in the face. As ever, his closeness made her heart race. Would she ever stop responding to him this way? She doubted it.

"You make it awfully hard not to be madly in love with you," she said.

He winked. "Ah, good. My malevolent plan is working."

"Oh, it is, is it?"

"Yes—and lest you have any thoughts to the contrary, I have a few strategies to keep it iron clad from here to eternity."

"Strategies, hey?"

Brian didn't answer with words. Instead he lowered his head and took her mouth in a soft, then deepening, increasingly passionate kiss. His fingers played beneath the hem of her shirt, tracing slow sensuous patterns across the sensitive skin of her lower back. She was breathless when they broke apart.

"Hm," she said. "I think your, er, strategies will be very effective."

Brian grinned. "If you like my strategies, just wait till you see my techniques."

Katelyn laughed, but felt almost weepy with happiness. How could this—how could *he*—be real? She smiled up at him. "Thank you."

"No," he replied seriously, "thank *you*."

Hand in hand, they headed back to Spring cabin to wake the kids and start the day that would kick off the rest of their run together.

Dear Reader,

Thank you so much for spending time with Brian and Katelyn. I hoped you enjoyed *Hook, Line & Sinker* immensely and that you'll visit River's Sigh B & B again soon. If the series is new to you, please check out the other books, *Wedding Bands*, *Hooked*, *One to Keep*, and *Spoons*. Also, watch for Aisha's story, *The Catch,* coming later in 2017.

I'd love to connect with you, so please visit www.evbishop.com, sign up for my newsletter, find me on Facebook or follow my Tweets (Ev_Bishop). On a similar note, reviews really help authors. If you'd be so kind as to leave a rating and a few words on GoodReads, your blog, Facebook, or anywhere else you hang out when your nose isn't in a book, I'd be thrilled! Thank you.

Wishing you love, laughter and great reads,

Ev Bishop

About the Author

 **Ev Bishop** lives and writes in wildly beautiful British Columbia, Canada. She is a long-time columnist with the *Terrace Standard,* and her articles and essays have been published in a variety of magazines and journals. Storytelling is her true love, however, and she writes fiction in variety of lengths and genres.

To see her growing list of published short stories, novels, and poems, please visit her website: www.evbishop.com.